Also by William H. Gass

FICTION

Middle C

Cartesian Sonata

The Tunnel

Willie Masters' Lonesome Wife

In the Heart of the Heart of the Country

Omensetter's Luck

NONFICTION

Life Sentences

A Temple of Texts

Conversations with William H. Gass

Tests of Time

Reading Rilke

Finding a Form

On Being Blue

Habitations of the Word

The World Within the Word

Fiction and the Figures of Life

EYES

Taken from *Hatred and Civility: The Antisocial Life in Victorian England,* by Christopher Lane. Figure 6.1, *Der Augenturm (The Eye Tower),* 1977. Copyright Dieter Appelt. Courtesy Kicken Berlin and the Pace/MacGill Gallery, New York.

EYES

Novellas and Short Stories

William H. Gass

Alfred A. Knopf

New York · 2015

THIS IS A BORZOI BOOK
PUBLISHED BY ALFRED A. KNOPF

www.aaknopf.com

Knopf, Borzoi Books, and the colophon are registered
trademarks of Penguin Random House LLC.

Art on page 152 © Photofest
Art on page 216 © 2014 Michael Hafftka (www.hafftka.com)

Library of Congress Cataloging-in-Publication Data
Gass, William H., [date]
Eyes: novellas and short stories / William H. Gass.—First edition.
pages ; cm
ISBN 978-1-101-87472-1 (hardcover : alk. paper)—
ISBN 978-1-101-87473-8 (eBook)
I. Title.
PS3557.A845E94 2015
813'.54—dc23

2014041957

Jacket photograph by Pete Thompson/Gallery Stock
Jacket design by Gabriele Wilson

Manufactured in the United States of America

First Edition

FOR MARY

thru thick and thin

THE POINT WHERE AN UNDERGROUND SPRING
SUDDENLY BURSTS TO THE SURFACE IS KNOWN AS AN
EYE. IT IS A PLACE OF MYSTERY, WHERE DRY GROUND
BECOMES SOAKED WITH LIFE-GIVING WATER, AND
NATURE GIVES US A GLIMPSE OF ALL THAT HAPPENS
OUT OF THE REALM OF HUMAN VISION.

—Jan DeBlieu

Contents

Appreciations

Four pieces in this group—"In Camera," "Charity," "Don't Even Try, Sam," and "The Man Who Spoke with His Hands"—first appeared in that sterling magazine *Conjunctions,* while the oddly authored "Soliloquy for a Chair" was published in *Tin House* and "Toy Chest" in *The Yale Review.* Thanks, too, to artists Michael Eastman and Michael Hafftka, as well as for the assistance of Catherine Gass.

In
Camera

Photo of the author by the author

1 THE STOCK

Mr. Gab didn't have that gift, though his assistant, who was supposed to be stupid but only looked so, would mutter beneath his breath, when annoyed by his tasks, "he had the gift, he did, did Gab." Mr. Gab spoke seldom, and then it was to shout at the steel shutters of the shop that were always reluctant to alter their position, whatever it was, and needed to be cajoled, flattered, then threatened. Or sometimes he spoke to the steam pipes, complaining of the knocking, complaining of the excessive heat they gave off when they had to be heated and of the odor that the steam brought to the nose through layers of paint resembling aluminum. Curls the graphs, he said with as close to a curse as he came.

Mr. Gab's shop was in a part of town so drably uninteresting robbers wouldn't visit even to case its joints, something Mr. Gab fairly certainly knew, and treasured, but he had these steel shutters left over from a former, more frequented, more luxuriant time, and felt obliged to use them. One could have guessed Mr. Gab's age from these small facts: that he thought of possible intruders as "robbers," and worried about being "glommed"—terms which have no present employment. The shutters, window-wide slats of steel in Venetian style, creaked as they descended, and no longer fit firmly together or overlay one another as they had been designed to do in some far-off factory; consequently, streetlights—lit to illuminate an empty avenue whose venerable storefronts were a menace even during the glare of sunny afternoons—would streak into the shop at night where Mr. Gab might still be sitting, long after closing, long after nodding bye-bye to his stupid assistant, staring at his prints in the darkness, prints that covered the pock-marked walls of the shop, displayed there like dead things hung from nails, as if slain while other prey were being hunted: while picking up fallen apples maybe (though he lived so far from the country), or rather if a brace of grouse were to fling themselves into the apple bag, or while gathering pignuts (models ago he'd sold his car) a pair of pigeons might creep into a handy box—that unlikely—while sorting buckeyes to find the feathers of a turkey, or, while pulling loganberries out of their briaries (though he wore no woolen sleeves), flushing a covey of quail instead—anyway—prizes inadvertently taken, mistakenly developed, proudly framed.

Mr. Gab certainly had his favorites. These were images he knew so intimately they were—well, not quite etched on the balls of his eyes. He needed only the least light to see them down to their last shades of gray: an Atget was frequently imagined to be the state of his street outside—Atget, the documentarian. Perhaps he'd decide on the Atget of an intersection, of *Angle de la rue L'homond et de la rue Rataud,* its cobbles moist, in late light, sky like sour milk, taken in the *quartier du Val-de-Grâce,* where on one wall a poster was papered to say un million, un million, a dozen times in a voice not ever husky. "Forever," Mr. Gab would allow himself sometimes to murmur: *cours de danse givre* . . . forever . . . though the "cours" is gone, "danse" is gone, even before the War arrived in a taxi, they were gone, gone, cobbles gone too, now, probably, building likely, gone, the lamp most certainly, gone, and the teeth of steel, like those of a large rake, that crossed the rue high above every head—sure, sure—that crossed the top of the image straight through the sour-milk sky and over the tree at rue's end—oh yes—gone, quite gone, even the tree whose feet were hid behind a low wall, deep in the shot where the road disappeared into a vee as though down a drain—ah well—cut by now, blown over, hauled off, firewooded, gone. Dear me.

"What a curb," Mr. Gab permitted himself to exclaim. At the Louvre . . . what did the advert advise and proclaim? Who could say? With the wall retreating, the posters defaced. What a glisten though! Still . . . the curb, the glisten, the deep recession of the street remained. Right outside there, beyond that barred door, beyond the shuttered window, lay Atget's modest little street still. Still . . . made of wavering lines of glis and shales of shine. The walk protected by posts. Mr. Gab did not dare to say aloud what he succinctly thought, as he looked out through his engraved eyes: I am Atget—the world is mine.

Only during the evening following work—Mr. Gab thought that way of it, thought of it as work—shortly after he had—well—dined, but before he went slowly to bed, unbuttoning the buttons down his shirt—well, his vest first—seeing the street or some other scene all the while the buttons went as buttons do, loose from their hole, not like released birds because it was shirt that was freed, the vest that flew loose, even if it clung to his slender frame like a woman in a romance to her equally handmade lover—no—the buttons like sentries would stay sewn in their useful line perhaps for an entire shirt life, vest time. In photographs, shirts do not get much attention.

He could of course have chosen to recall the elegant details of

Le Restaurant Procope's façade, the café's name like a decoration running along in front of the building's second-floor windows, each letter as bold as an escutcheon affixed to a wrought-iron balcony railing: GRAND RESTAURANT PROCOPE, and then, under the overhang, discreet as a meeting, the name again: Grand Restaurant Procope, no doubt no longer in business though one sign said *verte du vins pour ville*—oh the hanging lamps were like crowned heads, the walk lined with tables and paired chairs, the hour early, each empty—not the hours but the chairs—a busy day ahead of them, waiting to accommodate customers no longer alive.

Mr. Gab lived as many shopkeepers once did, both at the rear and above his establishment. He slept in a small loft a good size for bats that he reached by climbing the short stair that rose unsteadily from a corner of his kitchen, a kitchen of sorts, in whose foreshortened center Mr. Gab kept a card table and a ceramic cat. Breakfast might be an apple and an egg. Lunch—he frequently passed on lunch, though his stupid assistant ate lunch like a lion, growling over some sandwich distantly fixed. A sip of tea, a chewy biscuit maybe. Memories going back a long way. Mostly, though, he passed on lunch.

Days were dreary—oh yes—especially in a shop stuffed with gray-white gray-black photographs in cellophane sheets that had been loosely sidefiled in cardboard boxes, tag attached, maybe FRENCH XX or COUNTRYSIDE BRITISH or RAILROADS USA. He had three for trees: bare, leafed, chopped. On the walls, clipped to wire hangers that were then hung from nails, were his prizes, displayed so as to discourage buyers. Successfully. So far. For a decade.

Mr. Gab would have six or seven customers on a good day, which is what he would almost audibly say to them when they

entered, making the door ring—well it was a rattle really. His stupid assistant would answer most questions, show them the labels
on the boxes, wave at the walls hung with hangers, open a filing
cabinet or a case for those who fancied the pricier ones, explain
the proper technique for sliding a photograph out of its sheath-
ing, demonstrate the underhanded manner of holding it, or, with
palms gently placed at edges as if it were a rare recording, explain
how one could be safely examined.

The boxes were mostly of a conventional cardboard. They sat
on tables or beside tables or under tables as if they'd sat there
already a long time: the ink on the labels had faded; the paper of
the labels had yellowed; the corners of the labels were munched.
Covers were kept closed against dust and light and idle eyes by
beanbags, forever in the family, inertly weighing on the boxes'
cardboard flaps. The nails Mr. Gab had driven into the walls were
zinc'd, which made them suitable for fastening shingles, but you
couldn't have drawn one out without pulling, along with the
shank, large chunks of plaster. The wire hangers themselves were
in weary shape. So the pictures hung askew. As if holding on with
one hand.

Mr. Gab stocked several versions of the same photograph
sometimes. A round red sticker affixed to the wrap signaled a superior print, a green circle indicated one produced from the original
negative, but late in its life, whereas a yellow warned the customer
that the sheath enclosed a mere reproduction, however excellent
it might often be. His red version of rue Rataud was as fine as the
one conserved at the Carnavalet, but on the white rectangles with
their softly rounded corners which Mr. Gab had pasted to the
bottom of each envelope and where he identified the subject, the

photographer, the method, and the negative's likely residence, he had written about the less genuine image, below a yellow ball that suggested caution, the words "*trop mauvais état*," a little joke only scholars might understand and enjoy.

Mr. Gab's provenances were detailed and precise; however, years earlier an envious dealer had accused his rival (for Mr. Gab was then in a dinky shop across from him on another street) (and whom the envious dealer called "Grab," somehow sensing Mr. Gab's sensitivity about his name, though unaware that Mr. Gab had become silent in order to avoid being addressed by anyone as "Gabby") of accepting or otherwise acquiring (during midnight visits and stealthy trips) stolen property. How otherwise, the envious dealer complained, could one account for the presence, in prime condition, of so many rare and important photographs in such shabby shoebox circumstances. "Shoebox" was slanderous, certainly, though nothing had come of these allegations except a shady reputation, thought actually to be desirable in some circles.

A print's quality depended almost entirely upon its preservation of details, its respect for values. The fog-white sky of rue Rataud, in the version under its cautionary yellow dot, smeared the end of the street so you could not see how or where it turned, walls were muffled, and a hard light made the outlines of the cobbles disappear; while the red-tagged rue Rataud allowed the eye to count windows far away and discern a distant huddle of buildings. In the latter, the spiky rod, whose use he could not fathom, crossed the street in the guise of a determinate dark line; in the former it was dim and insubstantial, as if obscured by smoke. On red's verbose information label, Mr. Gab had written that his photograph had come to the United States in the luggage of Berenice

Abbott from whom he had received a few prime prints of other subjects. If interested, please ask. About the history of yellow, Mr. Gab offered nothing.

The stupid assistant was not sufficiently steeped, so when, as occasionally happened, a customer wished a little history, Mr. Gab would have to hold forth, not reluctantly with regard to the information, which he believed every cultivated person should possess, but reluctantly regards speaking—making noises, choosing words, determining the line of march for a complex chronology. From the box marked DECORATIVE ELEMENTS, for instance, another Atget might be withdrawn, and Mr. Gab could inform his customer that this view of some paneling at the Hôtel Roquelaure had been purchased from Atget by Georges Hoentschel—did he know?—the designer of the Union Centrale pavilion for the 1900 World's Fair in Paris; and subsequently in an archive of great richness and variety that Hoentschel had catalogued and published in 1908 before it was sold to J. P. Morgan who later donated the entire shebang to New York's Metropolitan Museum. Someone had dismembered a 1908 catalogue and this image—which you should please hold at its tender edges—is a limb from one of those dismemberments.

Mr. Gab did not usually remark the fact (since some found the fact disturbing) that the door was no doubt long gone, though the photograph was evidence of fine wood and careful workmanship; but because Atget had taken a portion of the decoration's portrait, the surviving image had increased in value at each exchange and become what Mr. Gab, in a rare moment of eloquence, called "a ghost worth gold." Nothing touched by this man's lens was lost, he said, each was elevated by its semblance to sublimity, even the dubious ladies of the XIXe arrondissement, three of them (two

leaning one peeking) from the traditional doorway, appetizing if
you ate mud, an example of which (not the mud but the unsavory
subjects) he, Mr. Gab, had in a box at the back of the shop marked
NUES, even though the women were decently dressed.

The light in the store, Mr. Gab's stupid assistant persisted in
judging, "was lousy." With the shutters closed, you could see how
dust-covered the front windows had become, while most of the
lamps were simply bulbs housed in coffee cans hung from wires
punched through their bottoms. A proper tungsten lamp throwing
the appropriately well-wiped light could be found at the rear of
the store—"don't call it a store," Mr. Gab always protested—where
anyone who wore serious eyes could contemplate in quiet a possible purchase. The assistant believed that the entire furnishings
of the store: the old oak desk where Mr. Gab presided, the swivel
chair, alike in oak, the rose-colored puff upon which he sat when
he was seated, the smeary windows, a door which uttered a need-
less warning, the faded façade from former days, which incorporated a large dim sign spelling P H O T O G R A P H Y in letters
that looked as if they wanted nothing to do with one another, the
scuffed and cracked linoleum floor, the pocked walls with their
swaying trophies, the trestle tables upon which the cardboard
boxes stood, or under which they hid, or beside which they huddled, the dumb homely handmade lamps that filled the room with
the rattle of tinlight, the tall stool in a back corner where the stupid assistant perched, the rug, instead of a door, which hung over
the entrance to Mr. Gab's private quarters: they were all meant to
deceive detectives and most untrained and idle inspection. For the
truth was—since the assistant harbored the same opinion as Mr.
Gab's once-a-time rival—the stock was stupendous, of varied kind

and exquisite quality, a condition which was quite unaccountable unless the prints had, at one time or other, by someone or other, been pinched.

The assistant, whose apparent stupidity was an effect of his seeming a suitable subject for Diane Arbus, knew, to cite one outré instance, that in a box at the back of the store, and in two Mr. Gab kept in a cleaning closet in his kitchen, were several beautiful pictures set in Sicily and shot in the early fifties by, of all people for Mr. Gab to have discovered, Enzo Sellerio: in particular one from Vizzini of the worn head and shoulders of a woman who had framed herself with a window that in turn was surrounded by rows and rows of descending roof tiles textured to a fare-thee-well—a woman whose gaze was one of total intensity, though her mouth expressed quizzicality, while on the sill lay an aristocracy of fingers, age infecting everything else—her fingers positioned as if she were emerging from the grave of days; then another taken through the flychains of a Palermo doorway so that a seated man, a horse and cart, a church front, and a couple are seen as if scrimmed by a blurring rain of o's; or the Chiesa Madre's quiltlike stairway viewed from above as it's being climbed by a herd of Paternò goats . . . well, where could this man who went nowhere, rarely to the edge of his neighborhood, have obtained work of this quality without hanky-panky of some kind? Without a lot of miscreation going on behind the back of every member of an honest public.

Oh . . . yes . . . Mr. Gab also had a very moving photograph—perhaps a tad mellow—of some trailer-camp kids in Richmond, California, that Ansel Adams had taken with Dorothea Lange's twin-lens Rolleiflex during the War, cropped and dodged according to his own account, and just how had that dramatic image made its way into a cello envelope and thence to a cardboard box in this silly little shop on Arsenal Avenue except if it were hiding out?

Mr. Gab was as silent about his system of supply as he was about everything else. He sold so seldom he may have been holding most of his stock for years, and in the same boxes too, long before his assistant became old enough to observe any rate of change. Nevertheless, from time to time a very big Russian-looking man in a very heavy Russian-looking coat, though not with a dead animal on his head, which would have made everyone take note, came with wild hatless hair to see, and apparently to consult with, Mr. Gab, going into his quiet private quarters for a little chat, carrying a case large flat and black. The Russian's big bass would soften as soon as his wide back disappeared behind the rug, which Mr. Gab held open for him as though they were entering a box at the theater. How are you this very day, my boy, the big man would thunder when the stupid assistant greeted him with a wince of recognition and a pleasant surprised smile. Annduh Missterr Gahb, my boy, is he ahbought? His accent, thick as his coat, was too eclectic to be genuine, and had been faked to cover a Russian one, the assistant thought. It was then, at the card table in the company of the ceramic cat, that the case would click open to disclose, the assistant imagined, a wondrous rarity, an August Sander maybe, filched from a German collector, a labor leader in an ill-fitting unpressed dark suit, throttled tie, intense vest, like those Mr. Gab wore, hair receding so it was now a headband, and those arms at his side ending in pugnacious little fists.

But when the assistant went later to look under Sander in the German box he found only the one which had been there through uncounted years: the hotelkeeper and his wife, Gastwirtsehepaar, around 1930, Tweedledum with Tweedledee, posed outside their vine-sided hostelry, she in her polka dot dress and frontally folded arms, he in bow tie and white shirt and hanky, a startle of patches against the compulsory black suit, including vest—black too—tucked under the coat like a head hid in a camera's hood—uh oh—there's one button missing, one out of four, too bad, the bottoms of the innkeeper's trousers hiked in an ungainly fashion above a pair of sturdy polished shoes, black as well, the innkeeper's arms clasped behind him so that the swell of his stomach would suggest to a hesitant guest hearty fare; well, they were both girthy full-fleshed folk as far as that goes, her eyes in a bit of a squint, his like raisins drowning in the plump of his cheeks.

What made August Sander's portraits so great—"great" was the appropriate word in the assistant's opinion—was the way his sitters made visibly manifest, like the backgrounds behind them, the lives that had shaped their pictured faces and forms, as though their daily occupations had drawn them there to be displayed for the camera with all the seriousness suitable to such a show of essential self.

If you were to look at the penetrating portrait Berenice Abbott made of Eugène Atget when he was a wispy-haired old man with sunken cheeks, a mouth relieved of most of its teeth, assertive nose, and intense eyes, you might get a whiff of Mr. Gab too, for he was ancient early, grew up to reach old in a hurry, and then didn't change much for decades, except to solidify his opinions, much the way Atget had, both men easily angered, both men hugging their habits, each short of speech, and patient as the stones Atget alone gelatinized. Mr. Gab disavowed color with the fervor of a Puritan, and nothing in the shop had a hue you'd want to name beside the dull brown cardboard and the pillow in his chair, because the walls were once a clean cream dirtied now to nondescription, and the lino floor was like a playing board of black/white squares, a design mostly seen unmopped in public toilets, while the rug he'd hung across the door to his digs was a tweed a fade away from tan.

Mr. Gab was a stickler. His ideal was the perfect picture taken on the wing with one shot, and allowed to emerge from its development like a chick its egg, so that one saw not just the subject supremely rendered but a testimony to the unerring fineness of the photographer's eye; an eye unlike the painter's, he claimed, because the painter constructed; the painter made up his image as if the canvas were a face; while the photographer sought his composition like a hunter his prey, and took it away clean, when it was found, to present in its purity, as the result of an act of vision, the sort of seeing no one else employed, what Mr. Gab called "slingshot sight." Painting took too long, sculpture of course was worse, and encouraged thinking, permitted alterations, endured changes of mind; whereas the photographer came, saw, and shot in a Rolleiflex action, in one unified gesture like waving off a fly.

Mr. Gab knew Atget bided his time, did and redid; he knew that Edward Weston pulled images like putty into weird unnatural shapes; he knew that Walker Evans cropped like a farmer, August Sander as well, who also staged every shot with theatrical calculation; that Man Ray was like Duchamp, an incorrigible scamp; that Ansel Adams dodged and burned and renovated; that even André Kertész, who possessed, like Josef Sudek, a saintly sensibility, had more than once employed a Polaroid . . . well, Mr. Gab didn't say very much about such lapses; he just threw up his hands, palms up/arms out, the way he did in the winter, salting his sidewalk, and said that it was beyond understanding that the same man who had taken, from an overlooking window, those pictures of Washington Square in a snow of fences—when? Nineteen seventy? well—in—anyway—a nearby year—it was dumbfounding that an artist of such supreme severity should have succumbed to Koda-chromania and taken, it was said, as if he had embezzled them, two thousand Polaroids, sinking for a time as far as Cibachrome, but genius was a dark cave full of flickers; who knew what the darkness might disclose? who knew, his hands said, washing themselves in the air.

Mr. Gab forgave, and forgave again, but certain photographers had too many counts against them, like David Bailey, to mention an outstanding instance, because he bandaged the body exposing only the legendary wound with its unlikely whiskers, or did the worst sort of celebratory portrait—Yoko Ono, for god's sake—or shot up the worst sort of scene—Las Vegas, can you imagine?—consorted with cover models, and had nudes blow chewing gum bubbles to match their bubbies or wear necklaces of barbed wire; then there was a hot lens like Irving Penn, who spent too much time in the studio, who worked for fashion maga-zines (advertising and news were also OUT), who photographed Marisa Berenson's perfect bosom and Rudolf Nureyev's perfect limbs because they were Berenson's boobs or Nureyev's calves, and did portraits of famous folk like Truman Capote on account of that fame, often in silly contrived poses such as Woody Allen gotten up as Groucho Marx (Mr. Gab vented exasperation), or did cutesy-pie pictures like that faucet Penn pretended was dripping diamonds, but almost worst, his malignant habit of pushing his subjects into corners where they'd be certain to feel uncomfortable and consequently conspire with the tormentor to adopt a look never before or after worn.

Nevertheless (for Mr. Gab was composed of contradictions too), Mr. Gab could show you (while complaining of its name) *Cigarette No. 69,* from a series Penn had done in '72, or a devilish distortion from the box marked NUES which Kertész had accomplished in 1933 as another revenge against women . . . well, it was admittedly beautiful, simply so, so simply blessed . . . he might mention the gracefully elongated hands pressed between the thighs, or draw attention to the dark button indenting the belly as if it were waiting to ring up a roomer on the fourth floor, the soft—oh yes—mound, also expanded into a delicious swath of . . . Mr. Gab's stupid assistant would have to say the word "pubic" . . . hair, a romantic image, really, in whose honor Mr. Gab's hands shook when he held the photo, because he'd feel himself caught for a moment in the crease of an old heartbreak (that's what an observer might presume), memories extended elastically through time until, with a snap, they flew out of thought like a pursued bird.

The customers . . . well, they were mostly not even browsers, but wanderers, or refugees from a bad patch of weather, or misinformed, even so far as to be crestfallen when they understood the Nowhere they had come to, but occasionally there'd be some otherwise oblivious fellow who would fly to a box, shove off the bag of beans, and begin to finger through the photos as you might hunt through a file, with a haste hope might have further hastened, an air of expectancy that suggested some prior prompting, only to stop and withdraw a sheet suddenly and accompany it to the light of the good lamp in the rear, where he'd begin to examine it first with a studied casualness that seemed more conspiratorial than anything, looking about like a fly about to light before indifferently glancing at the print, until at last, now as intent as a tack, he'd submit to scrutiny each inch with tight white lips, finally following Mr. Gab, who had anticipated the move, through the rug to the card table and the cat in the kitchen, where they'd have what Mr. Gab called, with a pale smile that was nearly not there, a confab.

Concerning cost. This is what his stupid assistant assumed. The meeting would usually end with a sale, a sale that put Mr. Gab in possession of an envelope fat with cash, for he accepted nothing else, nor were his true customers surprised, since they came prepared with a coat in whose inside pocket the fat envelope would be stashed. Consequently, it was a good thing the shop was so modest, the neighborhood so banal and grubby, the street, in fact, macadam to a fault, resembling Atget's avenues or stony lanes not a whit, not by a quick flip of light from a puddle or a flop of shade from an overhang, because the shop's stock was indeed valuable, and somewhere there was concealed cash with which, his stupid assistant surmised, Mr. Gab purchased further contraband, plus, if funds had been apportioned, a spot where lurked the money that tided Mr. Gab, his business, and his stupid assistant over from one week to the next (though their wants were modest) until, among the three who stepped inside at different times on an April day, a shifty third would paw through the box marked PRAGUE as if a treasure had been buried there, and then, despite nervous eyes and a tasteless cream-colored spring coat where—yes—the cash had been carried, buy a Josef Sudek that depicted Hradčany Castle circa 1915 under a glowering sky.

Mr. Gab really didn't want to let go of anything. His pleasure in a photograph, his need for it to sustain his sinking spirit, rose as the print was withdrawn and examined, and neared infatuation, approached necessity, as he and the customer, photo in front of them, haggled over the price. So Mr. Gab drove a hard bargain without trying to be greedy, though that was the impression he gave. Still, he had to let some of his prizes go if he was going to continue to protect his stock and ensure his collection's continued appreciation and applause.

Yes . . . yes . . . yes . . . the audience was small, but its appreciation was deep and vast, and its applause loud and almost everlasting.

Occasionally, as the assistant remembered, there were some close calls. A tall aristocratic-looking gentleman in expensive clothes and a light touch of gray hair chose a late afternoon to enter. Greeted by Mr. Gab in the usual way, he brusquely responded: I understand you have a photograph by Josef Sudek depicting two wet leaves. After a silence filled with surprise and apprehension, Mr. Gab replied with a question: who had informed the gentleman of that fact? He, by the way, he went on, was the owner of the shop; Mr. Gab was his name, while his visitor was . . . ? It is common knowledge in certain places, Mr. Gab, if it is indeed you, the tall man answered, and consequently has no more distinct location than a breeze. For some moments, Mr. Gab was unsure which of his two questions had been addressed. I shall, the stranger went on, show you my card directly I have seen the Sudek. *Two Wet Leaves,* he repeated. What period would that be, Mr. Gab said, somewhat lame in his delay. Though it was his stupid assistant who limped. And who did so now—limped forward in an aisle while Mr. Gab was making preparations to reply. His stupid assistant: smiling, winking one bad eye. His naturally crooked mouth turned his smile into a smirk. Later, Mr. Gab would gratefully acknowledge his assistant's attempt to Quasimodo the threatening fellow into an uneasy retreat.

But the man pushed forward on his own hook, looking sterner than a sentencing judge. You'd know, he said. You've got a print. *Two Wet Leaves.* Archival quality, I'm told. Nineteen thirty-two. You'd know. Then casting an eye as severe as a spinster's at the layout of the shop, he added: where shall I find it? (waving a commanding hand) where is it hid? The provenance of my photographs, Mr. Gab replied with nervous yet offended heat, is clear beyond question, their genuineness is past dispute; their quality unquestioned and unthreatened.

As if Mr. Gab's ire had melted the mister's snowy glare, he made as if to communicate a smile. The assistant tried various slithery faces on and did appear to be quite stupid indeed. I should think every photograph in this place was in dire straits, sir, the man said sternly, ignoring the reassurance of his own signal. As I remember, Mr. Gab managed, *Two Wet Leaves* is quite impressive. You'd know, the man insisted, beginning a patrol of aisle one, his head bent to read the labels of the boxes. I had such a print once in my possession, obtained from Anna Fárová herself, Mr. Gab admitted. Soooo . . . the stranger straightened and turned to confront Mr. Gab. And was it taken by sly means from Anne d'Harnoncourt's exhibit at the Philadelphia? Only from Anna's hand, herself, sir, Mr. Gab replied, now firm and fierce, and no other Fárová than

Fárová. As if there were many, the man said frowning, you would know.

Why not an Irving Penn? This insult was not lost on their visitor whose upper lip appeared to have recently missed a mustache. The many boxes seemed to daunt him, and it was now obvious that Mr. Gab would not be helpful. I have friends in Philadelphia, he said in a threatening tone. I understand the nearby gardens are nice, Mr. Gab rejoined. It was clear to the entire shop (and that included the china cat) that Mr. Gab had regained his courage. Was this freshly shaven man perhaps an officer of the law, the stupid assistant wondered, coughing now behind a stubby hand whose thumbnail was missing as David Smith's was in that portrait by Penn, the one in which Smith's mouth, fat-lipped and amply furred, is sucking on a pipe.

It was necessary to sidle if you wished to approach the wall, and sidle the tall man did, closing in on an image dangling there, gray in its greasy container. Is that, by god, a Koudelka, a Koudelka to be sure. His hands rose toward it. Not for sale, Mr. Gab said. Not for money. No need to remove it. But the deed was done. Slender fingers from a fine cuff parted the clip and slid the photo forth, balancing it under a blast of can light upon a delicate teeter of fingertips. Not for money? Then in trade, the man said, gazing at its darkly blanketed horse, and at the hunkered man apparently speaking to the horse's attentive head. Ah, what magical music, the man exclaimed, as if to himself. The grays ... in the horse, the street, the wall ... the tracks of light, the swirls and streaks of gray ... melodious as nothing can be. Unless it was Sudek himself, said Mr. Gab. The man's lengthy head rose from the picture where it had been feeding. Yes, he said, having taken thought. Only Sudek himself.

The fingernails are especially . . . Mr. Gab began, because he couldn't help himself. Ah, and the white above that one hoof, the visitor responded, entranced. Yes, the nails, the gesture of the hand, a confused puff of tail and that wall . . . such a wall. Hoofprints, Mr. Gab prompted. Dark soft spots . . . yes . . . and so . . . would you consider a trade, the man asked smiling—fully, genuinely—as he laid the cellophane envelope carefully on top of a cardboard box and allowed the print to float down upon it. I might have in my possession—if you have too many, you would know—a Sudek myself I'd be prepared to swap. I couldn't part— Mr. Gab broke off to repeat himself. Not for trade or sale, though, if the Sudek were fine enough, he, Mr. Gab, might be prepared to purchase . . . But were you to see the Sudek, the man said, point-ing toward his eyes . . .

It's a trap, Mr. Gab's assistant thought, for he only looked a bit stupid, especially with a little dab of spit moistening the open cor-ner of his mouth. It is the immersement, the immersement of the figures in their fore- and back- and floor ground, that is so amaz-ing, don't you agree? Mr. Gab, unsure, nodded. He's an entrapper, the assistant thought. I should show you the Sudek, the visitor said, no longer a customer but now a salesman. It sings, sir, sings. I'm willing to look at anything Sudek, Mr. Gab said, over his assis-tant's unvoiced series of "no"s. All right, the seller said, slipping his tall frame toward them. After reading Mr. Gab's expression, the man left abruptly, without leaving a clue to his intentions, and without closing the door behind him.

2   THE STUPID ASSISTANT

Had appeared at Mr. Gab's shop door years ago with a note from the orphanage . . . okay . . . from a welfare agency. The note was in fact in a sealed envelope, and the boy, who was at that time about ten or twelve, and wasn't yet Mr. Gab's assistant, hadn't an inkling of its contents. Nor did he care much. He was not then a very caring child. He had seen too many empty rooms filled with kids of a similar disownership of themselves as his. Mr. Gab looked at the envelope handed him and shook his head warily as if he could read through cream. He then conferred upon the child a similar gesture, as if he saw through him too—clear to his mean streak. Here at last, hey! he said. The kid had a pudgy bloataboy body. Half of him, the right half, though undersized, seemed okay; the leftover half, however, had been severely shortchanged. The head sloped more steeply than heads should, a shoulder sank, an arm was stunted, its squat hand had somewhere lost a finger, and the leg was missing most of its length. The child had consequently a kind of permanent lean which a thick woodsoled shoe did little to correct, though the fellow tried to compensate by pushing off with his short leg, and thereby tipping himself up to proper verticality. The result was that he bobbed about as though fish were biting, nibbling at bait hung deeply beneath whatever he was walking on—a sidewalk, lawn, shop floor, cindered ground.

The boy knew that he was being handed over. The lady with him had explained matters, then explained them again, and made silly claims that didn't fit what little he knew of his own cloudy history. This grouchy stranger, he was told, had been his mother's husband, but was not known to be his father. The identity of his father remained a mystery. The child's mother had not done a Dickens on him and died of childbedding, but had come down unto death with influenza when he was allegedly a month or two past the curse of his birth. Cared for by the state from then on. He went from wet nurse to children's home to foster parents back to children's home again. No one liked him. He was too ugly.

He appeared to be stupid, and most of what he did was awkward, to say the least. In close quarters he tended to carom. He learned that when you failed to understand something you were blamed for that, but that alone, thus escaping consequences. People would say: well, he didn't know any better; he's not all there. Mr. Gab called him "you stupid kid" from the very beginning, and never called him anything else, though he lived with Mr. Gab above the first shop (on the street of his envious enemy) like one of the family if there'd been a family, and in time ceased resenting the name, which was often sweetly drawled—hey-u-stew-pid—and eventually shortened to u-Stu, a result that u-Stu quite liked, though Mr. Gab pointed out that now his name was as out of kilter as u-Stu's stature and his gait.

In point of fact, there was really nothing the matter with his mind which had somehow scuttled to the right side of his brain when his deformities were being assembled, so when his head got lopped a little on the left, his intelligence remained intact, hiding safely a bit behind and a bit above his bright right eye, and looking out of it with the force of two whole hemispheres.

For his entire life, not omitting now, Mr. Gab's assistant had watched gazes turn aside, watched notice be withdrawn, watched courses alter in order to avoid the embarrassments of his body: the bob and weave of it, its stunted members, the missing finger, the

droopy eye, the little irreducible slobber that robbed his mouth of
dignity, and the vacancy of a look that lacked muscle; who wanted
to encounter them? face nature's mistake? pretend you were talking to a normal citizen instead of a mid-sized dope-dwarf? Kids
his own age were curious, of course, and would stare holes in his
shirt. Neither being ignored nor peered at were tolerable states.

U-Stu's speech had a slight slur to it on account of some crook-
edness at the left corner of his mouth and a bit of permanently
fat lip in the same place. Simpleminded, most thought him, if
they listened at all. He'd talk anyway. Ultimately he took pleasure
in producing discomfiture and awkwardness, embarrassment and
shame. It suited Mr. Gab to keep him around for the same reason.
And he liked the name "Stu" because he felt himself to be a loose
assemblage of parts that commingled in his consciousness like
diced carrots and chunks of meat in juice. A few, like Boombox,
the Russian furrier, would address him directly, but blarefully, so
they still wouldn't see him through the dust-up of their own noise.
After all, such folk had business with his master, as the assistant
was sure they thought Mr. Gab was. He, on the other hand, was
ugh! He was Igor. Who deals in eyes of newts. And brains of bats.
Stirs into pots the kidneys of cats.

At first the silence was stifling, Mr. Gab's directions terse, his
look stony; and his assistant was certain that this indifference
was an act to cover revulsion; but after a while Mr. Gab began to
see u-Stu's crooked mouth, saw the little bubbles of spit, heard
the slur, grew accustomed to the rockabyebounce, and accepted
u-Stew's absent finger as well as the nail that was never there,
not hammered off as had been, u-Stu believed, David Smith's.
Then, after further familiarity was achieved, the assistant became

invisible again, the way one's wife fades, or actual son recedes, seen without being seen, heard without hearing, felt without caring, even, when it was the wife, for her plump breast. This was okay in most minds because it was based upon acceptance. Like getting used to handling worms or disemboweling birds. Yet it wasn't okay to the assistant because the assistant felt he was in fact disgusting—quite—so that if you were to truly take him in you should continue to feel revulsion too: he hadn't been brought into the world merely to wobble, but to repel people by these means, and at the same time to remind them of their luck in having sailed all—not just portions—of themselves down the birth canal.

The first shop, though it had a finer front, had been much smaller, and the assistant, while yet too young to be much help, had to assist in sleeping, since Mr. Gab talked in his sleep, and snored like a roaring lion, and turned and tossed like a wave, and occasionally punched the air as if he were a boxer in training, so the boy had to shake Mr. Gab awake sometimes, or lie in the dark nearby, listen to his mumbles, and participate in the nightmares, which was one reason why the assistant said, in his own undertone, he has the gift, Gab has, the gift. The boy asked Mr. Gab if he had enemies he was defeating when he poked his pillow or flailed away at the night air, and this question helped Mr. Gab realize that their present sleeping arrangement wasn't salubrious. After some finagling, he found the space where they did their little business now, and there they established themselves, after making several trips (it was but a few blocks) to trundle cartons of prints on a handcart when it wasn't raining and if the coast was clear.

After the move, he slept in a sleeping bag at the back of the second store, at the border of Mr. Gab's quarters but not over the line, where a dog might have lain had they had one—art and dogs don't mix, Mr. Gab said (Mr. Gab squeezed his nose with a set of fingers whenever Mr. Wegman's name was mentioned), and the best kind of cat is ceramic. I shall be your guard ghoul, the assistant said, a remark which Mr. Gab didn't find funny, though he rarely laughed at anything; occasionally upon seeing a photo he would hoot; however u-Stu wasn't sure whether his hoot was one of amusement or merely derisory, so perhaps he was never amused, though he from time to time made such a noise.

U-Stu had facial hair on half of his face, and Mr. Gab, to u-Stu's surprise, would shave him. Half a beard is not better than none, he said. Because he believed for a long time that his assistant was too stupid to shave himself, certainly too stupid to live alone, take care of himself in any ordinary way, he shaved his adolescent; initially even cut the boy's meat; carefully combed his ungainly hair; pressed his few clothes with an iron he had heated on the stove; and tried to cook things that were easy to eat. Gradually, Mr. Gab realized that although his stupid assistant chewed crookedly, his chew was nevertheless quite effective, and despite the fact that the boy was short-armed (Mr. Gab always winced at this formulation), he could manage a knife and fork (he needed to lower one shoulder to pull his short arm to the front), and with his one good eye working overtime (as Mr. Gab probably thought), he could read, shave, look at pictures, and, with a control over his body that grew better and better, he could perform his characteristic bob-and-wobble much more smoothly. U-Stu soon learned to repair fixtures, sweep the store, replace photographs in their plastic sleeves, and return them properly to their cardboard files. Oh, yes . . . and ask visitors: muh I hulp you, shur?

Mr. Gab began by speaking to the boy (he had not yet received his promotion to stupid assistant) slowly, and a little loudly, as though the boy might be a bit deaf in addition, talking to him often, contrary to his habitual silence, plainly believing that such treatment was necessary for the lad's mental health, which it no doubt was, although no number of words could make him into a lad, because lads were always strapping. This loquacity, night and day it seemed, led the boy to believe that Mr. Gab gabbed, was a gabber by nature, so he would say to himself, almost audibly, he has the gift, he does, does Gab, as he went about his work which was each week more and more advanced in difficulty. He could see Mr. Gab's face wrestling with the question: what shall I say today—good heavens—and on what subject? Mr. Gab's slow considered ramblings were to be the boy's schooling. Perhaps, today, he'd want to learn about bikes. I want to know about my mother, the boy asked. Mr. Gab began to answer, almost easily, taken by surprise: she resembled one of Stieglitz's portraits of O'Keeffe. She was beautiful beyond the bearing of one's eyes. Such hands. Stieglitz always photographed her hands. Her hands. As if he had awakened, Mr. Gab broke off in great embarrassment, his face flushed and its expression soon shunted to a sidetrack.

Before that blunder—I want to know about my mother—Mr. Gab had spoken to the boy of many things. He always spoke as if chewing slowly, in the greatest seriousness, early on about school and how he, Mr. Gab, had struggled through classes here after his family had come to the States, having an unpronounceable name, and not knowing the language; about his sisters and aunts, mothers and grans, never of men, because men, he said, scorned him for his interests, and broke his Brownie; he talked about the time when he had begun work in a drugstore, learning from books how to develop his prints; about, after he had gotten canned for stealing chemicals, the days he had sold door to door—brushes, pots and pans—enduring the embarrassments of repeated rejection, once even attacked, his face mopped by his own mop by an irate customer (the sunny side of things was left dark); until, eventually, having marched through many of the miseries of his life (though leaving serious gaps, even his auditor was aware of that), the subject he chose to address was more and more often the photograph, its grays and its glories.

Beneath—are u listening, u-stew-pid-u?—beneath the colored world, like the hidden workings of the body, where the bones move, where the nerves signal, where the veins send the blood flooding—where the signaling nerves especially form their net—lie all the grays, the grays that go from the pale gray of bleached linen, through all the shades of darkening, deepening graying grays that lie between, to the grays that are nearly soot black, without light: the gray beneath blue, the gray beneath green, yes, I should also say the gray beneath gray; and these grays are held in that gray continuum between gray extremes like books between bookends. U-Stu, pay attention, this is the real world, the gray gradation world, and the camera, the way an X-ray works, reveals it to our eye, for otherwise we'd have never seen it; we'd have never known it was there, under everything, beauty's real face beneath the powders and the rouges and the crèmes. Color is cosmetic. Good for hothouse blooms. Great for cards of greeting. Listen, u-Stew, color is consternation. Color is a lure. Color is candy. It makes sensuality easy. It leads us astray. Color is oratory in the service of the wrong religion. Color makes the camera into a paintbrush. Color is camouflage. That was Mr. Gab's catechism: what color was. Color was not what we see with the mind. Like an overpowering perfume, color was vulgar. Like an overpowering perfume, color lulled and dulled the senses. Like an overpowering perfume, color was only worn by whores.

Grass cannot be captured in color. It becomes confused. Trees neither. Except for fall foliage seen from a plane. But in gray: the snowy rooftop, the winter tree, whole mountains of rock, the froth of a fast stream can be caught, spew and striation, twig and stick, footprint on a snowy walk, the wander of a wrinkle across the face . . . oh . . . and Mr. Gab would interrupt his rhapsody to go to a cabinet and take out one of Sudek's panoramic prints: see how the fence comes toward the camera, as eager as a puppy, and how the reflection of the building in the river, in doubling the image, creates a new one, born of both body and soul, and how the reflection of the dome of the central building on the other side of the water has been placed at precisely the fence's closest approach, and how, far away, the castle, in a gray made of mist, layers the space, and melts into a sky that's thirty shades of gradual . . . see that? see how? How the upsidedown world is darker, naturally more fluid . . . ah . . . and breaking off again, Mr. Gab withdrew from a cardboard carton called PRAGUE a photograph so lovely that even the stupid not-yet assistant drew in his breath as though struck in the stomach (though he'd been poked in the eye); and Mr. Gab observed this and said ah! you do see, you do . . . well . . . bless you. The stupid not-yet assistant was at that moment so happy he trembled at the edge of a tear.

Hyde Park Corner. This picture, let's pretend, is one of the Park speakers, Mr. Gab said, pointing at a hanger. What does it tell us? Ah, the haranguers, they stand there, gather small crowds, and declaim about good and evil. They promise salvation to their true believers. Mr. Gab went to the wall and took down his Alvin Langdon Coburn. Held it out for u-Stu's inspection like a tray of cookies or anything not likely to remain in one place for long. There's a dark circle protecting the tree and allowing its roots to breathe. And the dark trunk, too, rising to enter its leaves. In a misted distance—see?—a horse-drawn bus, looking like a stage-coach, labeled A1, with its driver and several passengers. In short: we see this part of the world immersed in this part of the world's weather. But we also see someone seeing it, someone having a feeling about the scene, not merely in a private mood, but respond-ing to just this . . . this . . . and taking in the two trees and the streetlamp's standard, the carriage, and in particular the faint diag-onals of the curb, these sweet formal relations, each submerged in a gray-white realm that's at the same time someone's—Alvin Lang-don Coburn's—head. And the photo tells us there are no lines in nature. Edge blends with edge until edgelessness is obtained. The spokes of the wheels are little streaks of darker air into which the white horse is about to proceed. But, my boy, Alvin Langdon Coburn's head is not now his head, not while we see what he is seeing, for he is at this moment a stand-in for God. A god who is saying: let there be this sacred light.

Mr. Gab would lower his nose as if sniffing up odors from the image. If the great gray world holds sway beneath the garish commerce of color, so the perception of its beauty hides from the ordinary eye, for what does the ordinary eye do but ignore nearly everything it sees, seeking its own weak satisfactions?

Such shadows as are here, for instance, in these photographs, are not illusions to be simply sniffed at. Where are the real illusions, u-Stu? They dwell in the eyes and hearts and minds of those in the carriage—yes—greedy to be going to their girl, to their bank, to their business. Do they observe the street as a gray stream—no—they are off to play Monopoly. Scorn overcame Mr. Gab, whose voice sounded hoarse. They have mayhem on their minds.

Finally, Mr. Gab had got round to the War. Mr. Gab's tour of duty—he was a corporal of supply—took him to Europe. In London he learned about the Bostonian Coburn. In Paris, he discovered Atget. In Berlin, he ran into Sander. In Prague . . . in Prague . . . Mr. Gab was mustered out in Europe and spent a vaguely substantial number of years in the continent's major cities. More, Mr. Gab did not divulge; but he did speak at length of Italy's glories, of Spain's too, of Paris and Prague . . . He took u-Stu on slow walks across the Charles Bridge, describing the statuary that lined it, elegizing the decaying, dusty, untouched city, mounting the endless flight of steps to the Hradčany Castle, taking in both the Černín and the Royal Gardens. They strolled the Malá Strana, the Smetana Quai, as well as those renamed for Janáček and Masaryk, had coffee in Wenceslas Square, visited St. Vitus Cathedral, and eventually crossed the Moldau bridges one word after another, each serving for two: a meaning in memory, an image in imagination.

When Mr. Gab returned to the States, he enrolled in New York's City College on the GI Bill, while working, to make ends meet, serially at several photography shops and even serving, during a difficult period, as a guard in a gallery. But now the gaps in this history of his grew ever greater, became more noticeable than before; details, which had been pointlessly plentiful about Prague buildings and Italian traffic, disappeared into vague generalities like figures in a Sudek or a Coburn fog, and most questions, when rarely asked, were curtly rebuffed.

But Mr. Gab did regale his pupil with an account of his trip in a rented truck to their present city, and u-Stu was given to understand, though the story did not dwell on cargo or luggage, that his cartons came with him, and, in Johnstown, of all places, were threatened by a downpour which forced him for a time to heave to and wait the water out, so sudden and severe it was, and how nervous he had become watching the Conemaugh River rise. The journey had all the qualities of uprootedness and flight, especially since Mr. Gab's account did suggest that he'd left New York with his college education incomplete, and a bitterness about everything academic, about study and teaching and scholarship, which only hinted at why he had abandoned his archival enterprise.

For in Europe, surrounded at first by fierce fighting, bombs made of blood and destruction, Mr. Gab had formed the intention of saving reality from its own demise by collecting and caring for the world in photographic form. There were footsteps he was following, or so he found out. Like Alvin Langdon Coburn he had been given a camera by an uncle. Like Alvin Langdon Coburn, he had crossed the sea to London. Like Coburn, he would tour Europe, though not with his mother, who was as missing from his life, he insisted, as that of u-Stu. In the footsteps of Mr. Coburn, possibly, but not in the same shoes, for he, Mr. Gab, hadn't had a father who made shirts, and died leaving his mother money. He hadn't found friends like Stieglitz and Steichen with whom he could converse, or exchange warm admirations. He sat in metal storerooms surrounded by supplies, and learned a few things about stocks and stores and shipment.

Unlike Johnstown's fabled inundation, but rather drip by drip, words entered Stu's ear, and filled his mind to flood stage finally; not that he needed to be instructed about the grimness of the world, or about what passed for human relations. Some of the words weren't nice ones. Mr. Gab kept his tongue clean, but now and then a word like "whore" would slip out. You will not know that word I just used, Mr. Gab said hopefully. Stu thought he meant the word "catechism" which indeed he didn't understand, but Mr. Gab meant "whore," which he proceeded to define as anyone who accepts money in return for giving pleasure . . . pleasures that were mostly illusory. There were shysters for mismanipulating the law. There were charlatans for the manufacture of falsehood. Quacks for promising health. Sharks for making illegal loans. Mountebanks to prey upon the foolishly greedy. Apparently, humanity was made of little else.

But there were, Mr. Gab assured u-Stu, the Saviors too. They bore witness. They documented. Eugène Atget had rescued Paris. Josef Sudek had done the same for Prague. August Sander had catalogued the workers of his country, as Salgado has tried to do for workers worldwide. Karl Blossfeldt, like Audubon, had preserved the wild plants. Bellocq had treated his Orleans whores with dignity. And how about Evelyn Cameron, who had saved Montana with her single shutter? Or Russell Lee, who photographed the Great Flood of '37 as well as the Negro slums of Chicago? Or consider the work of a studio like that of Southworth & Hawes, whose images of Niagara Falls were among the more amazing ever made. He, Mr. Gab, had but one of their daguerreotypes. And

Mr. Gab then disappeared into his room behind the rug to produce in a moment a group portrait taken in the Southworth & Hawes studio of the girls of Boston's Emerson School, and through the envelope, which Mr. Gab did not remove, u-Stu saw the identically and centrally parted hair of thirty-one girls and the white lace collars of twenty-eight.

Mr. Gab went on to extol the work of Martín Chambi whom he had available only in a catalogue produced for an exhibit at the Smithsonian (so there were an unknown number of books behind the rug, perhaps in that closet, perhaps in a shelf above the boxes). Although Mr. Gab was capable of staring at a photograph uninterruptedly for many minutes, he had the annoying habit of flipping rapidly through books—dizzying u-Stu's good eye, which could only receive the briefest tantalizations of an apparently magical place, set among the most remote mountains, Mr. Gab called "Macchoo Peechoo"—until he reached the photo he was searching for. There, there, Mr. Gab said, pointing: a young man in a most proper black suit and bow tie was standing beside a giant of a man clad in tatters, a cloth hat like an aviator's helmet in the giant's hand, a serape draped over the giant's shoulders—and—and around the small man's, a huge arm finished by fingers in the form of a great claw. The little fellow is the photographer's assistant, Mr. Gab informed his. Who, u-Stu saw, was gazing up at the face of the giant with respectful incomprehension. But one was mostly drawn to the giant's patched and tattered shirt and baggy trousers, to the barely thonged feet that had borne much, and finally to the huge stolid countenance, formed from endurance. Shots of shirts were rare.

Not all of Mr. Gab's enthusiasms were trotted out at once. They were instead produced at intervals involving months, but each was offered as if no finer effort, no better example, could be imagined. Yet u-Stu came to believe that the artist Mr. Gab called P.H. (Ralph Waldo was the other Emerson) was dearest to him, after one afternoon being shown (again from the cache in the kitchen) a simple country and seaside scene: a crude sailboat manned by three, and oared as well, under way upon a marshy watercourse, the rowboat's big sail, with its soft vertical curves and pale patches, in the center of the photograph, and to the left where the reeds began, though at the distance where there had to be land, a simple farmhouse resting in a clump of low trees, a trail of chimney smoke the sole sign of occupancy.

Every photograph by its very nature is frozen in its moment, Mr. Gab said, but not every photograph portrays stillness as this one does. The sail is taut, smoke is streaming away toward the margins of the picture's world, and the postures of the oarsmen suggest they are at work; but there is little wake, the surface of the water is scarcely ruffled, not a reed is bent, the trees are without leaves, and the faint form of a small windmill shows the four blades to be unmoving. Nevertheless, it is the lucency of the low light, the line of the sail's spar, which meets on one side a shoreline, on the other a small inlet-edging fence, which holds the image still; it is the way the mast runs on into its reflection, and the long low haze stretched across the entire background at the point where earth and air blend, where the soft slightly clouded sky rises; it is the relation of all these dear tones to one another that creates a serenity which seeks the sublime, because it is so complete. Complete, u-Stu, complete.

Look. In this work, the house, the boat, the rowing men have no more weight than the boat's small shadow on the pale white water, or the bare trees and stiff reeds, because all are simply there together. Equals added to equals yields equals. One can speak one's self insensible about the salubrious and necessary unity of humankind with nature, u-Stu-u, yet rarely enable your listener to see how the solitude, the independent being, of every actual thing is celebrated by the community created through such a composition. The light, coming from the right, illuminates the sides of the house in such a way it seems blocky and dimensional, as the boat does; however the sail, the sky, the water, and their realms, though made of a register of curves, are otherwise, and flat as a drawn shade.

At exam time, Mr. Gab would cry out: what have I been saying? What have I said? Every player is made a star when the team succeeds as a team, Stu promptly answered, whereupon Gab lost his mister and his temper at the same time, complaining of the comparison, and refusing (as he regularly did after exams) to speak to his help, who had been relegated a rank.

In this bumpy way his education proceeded, but it had an odd consequence. Stu's experience was made by someone else's words; his memory, formerly poor, was reluctant to linger on an early life that had been a bitter bit of bad business; so he adopted another person's past, and he saw what that other person said he'd seen. He kept house in another's household, and adopted points of view he never properly arrived at. Who could blame him? Would not each of us have done the same? Why not change residences when the skin that confined you was a bitter bit of bad business?

His fingers licked him through the pages of Mr. Gab's dozen or so books of photography, mostly limited to Mr. Gab's narrow enthusiasms; however there was a recent Salgado which rendered the stupid assistant weak in one knee, though he'd been told messages were for Western Union not for artistry. Such marvelous messages though—these Salgados proved to be.

Stu started stepping out—a phrase to be used advisedly. He obtained a card at the local library, shoplifted a few fruits, and sat in sun-filled vacant lots, deep in the weeds, happy with the heavy air. In the library he began examining the work of the two painters Mr. Gab admitted to his pantheon: Canaletto and Vermeer. In the shops he slyly added to his meager stock by stealing small fruits: figs, limes, kiwis, cherries, berries. In the weeds, feasting on his loot, Stu would imagine he lived in an alternative world, and he'd scale everything around him down, pretend he was hunkered in a photograph, where woods were black and white and pocket-sized. In the library he was eyed with suspicion, and Stu felt certain that only the librarians' fear of a lawsuit let them lend what they did lend to him. In the open-air market, they knew he was a thief past all convicting, yet they hadn't caught him yet, it was a public space, and they begged for the crowds that concealed his snitches with distracting blouses and billowy shirts. Shirts ought to receive some celebration. But he was soon run out of his weedy lot by a puritanical cop.

It was about then that Mr. Gab expelled Stu from his sleeping post, and he formally became Mr. Gab's assistant. Mr. Gab had never paid his assistant a wage, not a dime, nor had he bought him anything but secondhands; even the comb he let Stu have had been run through many an unknown head of hair. Mr. Gab was frugal, probably because he had to be, so their diet was repeatedly rice and beans. He moved his assistant into public space and a rooming house run formerly by Chinese, or so the Chinese who ran it now maintained. It had brown paper walls, a cot and a chair, a john down the hall, a window without a blind, a throw rug which—to expose a splintery floor—would wad itself into a wad while you watched. You can keep this job if you want it, Mr. Gab announced, and I'll pay you the minimum, but now you must take your meals and your sleep and your preferences out of here—out—and manage them yourself.

At first the new assistant was wholly dismayed. What had he done, he finally asked. You've grown up, was Mr. Gab's unhelpful answer. You go away, god knows where, and look at god knows what, color and comic and bosom books. Actually, it was as if Mr. Gab were clairvoyant and knew that his assistant had come on a book by Ernst Haas called *Color Photography* in the same local library where he had obtained his volume of Vermeer, and been subsequently ravished, just as Mr. Gab feared. But if Vermeer was photographic, Haas was painterly. Stu was sure Mr. Gab would say, very pretty, very nice, nevertheless not reliable. The object is lost, can you find it? torn posters and trash—that's the world? and how far into a flower can you fall without sneezing?

Reality is made of nouns not adjectives, Gab shouted at the wall where his nouns sat in their sacred gray desuetude.

The stupid assistant suspected that Gab had listened to what was going on in his stupid assistant's head, and heard objections and reservations and hesitations and challenging questions, both personal and educational, particular and theoretic. Then said to himself: this Stu should go elsewhere with these thoughts. Ernst Haas had photographed some flowers through a screen, making romantic a symbol of romance; through an open oval in a dark room, like the inside of a camera, he had rendered a bright café scene so its reality seemed an illustration in a magazine; he'd snapped a cemetery bust at night as if the head had leached the film and raised a ghost; and Mr. Gab would certainly have denounced these startling images as mere monkey business, had he seen them: the cropped stained glass from Cluny, too, glass heads looking like stone ones in a dismal darkness, a regiment of roofs in Reading, the silhouettes of fishermen fishing in a line along the Seine; but the assistant could remember now, Sudek's magical garden pictures, with their multiple exposures, dramatic angles, and cannily positioned sculptures, and he found himself thinking that it wasn't fair, it wasn't fair to be so puritanical, to live with a passel of prejudices, even if each enthusiasm that was denied inspection intensified the believer's devotion.

Mr. Gab's exiled assistant came to work just before ten each morning like a clerk or a secretary, but if mum were Mr. Gab's one word, he would not utter it. Between them, throughout the day, a silence lay like a shawl on a shivering shoulder. In the flophouse where the assistant lived now there was plenty of jabbering, but he couldn't bear the cacophony let alone find any sense to it. In his room the world had grown grossly small. The window framed an alley full of litter. The brown paper wall bore tears and peels and spots made by drops of who knew what—expectorations past. Yet in such stains lay lakes full of reeds and floating ducks and low loglike boats. Instead of the sort of wall which furnished a rich many-toned background for so many of Atget's documents: instead of the cobbled courtyard that the remainder of the photo surrounded, shadowed, or stood on; instead of gleaming disks of stone with their dark encircling lines; instead of the leaves of trees in a flutter about a field of figures; there might be—instead—a single pock, the bottom of it whitish with plaster: that's what he had to look at, descend into, dream about, not a rhyming slope of rock, its layers threaded and inked; not the veins of a single leaf like roads on a map, or a tear of paper resembling a tantrum—his rips didn't even resemble rips—or faded petals that have fallen like a scatter of gravel at the foot of a vase; not an errant flash of light centered and set like a jewel: instead he had a crack, just a crack in a window, a cob's web, or that of a spider, dewdrop clinging like an injured climber to its only rope of escape; not a clay flowerpot given the attention due a landscape; not a scratch on the hood of some vehicle, not directional signs painted on the pavement, instructions worn by the wheels of countless cars; not a black eye enlarged to resemble the purple of a blown rose. These were the images in his borrowed books, the material of his mind's eye, the Lilliputian world grown taller than that tattered Peruvian giant.

Even Mr. Gab's heroes, even Josef Koudelka, had devoted at least one frame, one moment of his art, to a slice of cheese, bite of chocolate, cut of fruit that had been strewn upon the rumpled front page of the *International Herald Tribune* to serve as a still life's prey—a spoiled fish—a party of empty bottles. That's okay, he heard Mr. Gab say, because such a shot records a lunch, a day, a time in the world. I want that, u-Stew-u, I want the world, I don't want to see through the picture to the world, the picture is not a porthole. I want the world *in*—you see—*in*—the photo. What a world it is after all! Am I a fool? Not to know what the world is; what it comes to? It is misery begetting misery, you bet; it's meanness making meanness, sure; it's calamity; it's cruelty and greed and indifference; I know what it is, you know what it is, we know how it is, if not why—yet I want the world as it is rescued by the camera and redeemed. U-Stu-u. Paris is . . . was . . . noisy, full of Frenchmen, full of pain, full of waste, of *ordinaire;* but Atget's Paris, Sudek's Vienna, Coburn's London, even Bellocq's poor whores (I never showed you those ladies, you found out and stared at that filth yourself), Salgado's exploited, emaciated workers are lifted up and given grace when touched by such lenses; and every injustice that the world has done to the world is forgiven—*in* the photograph—in . . . in . . . where even horse-plopped cobbles come clean.

But what about, the stupid assistant began, what about Haas's *Moreno,* a photo full of steps, the dark woman walking toward a set of them, her black back to us, the red and white chickens standing on stairs . . . they'd all look better gray, he was sure Mr. Gab would say. Or the lane of leaves, that lane of trees beside the Po, or the Norwegian fjord photo, Mr. Gab, the faint central hill like a slow cloud in the water, what of them? what of them? So what, he replied on behalf of Mr. Gab who was somewhat cross, when one can have Steichen's or Coburn's streetlamps, spend an evening full of mist and mellow glisten, bite into an avenue that's slick as freshly buttered toast.

But Mr. Gab, do you dream that Sebastião Salgado wants anyone forgiven: are the starving to be forgiven for starving? are those scenes from Dante's hell (the hell you told me about) redeemed because the miners of Serra Pelado's gold—worn, gaunt, covered with mud and rags—are, through his art, delivered from their servitude and given to Dante? am I to be forgiven for my deformities? my rocking, as if I were indeed the baby in the tree, is it okay? If cleverly clicked? o yes, Mr. Gab, you're right, I did peek at the fancy girls, and I was toasted by one in striped tights and a bonnet of hair who raised to me a shot glass of Raleigh Rye, but so many of them, sad to say, had scratched-out faces, only their bare bodies were allowed to be; while Bellocq too, by the book, was said to be misshapen . . . not quite like me; but he didn't dwarf himself, I bet, and behaved himself with the girls because he understood his burden; just as it's true, I didn't do me, someone else, perhaps yourself, Mr. Gab, did, but I was not a party to the filthy act that made me, or to the horror of having insufficient room in an unsuitable womb; I didn't mangle myself, suck the nail from my own thumbs, shorten my stature, wound my mouth; yet daily I inflict them on others; I wobble along on my sidewalk and all those passerby-eyes flee the scene like shoo'd flies.

Should Salgado—u-Stu-u—Mr. Gab rejoins, should he then forget his skills and just picture pain picture human evil picture human greed picture desolation picture people other people have allowed to become battered trees made of nothing but barren twigs, picture many murdered, meadows murdered, hills heaved into the sea, sand on open eyes, the grim and grisly so that it approaches us the way you do on the street, so we will look away, even cross against traffic in order to avoid any encounter, because the overseers of those miners don't care a wink about them, never let their true condition sneak under a lid, form a thought, suggest an emotion—unless there is a fainter, a sluggard, a runaway—no more than the other workers, who sweat while smelting the ore, give the miners time, since no one thinks of the smelters either, the glare oiling their bare chests, no more than those who stamp some country's cruel insignia on the country's coins or dolly a load of now gold bars into a vault think of anyone else but their own beers and bad bread and breeding habits.

But Mr. Gab, sir, when I look at that huge hole in the earth, and at those innumerable heads and shoulders heavy with sacks of dirt like a long line of ants on paths encircling the pit that their own work has bit into the ground, just as you and Dante said hell's rungs do; against my will, I see something sublime, like the force of a great wind or quake or volcanic eruption.

Yes, u-Stu-u, because u have a book in hand, u aren't in the picture, u are thousands of miles from Brazil, u wear clean underclothes (I hope and suppose), but can u now reflect on your own sad condition, as molested by fate as they've been, those poor workers, because who of us at the end of the day goes home happy? do you go to your room and laugh at its luxury? You saw—it's less than the whores of New Orleans; don't you still see trash from your window, and stains on the wall and through a pock or two if you peer into them won't you encounter again that unearthed creature covered with a silkskin of mud, a man who a moment before the photo was in a long climbing line up the laddered side of one of hell's excavations, and won't you continue to find behind him, and free of misery's place in the picture, another man in shorts and a clean shirt studying a clipboard? and what are we to think of him, then? and what are we to think of ourselves, and the little gold rings we wear when we marry?

Starve the world to amuse a few. That's man's motto. That sums it. But now Mr. Gab's assistant didn't know—couldn't tell—who was supposed to have said it.

Alvin Langdon Coburn came up. After a day of silence, his name seemed a train of words. Alvin Langdon Coburn. As if Mr. Gab had really been talking with his assistant as his assistant had imagined. He was holding a paperback copy of Coburn's autobiography. With a finger to mark his place, Mr. Gab gave it a brief wave. I shall read u-Stu what Alvin Langdon Coburn wrote about those who do dirty tricks with their negatives. Mr. Gab's voice assumed a surprising falsetto. His assistant had never heard him read aloud out of a book before this moment—a moment that had therefore become important. "Now I must confess I do not approve of gum prints which look like chalk drawings . . ." Mr. Gab interrupted himself. P.H. was equally fierce and unforgiving, he said. ". . . nor of drawing on negatives, nor of glycerin-restrained platinotypes in imitation of wash-drawings as produced by . . ." You won't have heard of this guy, Mr. Gab added, letting disdain into his voice like a cat into a kitchen. ". . . Joseph T. Keiley, a well-known . . ." Well known, well known—not anymore known than a silent-film star. ". . . American photographer and a friend of Alfred Stieglitz." They all claimed to be that—a good, a fond friend of Stieglitz. Let's skip. ". . . I do not deny that Demachy, Eugene, Keiley and others . . ." Heard of them, have we? Are they in the history books? are they? take a look. ". . . and others produced exciting prints by these manipulated techniques . . ." Bah bah bah-dee-bah. Here—"This I rarely did, for I am myself a devotee of pure photography, which is unapproachable in its own field." Unapproachable, you hear? Pure. That's the ticket. That's the word. Unapproachable. He snapped the book shut and sank back into a silence which said something had been proved, something once for all had been decided.

3 FROM THE STOOL
OF THE STUPID ASSISTANT

During the long empty hours between customers, Mr. Gab sat at his desk at the front of the shop and drowsed or thumbed through the same old stack of photographic magazines he'd had for as long as his assistant had been near enough his paging thumb to observe what the pages concerned. Most of the time Mr. Gab sat there with the immobility of a mystic. Occasionally, he'd leaf through a book, often an exhibition catalogue or a volume containing a description of the contents of a great archive, such as Rüdiger Klessmann's book on the Kaiser Friedrich Museum, over whose pages and pictures he'd slowly shake his head. Once in a while, his back still turned to his assistant, he'd raise a beckoning hand, and u-Stu would leave his stool in the rear where he was awkwardly perched while trying to read books slender enough to be steadily held by one hand, and come forward to Mr. Gab's side where he was always expected to verify, by studying the picture, Mr. Gab's poor opinion of the masterpiece.

The beckoning finger would then descend to point at a portion of a painting; whereupon Mr. Gab would say: look at that! is that a tree? that tangle of twigs? The finger would poke the plate, perhaps twice. It's an architect's tree! His voice would register three floors of disgust. It's a rendering, a sign for a tree; the man might as well have written "tree" there. Over here, by "barn," see "bush." And the fellow is said to be painting nature. (It might have been a Corot or Courbet.) See? is that a tree? is that a tree or a sign, that squiggle? I can read it's a tree, but I don't see a tree. It is not a tree anyone actually sees. Twigs don't attach to branches that way; branches don't grow from trunks that way; you call those smudges shade? To a simp they might suggest shade. To a simpleton. There's not a whiff of cooling air.

The finger would retire long enough for the assistant to make out an image and the book would snap shut like a slammed door: I am leaving forever, the slam said. A fake crack in a fake rock from which a fake weed fakes its own growth, Mr. Gab might angrily conclude: we are supposed to admire that? (then after an appropriate pause, he'd slowly, softly add, in a tone signifying his reluctant surrender to grief) that . . . ? that is artistry?

The assistant spent many hours every day like a dunce uncomfortably perched on a stool he had difficulty getting the seat of his pants settled on because it stood nearly as high as he did and furthermore because the assistant was trying to bring a book up with him held in his inadequate hand. Once up, he was reluctant to climb down if it meant he'd soon have to climb up again. So he perched, not perhaps for as long as Mr. Gab sat, but a significant interval on the morning's clock: with a view of the shop and its three rows of trestle tables topped with their load of flap-closed cardboard boxes adorned by beanbags as if they were the puffy peaks of stocking caps. The tables appeared to be nearly solid blocks since so many containers were stored underneath each one where with your foot you'd have to coax a carton to slide sufficiently far into the aisle to undo its flaps and finger through its contents. ROME I.

But Mr. Gab or his stupid assistant, whoever was closest, would rise or fall and wordlessly rush or rock to the box and lift it quickly or awkwardly up on top of the ones on the table, deflapping it smartly or ineptly and folding the four lids back before returning to chair or stool and the status quo. Mr. Weasel would occasionally come in and always want a box buried beneath a table in the most remote and awkward spot; but at least he'd pick on a container up front where Mr. Gab would have to say good day in customary greeting and then push cartons about like some laborer in a warehouse to get at PARIS NIGHTLIFE or some similar delicacy that Mr. Weasel always favored.

Customers who came to the shop more than once got names chosen to reflect their manner of looking or the shapes they assumed while browsing, especially as they were observed from the stool of the stupid assistant. Weasel slunk. He was thin and short and had a head that was all nose. His eyes were dotted and his hair was dark and painted on. The first few times Weasel came to the store the stupid assistant watched him carefully because his moves produced only suspicion. After a number of visits, however, the Weasel simply became the Weasel, and the stupid assistant shut down his scrutiny, or rather, turned it onto his page.

Part of the stupid assistant's education was to study books which Mr. Gab assigned, not that they ever discussed them, and it would have been difficult for Mr. Gab to know, ever, if his assistant was dutiful or not, or was reading filth and other kinds of popular fiction. When he thought he had caught the Weasel, u-Stu was wading through Walter Pater. And Pater held a lot of water. U-Stu was wading waist-deep. Mr. Gab had not recommended any of what the assistant later found out were Pater's principal works, but had sent him to a collection of essays called *Appreciations* where u-Stu learned of Dryden's imperfect mastery of the relative pronoun, a failing he misunderstood as familial. All Mr. Gab asked of his assistant regarding the works he assigned (beside the implicit expectation that it would be u-Stu who would withdraw them from the library, now he had his own card) was that u-Stu was expected to select a sentence he favored from some part of the text to repeat to Mr. Gab at a suitable moment; after which Mr. Gab would grunt and nod, simultaneously signifying approval and termination.

It was not clear to u-Stu whether there were designs behind Mr. Gab's selections, but *Appreciations* contained essays on writers whose names were, to u-Stu, at best vaguely familiar, or on plays by Shakespeare like *Measure for Measure* for which slight acquaintance was also the applicable description. The first essay was called "Style" and u-Stu supposed it was Mr. Gab's target, but, once more, the piece was larded with references that, from u-Stu, drew a blank response of recognition. U-Stu resented having his ignorance so repeatedly demonstrated. To Mr. Gab he said: "this book is dedicated to the memory of my brother William Thompson Pater who quitted a useful and happy life Sunday April 24, 1887." Quite to the quoter's surprise, this sentence proved to be acceptable, and u-Stu was able to return the volume a week ahead of its due date.

This is not to say that u-Stu didn't give it a shot, and in point of fact he was in the middle of trying to understand a point about Flaubert's literary scruples (all of Mr. Pater's subjects seemed to be neurotic) when his head rose wearily from the page in time to see the Weasel slip a glassine envelope, clearly not their customary kind, into the stock of a cardboard box labeled MISCELLANEOUS INTERIORS. Skidding from his stool he rocked toward the Weasel at full speed. Sir, he said, sir, may I help you with anything; you seem to be a bit confused. This was a formula Mr. Gab had hit upon for lowering the level of public embarrassment whenever hanky-pankies were observed. However, as u-Stu took thought, as Mr. Gab turned to locate his assistant's voice, and as the Weasel looked up in alarm, u-Stu realized that the Weasel, so far as he had seen, was adding to, not subtracting from the contents of the container. Had u-Stu perhaps missed an extraction? Was this the latter stage of a switch?

It's all right, Mr. Stu, Mr. Gab said urgently. Mr. Grimes is just replacing a print for me. Oh, said Mr. Stu, stopping as soon as he could and calming his good eye. Mr. Grimes, the Weasel, winked in surprise and backed away from Mr. Stu in the direction of the door. Something is up, Mr. Stu thought, thinking he was now Mr. Stu, an improvement surely, a considerable promotion, a kind of bribe, but an acceptable one, coming as it did at long—he thought—last. But what was up? what? Mr. Stu retreated to his stool and Mr. Grimes slid out of the shop with never a further word. In fact, Mr. Stu couldn't remember a first word. But he'd been inattentive while tending to Walter Pater's work, and to the peevish Flaubert, who had just vowed, at the point Mr. Stu had reached in his reading, to quit writing altogether.

Mr. Gab's back was soon bent over MISCELLANEOUS INTERIORS. From his stool where he was perched once more like some circus animal, Mr. Stu couldn't see a single interesting thing though he knew that rummaging was going on. He felt in his stomach a glob of gas, a balloon filled with rising apprehension. Mr. Gab, having done his dirty work, returned to his desk empty-handed, allowing the store to become as law-abiding as before. With his Pater closed, Mr. Stu, as he would from this morning on be called, began to fill the back of Mr. Gab's head with his own thoughts, enjoying a vacation in another body, even old Mr. Gab's, which had to be a low-rent cottage in a run-down resort, but—hey—several limps up from the ramshackle where he currently was.

Other eyes, both reasonably well off, saw through gray glass into the street where the world would scarcely pass. He imagined he was sixteen, which was perhaps his age. He had the legs of that Caravaggio cupid which had so exercised Mr. Gab when he'd come upon them the other day in Rüdiger Klessmann's catalogue of the paintings in the Berlin Museum (remember that liar's name, Mr. Gab had commanded). Naked, the kid was. Very naked. A pornpainting, Mr. Gab said in sentence. It is written here that this is the figure of a boy about twelve. Sitting on a globe. The posture is contorted, but not like Mr. Stu on his stool, Mr. Stu thought. Look, this Klessmann fellow says that every wrinkle and fold of the skin is reproduced with the utmost realism. Ut-most. Look. What do you see?

U-Stu saw a cupid with arms and thighs wide apart, as wide as full sexual reception might require, and musculated like a twenty-five-year-old wrestler, though wearing the weenie of a boy of six, one nipple showing in a swath of light which flew in conveniently from the left to dispel a general darkness; in fact to fling it aside like a parted robe and reveal a creased and belly-buttoned stomach below a strong broad chest where the nipple lay, as purple as a petal fallen from a frostbitten rose (Mr. Gab had said as if quoting). The head, however, bore a leering drunken grin as salacious as they are in Frans Hals. Those huge thighs, though, Mr. Gab fairly growled, how are they rendered? See the way they are rounded into a silk-soaked softness? (Was he quoting still?) An amazon in the guise of a baby boy. Holding the bow of a violin!

What allegorical gimcrackery! But no! another masterpaint, Mr. Gab announced, as if introducing a vaudeville act. And Klessmann dares to call this pornographic pastiche realism!

Caravaggio was simply a ruffian. His darks were merely dramatic, his colors were off, his attitudes appropriate to saloons. He was a pretender in front of reality, and reality had made him a murderer and a convict. Tenebrist indeed. Remember that word. (His assistant tried, but he understood it to mean "tenuous.") Mr. Gab could be relentless. Carrahvaggeeoh, he'd growl. For him darkness is never delicate. Carrahvaggeeoh didn't understand what a shadow was—an entire region of the world. Ah . . . we know where to go for shadows.

By now Mr. Stu was able to interpret Mr. Gab. Realism—truth—was the exclusive property of the photograph. He regularly ridiculed paintings that presented themselves as lifelike. About trompe l'oeil compositions he was particularly withering. What kind of streetcar accident has caused this rabbit, that jug, this—hah!—hunting horn, that—hah!—hat, that knife, that—hey?—horseshoe, and that key—a key!—those two dead birds?—to hop to run to fly to get carried in a carriage to see the smash, rehear the crash, and enjoy the bloody scene? What drew them to this place? These dots of detail? That's the real? reality is a stupid collection? trophies of a scavenger hunt? Whose eye would they fool?—hey?—whose?

Mr. Stu, now in the guise of Caravaggio, stretched his grand legs wide, even if he wouldn't fool anyone, and flaunted his cute little sex. Those few who might pass would never look in. Anyway. He wondered, as he had so often, what it would be like to be ordinary and have had an ordinary childhood, not one in a

Home where everything had to imitate shoes in a line. And nothing had ever been his: not his bed or blanket, the table at which he drew, not a wall, not a window, not a fork or spoon, lent instead, shared, maybe his underclothes had been his, but only because they wouldn't let anyone else soil them. He'd left with the clothes on his back as the cliché maintains, so they had to be his: his shoes, and his socks and his bulbous nose. Even now his room was rented, his books were borrowed, his stool belonged to his employer, as did the boxes of photographs, presumably they weren't all stolen. At the moment, though, he owned a violin and sat heavily on his own globe.

He'd noticed how Mr. Gab did it: how he studied a picture (this one, another Sudek, had showed up out of the blue to be held under Mr. Stu's nose) until he knew just where the darks went (had he bought it from that haughty high-hatter? that would not have been wise); dark filling almost the whole road except for the wet and glistening dirt that still defined some wagon tracks (the temptation would have been far greater than for another piece of cake), the sky, too, setting with the paling sun, and walls and buildings nothing but edges, tree trunks rising into the dying light, crisp and unconfused (had it been dropped off by the Weasel? God forbid), rows of insulators perched like birds for the night on faintly wired poles, but so composed ... made of mist ... composed so that the bushes at one end of the panoramic rhymed with the tree limbs at the other; thus the blacks beneath held up the grays above, so the soft glow of the failing sun, which could be still seen in the darkening sky, might lie like a liquid on the muddy lane ... and Mr. Gab would inhale very audibly, as if a sigh had been sent him from somewhere, because only once had the world realized these relations; they would never exist again; they had come and gone like a breath.

An image had been etched on an eye.

Mr. Stu had made Mister, all the same, even if he didn't have a childhood; and he had a job—a job that was his job, no one else's, as stooled to its heights as an accountant's—and he had his own room even if it was rented, even if it was paid for by his father figure; and he had a market where he could swipe fruit, a weedy field to sit in now and then, a library card for borrowing books; and a worry which was ruining his reveries. If the cops got Mr. Gab, what would become of Mr. Stu? No job then. No room. He could read in the weeds. But the authorities didn't like the appearance it gave the neighborhood when he flopped down in the empty lot and looked up at a clutter of clouds or saw inside a deeply receding blue sky a scented silent light.

With Walter Pater parked, Mr. Stu settled on his stool and set his sights on the back of Mr. Gab's head, and bore into it with his whole being until he felt he was looking out into the empty sun-blown street where now and then a figure would pass, moving more often left than right, while he wondered what was to be done, what he should do to defend them from the calamity that was coming. After closing, after, as he imagined, still wholly inhabiting Mr. Gab, he'd taken that body to bed in the Chinese flophouse where Mr. Gab's somewhat resourceful assistant had found a curtain made of mediocre lace at the market—near that stall from which, by using the crowd, he'd appropriated fruit—just a cloud of thread to tack to the wall above his window so that now when Mr. Gab's hand drew the curtain the room grew gray and a few of the city's lights spangled the frail netting where, bed-clothed, u-Stu in the garb of Mr. Gab could still see, till sleep, a kind of sky, and pretend he was napping in the weeds or smelling space like a moth; so after closing, Gab gone to the flop, what was left of Mr. Stu would go through the boxes one by one and systematically, if there was a system, hunt for pictures that were likely pilfered in order to hide them . . . yes, by reswapping bodies for the task, putting Gab back in his own boots—maybe too many switcheroos to seem dreamable—and subsequently to slide the suspicious photographs into such other boxes as he'd have collected under his so far fleabagless bed, where no one would ever think to pry, thus cleansing the premises of the taint of loot and securing the safety of what was looking more and more like a possible life.

He swore that were he able to do it, he would work earnestly to improve himself during the remaining existence he'd been given, giving up both fruit and stealing; he'd pass out flyers to stimulate the store; he'd memorize a new word every day and read it—one two three four—like a regiment on the march; he'd—

What, though, could be done about the ones which perched in plain view upon the walls, yet tried to lie about their presence like the purloined letter, even though they could be seen to be what they were: Koudelka, in an instant, glorious, an icon worth worship, or an Emerson, swimming in silence through reedy weeds, or that damn Evans with the foursquareface outstaring stone, or the Abbott tucked away near the rug-hugged doorway; because Gab would feel their loss even if Mr. Stu just replaced the prints and not the hangers; put up at some risk a Harry Callahan or Marc Riboud instead, since who knew if Gab had thieved them too; he'd feel their loss like a draft through a door left ajar, the hairs on the back of his neck would whisper their names in his ears; yet the

Koudelka, the Feininger had to go, guilt could not be more loudly advertised. Looking at *Lake Michigan* Mr. Gab had muttered place-ment, placement, placement, three times, u-Stu supposed, to honor the three figures standing in smooth lake water, water which merged imperceptibly with a grayed-over sky, three figures per-fectly decentered, and the wake of the walking bather . . . well . . . as if there'd been some calculation . . . if not by nature than by Callahan . . . alas, not a serious name. Yet Callahan, said Mr. Gab, would do.

He could not spirit these evidences from their walls. Suppose he could persuade Mr. Gab to squirrel them away in some quiet sequestership of his own where they couldn't be seen let alone seized let alone certified as Grabbed by Gab. In so doing, in going along with Mr. Stu's suggestion, wouldn't Mr. Gab be confess-ing to his crimes? Then, though, if he did that, perhaps he'd be relieved of his reticence. What stories Mr. Gab could tell about each one—Cunningham's magnolia, that late Baldus, or Weston's two shells—how he had found them, stalked them, and withdrawn them from the owners' grasps (even slipped them out of their countries) as if they were already as much his as his hand was his, leaving a handclasp to wave farewell to their properties.

At first, of course, u-Stu's head, heart, conscience were all firmly set against the notion, voiced by their enemy from the earlier street, that Mr. Gab's stock contained stolen articles. His mind could not figure out how Mr. Gab might have managed. He seemed taciturn not sly, blunt and biased not crafty or devious, and it was difficult to envision Mr. Gab as young, vigorous, and thievish, climbing walls like a lusty vine, seeping like pulverulent air (his word to work on for the day) under doorframe or window sash; yet so quick-fingered as to pry open cases in a wink, slip a photo from its frame in a trice, and then to saunter carefree and concealing from a museum or pretentious shop straight through customs declaring only a smile and a bit of a cough. Nor had he the heart to imagine Mr. Gab to be no more than a fence for those more slick and daring than he—as if Weasel were—what a laugh; yet appearances were deceiving, who knew better than he how that was, for he, Mr. Stu, no longer the Stupid Assistant, never had been, only looked so, on account of his one cross eye and leaking lip. Conscience . . . well conscience made a coward of him. Made him fear a fall. From his stool of course. From his room, job, only relation. Because he actually would have loved to believe that Mr. Gab was a Pimpernel of prints. He knew that conscience, if it had to compete with pride, wouldn't stand a chance, and could be cowed into silence. So that to have the prince of purloiners for a pa . . . well . . . that would be okay. That would be quite all right.

He might have to get used to some such idea. Evidence was more prevalent than fingerprints. There was that envelope postmarked Montreal in which the Baldus was, contrary to custom, still kept: an absolutely perfect albumen silver print of the train station at Toulon, with the Baldus signature stamp lower right; the envelope carrying the capital letters CCA outlined in red on its front flap: rails running straight through the glass-gated shed into the everlasting; the envelope dated in a dark circle May 1, 1995: about a foot and a half wide, the sky, as almost always in Baldus, kept a clear cream, the scene so crisp as to seem seen through translucent ice; the print in heavy plastic slid between tough protective cardboard: uncluttered, freight cars parked in place, not a sight of mortal man as usually, in Édouard Baldus, was the case, a document that documented as definitely as a nailed lid; but now, so overcoated, the thing bulked in the box it was shoved in, crying out to the curious.

What a quandary. Surely Mr. Gab would see the wisdom in such a gleaning of the incriminating prints whose very excellence made them enemies, and surely he would understand, in such circumstances, the good sense in ceasing for a time to acquire anything more that might entrap Mr. Gab against his will in the terrible toils of the law; yes, surely he would have to recognize how wise it was to heed these warnings, to back off and go double doggo; but Mr. Stu knew that Mr. Gab would bite on that Sudek if it were offered, that he could not resist Quality which overcame him like a cold; because what he understood to be Quality was all that counted in the world, Mr. Stu had come to grasp that. Not warmth, it threatened the prints; not food which merely smeared the fingers; not leisure, for where would an eye go on vacation but to its graphs—to bathe in their beauty as if at a beach? Not shelter since his pictures furnished him his bricked lanes and cobbled streets, damp from rain, and all his buildings defined by shade and the white sky and the dark freshly turned fields and the veined rocks and river water frozen while falling into a steaming gorge; not a woman's love, since the photos gave up their bodies ceaselessly and were always welcoming and bare and always without cost—after, once, you had them; further than that there was the flower petal's perfection, the leaf's elemental elegance, the militancy of rail and vagrancy of river line, rows of trees, a hill, a château, a vast stretch of desert dotted with death and small mean rocks. Mr. Stu had a dim hunch about how, for Mr. Gab, they had replaced his mother's flesh. I touch you. You touch eye. That eye owns the world.

So what to do. Just broach the subject? Just say: I think, Mr.

Gab, we should take these precious ones away for safer keeping. There are robbers out there looking for swag. The richness of your stock might get about, remarked here, mentioned there, whispered around until the information reaches the wrong ear. And then in the night when you are asleep up there, wherever it is, some thug may force his way in, easy enough even if the shutters are shut and the door is locked; these days they have pry irons and metal-cutting torches and lock picks and credit cards they cleverly put to illegal use. Mr. Gab, is that you, sir, someone said, startling Mr. Stu out of his thoughts as though they were dreams. We, sir, are the police. You have been denounced.

4   THE DAY OF RECKONING ARRIVES

I've—?

You have been informed upon.

Mr. Gab gave Mr. Stu a look of such anguish and accusation his assistant's heart broke. Mr. Stu felt his blood was draining from him and put his hand to his nose. Then Mr. Stu returned Mr. Gab's anguish with his own, a pitifully twisted expression on an already twisted face. Mr. Gab immediately knew his suspicion was false and unfounded; it had followed the awful announcement as swiftly as the sting from a slap; there had been no time to take thought, show sense, conceal his feeling. He realized how horribly he had wounded his adopted kid, his loyal assistant whom he'd helped from the Home and taught to grow up, reaching the rank of Mister. Mr. Gab understood now that he'd left a son a second time. Whose only mistake was being born. Or being in the neighborhood when Mr. Gab was nabbed.

We have a warrant.

A warrant?

To search your shop and to remove these boxes and place them in our custody while they are examined. It's been alleged you have been in receipt of stolen goods.

Mr. Gab tried to rise from his chair by pushing at its arms with his fists. I have no receipts. Long ago they each arrived, these photographs, like strangers off a boat, you understand. There are decades of desire boxed here. Though they are good photographs. I admit that. Good. It makes for envy in others. But he was not speaking to the detective who had probably been chosen for the job because he didn't look like a detective is supposed to look, because his look, now, was deeply troubled too. And it made his figure seem puny, his hands small, his nose abruptly concluded as if it had once fallen off. Mr. Gab was not even attending to himself. He was being borne down by a lifeload of anxiety and a moment of misguided distrust.

It is said these boxes are full of stolen pictures.

They are mine. My prints. They live here.

These pictures may not belong to you.

They are prints not pictures. They are photographs not pictures. They are photographic prints.

They may not belong to you.

They do. They belong. In these, of all boxes, they belong. But Mr. Gab was not attending to the officer either. Bulky men were entering the shop, one by one, though they had begun trying to enter two by two. The detective held forward a folded sheet with an insecure hand. Out in the street, Mr. Stu saw the Russian without his hat—his hair, in the sun, shining from the effort of a thick pomade. The bulky men wore overalls with a moving-company logo on them. Here is the writ that empowers this, the detective said, beginning softly but adding a hiss by the end. He sensed he was not impressive. He shook, again, his folded paper. Mr. Gab still sat as solemn as a cat and seemed to be registering one blank after another. The warrant was placed in his lap. This gives us the right to remove (the man waved) and to search the premises. If the allegations—which I must tell you come from high up—powerful government agencies—if they are unfounded, these materials will be returned to you. You shall be receipted.

Receipted? At that, Mr. Gab gathered himself. The paper slid to the floor as he rose. For the first time, he seemed to be taking in the police and the moving men. These are my eyes, and the life of my eyes. One man bore a puzzled look but picked a box up in his arms anyway. Bring in the hand trucks, somebody said. You are using Van Lines? There will be a complete and careful inventory, the detective reassured him, looking intently about the store. Maybe you will finally learn what you have. Then he peered at Mr. Gab. You understand, sir, that later we shall want to speak to you at length. A hand trolley stacked with a box at its top marked PRAGUE rolled out. PARIS NIGHTLIFE went next.

MISCELLANEOUS LANDSCAPES followed.

There are not a lot of these prints left, Mr. Stu heard himself say.

Why don't you help us by taking those pictures on the hangers down, the detective suggested to Mr. Stu. That way, nothing will get bent or soiled. So Mr. Stu did. First finding an empty carton to keep them in. Which took time because he was bloodless as a voodoo victim, and the bulky men and their boxes were in all the aisles. The enormity of everything took his blood's place.

One of the movers stopped for a moment to stare at a photograph Mr. Stu was about to unfasten. How dare you, Mr. Stu shouted. The burly man shrugged and went about his business. No one else cared.

Mr. Gab no longer protested. He simply stood beside his desk and chair and with an empty gaze followed the men as they pushed their trolleys past him. Mr. Stu made out a truck parked at the curb. Against its pale gray side the Russian figure leaned. As each box was loaded into the rear of the truck, he wrote something on a clipboard. Mr. Stu suddenly thought: where are his witnesses? Every transaction took place in the back, behind the rug, between the two interested parties, and was always in cash, Mr. Stu had been given to understand. There weren't any records. What could they prove?

Mr. Stu rocked into the movers' doorway. You shit from a stuffed turkey, he shouted, though it was doubtful the Russian understood him, he hardly looked up from his list. Turkey turd, yeah! A big moving man easily hipped him out of the portal. We'll get you guys, he later feared he had u-stupidly said. Mr. Gab's position or posture hadn't altered. His eyes were unnaturally wide and seemed dry. Why was his face, then, so wet all over? One aisle of tables was vacant. How strange the shop seemed without its brown boxes. Now the entering men with their empty trolleys went down the open aisle and returned to the street through one that was solidly cased. Wire hangers lay in a tangle on the trestle tops. The big moving men were tossing the beanbags on the floor, often in fun. Mr. Stu thought of saving several of the displayed photos by concealing them under his shirt, but the detective had two public eyes on his every move. The toe of one of Mr. Gab's shoes was on a corner of the warrant. Tears were sliding from his eyes in a continuous clear stream.

Evidence, Mr. Stu feared. They had evidence aplenty. Who had owned the Julia Cameron before it had come to hide and hovel here? she who specialized in wild hair and white beards? about whom he'd read had breathed the word "beautiful" and thereupon died, her photographs "tumbling over the tables." Was this an orphanage Mr. Gab ran, and were all these wonders children who had wandered or run away from their homes and families to find themselves in alleys and doorways and empty squares instead of warming hearthsides and huggie havens. No, they all had owners once and, Mr. Stu feared, had been—as if by fairies—stolen. Picsnapped. So they'd be traced—every trade and traduction. And then what? Mr. Gab's presence in the town nearest his lordship's estate, his lodging at the inn, his visit to the household—each would count against him; his travels to Paris at opportune times, his many friends in the army who might turn up a bit of art here and there for some of the crown's coins, complaints from shops about losses they had suffered shortly after his employ—they would surely count against him too; oh so many collaborators, filchers anonymous, partners in crime, many of whom would be still around to testify, and, for a break from the court, would see no need to lie. The prospect before Mr. Stu and Mr. Gab, Mr. Stu decided, was nothing short of calamitous. That was what he had thought to call it before: calamitous. In any case, and the awful moment came back to him like a bad meal, Mr. Stu could hardly work for a man who was so immediately ready to suspect him; who believed he might be a traitor, a child sent by society to win his trust, trip him up, and dispatch him to jail.

Mrs. Cameron was a woman of good character, and did not retouch, Mr. Gab had once confidently claimed, but she was far too social in her choice of subjects. Social might have been a good idea, Mr. Stu now wanted to say to Mr. Gab. Friends in high places might have stood Mr. Gab in good stead. Tennyson. Darwin. Could come to the rescue. Attest to Mr. Gab's character. Honest fellow, as trustworthy as a hound. His museum was being removed, his life looted. Such a painful wrench and one deceitfully turned. The Russian—and Mr. Stu now saw his blurry figure counting boxes as they were taken off to jail—might have been an Albanian in disguise. He might be wearing that goo to fool Mr. Gab and Mr. Stu into thinking him sufficiently shiny to do business with. In reality, he was probably some Fed who lived in town with wife and child.

What's back there, the detective said, as if asking permission when he wasn't, and pushing the rug aside to see. Kitchen, came his voice again. George, he shortly cried. One of the busy big men turned away from his work and went to join the detective out of all sight. They will surely find the special treasures, Mr. Stu thought. Soon enough the big man returned carrying within both arms a large box clasped against his chest. What's this, the detective asked when he reappeared. It has no label. Tell Amos to list it as "Kitchen Closet," he shouted after Shoulders as Shoulders bore his burden out.

Mr. Gab's eyes ran without relief.

It's terrible. Why do you have to take everything, Mr. Stu asked desperately. Can't you see how awful it is for Mr. Gab?

What?

Mr. Stu tried to speak more clearly—slowly and precisely as, in the Home, he had once been taught. By switch and rule and ruler.

Order of the court, seized on suspicion, the detective finally said, leaving the place himself. The walls were bare except for the shiny zinc heads of the roofing nails. The tables sheltered nothing under them now, while the emptied tops merely supported that absence, and reflected the glare of canned bulbs through a mist made of shoe-scuffled dust. The air though was heavy, and Mr. Stu felt the trestles groan. Then the men with their big damp backs were gone. The truck was driven off, and the detective and his Albanian henchman vanished as though they'd become street trees.

Mr. Gab was where he'd been the entire time, still painfully silent, his face oozing away into grief, perhaps not to return. Mr. Stu, out of a need to soften the barrenness about them, slowly turned the cans off, so only the late-afternoon light, made gauzy by the dirty window it oozed through, illuminated the room. Then Mr. Gab moved to *wreeeeek* the shutters down. Here and there a streak of sun would reach deeply into the darkness of the shop. What are we going to do? Mr. Stu spoke to himself more clearly than he spoke to strangers. At least you have those photographs engraved on the balls of your eyes.

Don't accuse me, Mr. Gab finally said, smearing his face with a shirtsleeve. What evidence can they have—from that fellow, I mean, Mr. Stu ventured. I gave him the slip, Mr. Gab said slowly, separating the words with consternation. He wanted a receipt for his cash. So I gave him the slip. He'll have a— Well, maybe not, Mr. Stu said and received a bleak look for his pains. Not the first times, but the last time. Then I gave him one. Still, Mr. Stu persisted, you couldn't have known— I knew, and he knew I knew, Mr. Gab said firmly. It was a Lange I had to have. A face of pain—pale gray—as if—a face worn wooden by a wind. I'm sorry, Mr. Gab added. They've taken away my beauties, but I've taken away your world, u-Stu, as thoroughly as they've taken away mine. Mr. Gab wavered when he walked, a pushover who now resembled the old rug he had hung for a door.

Mr. Stu sat carefully in Mr. Gab's chair. It was not all that comfortable. Slivers of sun, as though from a fire at their front door, raced through the shutters and ran up the rear wall, now wholly exposed, the faint shadow of a table against the plaster like a patch of unsunburned skin. When someone passed by on the sidewalk, the pattern palpitated. It was true that Mr. Gab didn't have much of a life. He sat in this not very comfortable chair most of every day, letting his eyes lie idle or roam randomly about like a foraging pooch, thinking who knew what thoughts, if he thought any, and if he thought any, who knew that either. Now, and even more often then, Mr. Gab would reluctantly help a customer, and once in a great while do a bit of business behind the rug where the rug quite muffled the doing. You'd have to account it a life overflowing with empty. But that life had better prepare to be so much worse, and embrace mere absence like a lover. Nevertheless, who knew how to count these things: the quality of an existence—especially when you compared it to the meager stuff that took place in the deranged world outside—in walking these formerly narrow aisles, talking occasionally, eating meagerly, drinking rarely, sitting rudely on a board seat long hours, leafing a leaf from an out-of-date mag, arguing with an image in a catalogue, watching faint figures pass?

Mr. Stu let his eye run back and forth along the light like a squirrel on a wire. His life wasn't a winner either. Yet he had a job, a room, a library card. And he could open a book as if it were a door and disappear. He could inhale air in his weedy lot. He could look. He'd even learn. Yet he'd already found Sundays a stretch. He was supposed to stay home and pretend to be a person of substance in that slummy brown shoebox space of his. Itemize the alley. When the walls were whisked away? When the window went, what could he count? When his little box of belongings was put on the sidewalk outside, what would he manage? Mr. Gab, Mr. Gab, what were they to do? And when they took Mr. Gab downtown for questioning, and found what they would find in box after box, folder after folder, plastic pocket after pocket, how could either of them stand it? . . . endure it? . . . live through it? It was . . . awful . . . unrelievedly . . . foul. Mr. Gab reappeared with a bundle. He wore, for once, a wry smile. Quick as a cat Mr. Stu vacated the chair.

There are signs the dick went up the ladder to my loft, Mr. Gab said, but the dick missed this, wrapped in a sheet, under my cot. He held it out as you would a tray of sweets. There was a great wad of sheet to be clumsily unwound before a photogravure, rubber-banded between cardboards for its protection, was released. Mr. Gab put the print where a streak of sunlight crossed a trestle so they could see it. An Eastern moment, Mr. Gab said softly, and Mr. Stu saw the most beautiful silklike scene he'd ever, which Mr. Gab explained was a Stieglitz from 1901 called *Spring Showers*. Composed by a god, Mr. Gab whispered, as if the detective might overhear. He also spoke in awe, Mr. Stu knew. Like an oriental hanging, Mr. Gab said, as though the mottled gray surface was that of cloth. Less than half a foot wide, a foot tall, made almost solely of shadow, Mr. Stu saw there in the dimness a street sweeper in wet hat and wet slicker pushing a wide broom along a wet gutter toward the photograph's wet left edge. Despite Mr. Stu's despair the image made him feel good for a moment, then worse. Just off-center, though on the same side as the sweeper, so that the right two-thirds of the picture was empty of everything except some soft faint shapes that represented traffic on the street, there grew a sidewalk tree with a gently forking trunk protected, perhaps from being pissed on, by a round wrought-iron fence whose pickets were thin as sticks. Surrounded by the sweetest vagueness, the tree rose from the walk on its own wet and wavy shadow as though that dripping shadow were a root, easing toward its dim thin upper limbs, which were dotted with brief new leaves and one perched bird, to faintly foliate away in indistinctness, though there were hints that tall buildings might block you if you entered the background, as well as shimmers that signified some moving vehicles, and the loom of a large ornamental urn—was it?—the viewer could not be sure.

What was certain was the photograph's depth, its purity, its delicacy. And the silken faintly hazy and amorphous gray that made up most of this small and simple streetside scene was the most beautiful, most comforting, most expressive quality of all. It was everywhere as wet, Mr. Stu realized, as Mr. Gab's face had been before his sleeve had swabbed it. Gloom began descending like a jacket hood, because his admiration could not keep misery away, not for long. Beauty eventually increased the pain. Perhaps not in better days. Mr. Stu understood incompleteness for he was plete aplenty. Mr. Gab understood loss because he was its cause as well as its victim. Pictures someone had taken, he'd taken, taken and hid. Now these prints had been wrenched from him in turn, and were nowhere where they might be gratefully seen—pictures that had been selfishly sequestered, then put like bad kids "in custody," to be examined by eyes that were mean and sharpened by the crude rough looks of criminals.

His shoulders in such a slump they ceased to be, Mr. Gab

went with his treasure through the carpet again. Part of the rug had pulled from its tacks so that now its hang was uneven. It bore a diamond design that Mr. Stu had never noticed before, cut deeply into its pelt. In better days he would have dreamed it outlined a playing field where figures the size of small ants might run about. Throughout the shop sunlight flickered for a moment. Someone was passing. In better days the store would still be open. Mr. Stu thought that when masses were made of mist and shadow, as they were in Stieglitz's painterly picture, and loomed without any consequences caused by bulk or weight, they possessed their own kind of being, and that the photograph, which had so little that was definite in it, nevertheless presented us with a whole world made of fragility and levitation. What would it mean to a man to have made such—there was no other word for it—such beauty? to have drawn it in through rainwatered eyes? to have captured it in a small now antiquated box? brought it to life almost amniotically? (another from his daily assignment of words) and sent it forth in the style of a far-off culture that he had learned about solely from photographic samples. Would it fill his life with satisfaction and achievement, or would it sadden him, since a loveliness of that kind could never be repeated, could never be realized again?

Mr. Gab had treasured his collection. However acquired. He had gathered good things together that had perhaps been stolen and dispersed once already. He had achieved an Archive, made his own museum in the midst of a maelstrom. Didn't that count? So Mr. Stu thought maybe Mr. Gab could say he hadn't known they were anyone's legitimate possessions any longer, but were the spoils of war, refugees of slavery, expropriation, and murder. Of course they could be returned to their proper homes if they had any, as long as it was their real wish to be rehung on the dour walls of grandiose old estates with their long cold halls given over to stuffily conventional family portraits and other tasteless bragging, to languish in the huge mansions or palaces they'd come from, or to sit in shame propped up on some lectern like a speech no one would give and no one would wish to hear; that would be okay, provided there'd be no further punishment for Mr. Gab, since he'd had pain enough from his loss to surpass that of most lovers. Lover: that was right, because who, Mr. Stu surmised, had looked at them as though they were gray lace, who had weighed a shadow against a substance, a dark line against a pale space, the curvature of a street's recession against the forefrontal block of a building, so as to feel the quality of judgment in every placement, the rightness of every relation, and how these subtle measures made the picture dance with the ideal gaiety of an ideal life.

We pass through frames, Mr. Gab had said. We walk about our rooms, our house, the neighborhood, and our elbow enters into a divine connection with a bus bench or bubbler in the park, a finial, a chair or letter lying on a hall table, which is, in an instant—click—dissolved. The nose, the earlobe, the bosom, the elbow, the footfall, the torso's shadow pass in and out of awkward—in and out of awful—in and out of awesome combinations just as easily as air moves; the sublime, the suddenly supremely meaningful and redemptive moment is reached, achieved, left, dissolved into the dingy, only, in a few frames further, to connive at more communities. It is grace and disgrace constantly created and destroyed. The right click demonstrates how, in an instant, we, or our burro, or our shovel, or our eye or nose or nipple, were notes in a majestic symphony. A world of self-concerned things is suddenly singing a selfless concerned song: that was what the fine photographer, over and over, allowed to be *seen* in solemn apology for what should have been *heard.*

Nothing had been heard from Mr. Gab in quite a while, though Mr. Stu hadn't counted breaths; however his employer's retreat should not have been surprising since he'd just lost a wife, more dear than life, to a bunch of hand trolleys. He'd been in the dark on his garret cot sobbing like a sad child, Mr. Stu bet, why not? In a room fixed to the top of a shabby ladder like a squirrel's nest in a tree; what could be sillier than where it was? and Mr. Stu had wanted to laugh when he first saw the way the ladder led up through a hole from which coal could once have dropped. Perhaps Mr. Gab could be comforted by the darkness since it might suggest an end to things—no more moving men moving his treasures out, treasures to be treated like contraband—less anxiety, fewer humiliations—dark at midday was what this day deserved—so perhaps he'd been somewhat slightly—well, not reassured—but protected from any additional pain, such as being pierced through and through by his unwarranted suspicion of his former employee, Mr. Stu, a feeling that had been turned on—click—like a light, when the strange man had said the phrase—the curdling phrase—"informed upon."

You have been given up, Mr. Gab. We gotcha. Dead to rights. We got yer goods too. Yer a looter, a despoiler, a thief, a fence, a flown-away father, an ungrateful and suspicious boss. Now you'll have to bear your loss like just desserts. Go to bed like your boy has, time upon time, to cry inside the pillow till the pillow flats. Go to bed like your boy has, countlessly, to imagine the bitter oncoming day. When you will walk about a barren store. When you will begin to miss me. When you'll be invited to "come down-town." Go to bed like your boy has, heart beaten by shame, sore and in despair he is alive. Go to bed like your boy has, angry at all, alone as a bone that has lost its dog. Head screams aren't effective. Head howls aren't effective. Headlongs aren't worth a damn. Seek some solace in the fact that you aren't being gnawed on at the moment, not being yelled at, at the moment, not being guffaw'd, not being always, at anything, the worst, to be the basket into which everything is eventually tossed. Seek solace we advise . . . seek solace, don't we say? The one photograph that remains, had it been unshrouded and claimed, would nonetheless have been engraved on your weeping eyes.

Mr. Stu felt a wadded sheet at his uneven feet. He picked it up, to unwrap and refold, only to find his arms weren't long enough, so he spread it out on a trestle where bright slivers of sunshine from the shutters fell in lively white streaks. Mr. Stu drew a roll of masking tape from Mr. Gab's desk drawer, tape Mr. Gab used now and then to repair boxes, and began to block out the light, initially not easy because it bled through the thin tape, and it took several layers to make the glow even faint. By biting the tape into thin strips and making its stickum cling, Mr. Stu gradually darkened the room. Now there was only a halo to see by. It ran around the rug and apparently came from a light in the kitchen. Bring a pin, Mr. Gab, please, Mr. Stu called out. Though he thought he heard in his head the beating of a desperate heart, Mr. Stu boldly drew back the rug and entered the kitchen where he found, after a few minutes of pawing about in drawers which otherwise yielded little in the way of contents, a roll of stout picture wire. Bring a pin, Mr.

Gab, please, Mr. Stu shouted up the ladder at the hole that was even darker than the inside of a hose.

Mr. Stu was feeling his way to his idea. He realized, while groping between trestles, that he was performing the steps of his project in the wrong order. Consequently it was with difficulty that he found the nails he wanted on opposing walls, and with difficulty that he finally fastened one end of his wire to a conveniently big nail, and with difficulty that he unrolled the wire—held over his head—to the other side and found another roofer to wind his wire around, allowing the remainder of the roll to dangle. Now he had a firm line across the room to fling the sheet over, but he was unsure of what came next. Bring a pin, please, Mr. Gab, he called, suddenly weary and useless.

It took some time—and after the slow return of resolution—to hang the sheet, though he should have been more expert, having hung a lot of laundry out to dry in his day, even standing on a short stool to do his pinning when the line was beyond his reach. He stared into the dark, making nothing out. What's the idea, Mr. Gab asked. They stood in pitch now that Mr. Gab had turned the kitchen light off. I just thought we might—. Mr. Stu began. Ah, of course, you've occluded the shutters. Tape, Mr. Stu said. Something to do. You might have thought I was crying, Mr. Gab said. I was not. I was at a loss even for that. I didn't, Mr. Stu said, think. You might have thought I was huddling, Mr. Gab said. I was not. I was too tired to lie down. I didn't, Mr. Stu said. There is nothing for my eyes to adjust to, Mr. Gab said. It's as dark as the hole in a hose, said Mr. Stu.

They both stood without the whereabouts of the other. Say something more so I'll know where you are, said Mr. Gab, clearing his throat as if he were warning a boat about a shoal. I thought if we pinholed a bit of the tape, we'd get here, on this sheet you can't see, a bit of picture. Something to do, said Mr. Stu. Mr. Gab bumped gratefully into his desk. Mr. Stu heard its drawer being withdrawn. I've a hatpin here somewhere. Rats—ouch. No. I didn't stick myself, just thought I might have. Mr. Gab had to get close up because the tape on the shutters was barely visible even close up. If I were to put a hole, say, here—what—

Suddenly there was a faint loose smear on the sheet. Needs to be closer up, was the opinion of Mr. Stu. Needs to be farther back, Mr. Gab decided. In the sheetlight it was easier to find the tightly fastened wire and unwind it from its nail, Mr. Gab doing one side, Mr. Stu the other. They moved in concert slowly toward the rear of the room, watching an image grow and slowly brighten. Now, cried Mr. Gab, and they both scrabbled for nailheads, feeling the wall gingerly as though it were flesh not their own, holding the wire as high as they could, which wasn't very, in Mr. Stu's case, because the sheet dragged on his left side. Shouldn't let it get dirty, Mr. Gab said in his familiar cross voice which was suddenly reassuring. The sheet, however, hadn't hung clear for many feet before it rolled over tables and caught on their crude edges. The image, now rather sharply focused, ran like a frieze across the top of the screen, but then the sheet tented toward the front of the shop as though there were a wind gusting from its rear and filling it out like a sail.

Without a further word needed, Mr. Gab and Mr. Stu began to shove the tables—not an easy thing to do—toward the sides of the store so there'd be a space for the sheet to hang and its image to cohere. Sawhorses don't roll; they wouldn't even skid;

and beanbags were treacherously everywhere. Mr. Stu knew not to curse, but he nearly cried. It was futile. Why were they doing this? What had his idea been? Mr. Gab would go to prison. Mr. Stu imagined this might take place tomorrow. And homeless Mr. Stu, whose deforming birth marks bespoke bad begetting, would get the heave-ho from every eye, from every back a turn, and even from those on pleasant picnics.

Quickly, quickly, your stool, Mr. Stu, you mustn't miss this. Mr. Stu dragged his perch awkwardly forward. Beanbags bore him malice. Mr. Gab had turned his chair to face the screen, and there . . . and there . . . there was their street, clear as clean water. There bloomed a building of red brick. Of a deep rich rose they had never before seen. It was . . . it was as if the entire brick had been hotly compressed the way the original clay had been, yet each brick was still so supremely each because the mortar between them was like a living stream, and the pocking was as crisp as craters photographed from space, individual and maybe named for Greek gods. Where the brick encountered a lintel of gray stone, the contrast was more than bugle calls in a basement. The gray had a clarity one found only in the finest prints. Mr. Gab's hand rose toward the scene in involuntary tribute. Where the glass began its passage through the pane, light leaped the way water encircles the thrown stone, though now they were seeing it from below like a pair of cautiously gazing fish. Further on, in the darker parts, were reflected shades of such subtlety that, still a fish, Mr. Gab gaped.

The sheet bore creases of course. It would have to be ironed. The hang of the cloth over the wire could use some adjustment, perhaps a little weight attached to the bottom edge might improve the stretch, and the wire itself might be profitably tightened. Nevertheless, toiling in the dark, they'd done a good job.

We'll keep watching. Someone will be along soon. In a red sweater maybe. How would a red sweater look passing that brick, Mr. Gab wondered. Such a spectacle. Well, Mr. Gab, it *is* upsidedown, Mr. Stu said. I should say "thank you" to you, Mr. Stu, Mr. Gab said. You've given me quite a gift. And upsidedown will be all right. Like reflections from water. We shall adjust. I guess it will be, Mr. Stu said, but not even his ears knew whether he spoke in earnest agreement or out of sad acceptance of it. It . . . it's colored through. Yes, Mr. Stu, and what colors, too. Have you ever seen such? And look at the contours, so precise while staying soft and never crudely edgy. Never . . . you know . . . I never saw this building before. I never observed our street. We might wash the window—that bit in front of the pinhole, Mr. Stu suggested. Splendid idea, Mr. Stu, agreed Mr. Gab. But it *is* upsidedown, Mr. Stu ventured. They gave one another looks which were gifts not quite accepted. In color, Mr. Stu reminded. Sweet as rainbow ice cream, insisted Mr. Gab. A car . . . a cab . . . flashed by. The chariot of the sun, Mr. Gab exclaimed. Oh, Mr. Stu, this will indeed do. The bricks reddened to the color of rare roast beef. It will do just fine.

Charity

Dear Sir/Madam,

I understand you have helped people like myself in the past and I would like you to consider helping me at this time. My situation has changed drastically in the last several years and I have lost all that I have with the exception of my home. At this writing I have after all this time just started a part time position with the hope that will eventually lead to a full time employment.

The reason I am writing you this letter is I am in desperate need of money to replace my roof so that I may continue to have a roof over my head. I have struggled to do repairs but have run out of money to complete the roof.

I understand that you may have been in a similiar situation some time in your life and my promise to you is "I will in turn help someone as you have helped me, once I am financially stable". All I need is $7900.00 to replace the roof and will be in your debt should you find it in your heart to help me.

You may personally contact me at ███-███-████ between 3pm and 5pm Monday thru Friday as I am working other hours and a friend accepts my calls if I am not available.

My gratefull appreciation in advance.

Sincerly

Actual begging letter to author; only the name of the writer is deleted.

Hardy held the can firmly in his fat little fingers. He was old enough to be ashamed of the label: a cheap brand of brown bean soup—or was it chili? He slipped from his seat and walked warily to the front of the room where he placed the soup, facedown, on the heap of cereal boxes, pasta packages, and miscellaneous tins of mixed fruit, Spam, creamed corn, sauerkraut, sugar peas, and sardines. He heard jingling behind him that sounded like loose change. And the patterpad of sports-shod feet. This shouldn't be happening on K Street. He began walking as rapidly, as purposefully, as vigorously as he could. A dark arm swung itself alongside him. Sir. Sir. It said. Some kids had come with two cans or one bag of rice and one round box of quakered oats. We've already given—in my homeroom—quite a lot, Hardy's father felt he had to remind his son. I have to set an example for the kids—in my own homeroom—show benevolence. But—you know—we're not here to feed the world. We can take on—through my homeroom—just one unfortunate—one less unfortunate—one deserving family per year. Sir. Whatever change you have would be helpful. Hardy could hear the coins the man had already commanded jingaching-ing in a pocket, chinging because the extorter had to be loping to catch up with his extortee. Maybe the sound was meant to prime the pump. Hatcheck girls put a bill or two in their tip glasses for the same reason. She said if you must you must but you must promise to stop your begging, poor boy. The face alongside him had huge eyes. Pupils dark as dirty dimes. On bright hard paper. It was not coins but chains that were jingling. Hardy was offended by a row of square white teeth, plump moist lips, bumpy black skin that needed a bit of sanding. The man—the panhandler—had short stiff hair like a brush all business. A little change will do a lot of good here. Hardy looked straight ahead at the hollow of her throat so he saw her breast out of the corner of his eyes when she pulled aside her bra the way he caught sight of the box of fig newtons among all those bags and cans, and surprised himself, even at that age, by experiencing desire's definite tug. He judged himself cowardly. He couldn't confront. He was consumed by anger, cornered on a big street. Was the world without shame? Running alongside him like another train. At goddamn noontime. Hardy hastened back to his desk and sat with solemnly folded hands while others went forward to deliver their contributions. The class had already recited the Pledge of Allegiance. The pledge scarcely bound you beyond a single day; it could no more be counted on to last than the visit of a fly, because it had to be renewed so frequently, like a magazine subscription that ran for five minutes. Allegiance must surely lapse altogether during weekends. There were kids in the class, poorer than any probable beneficiary, who had brought ostentatiously large bottles of juice or packages of cookies featuring biggish pictures of the plump round toothsome sweets, cut open (in their pictures) to show they were full of filling. He was daily made aware he had no secretary; one of the few in the firm to be without such a sign of success; but he slit the envelope deftly nevertheless and angrily blew it open. I'm not paid for this. How could Hardy claim he had no change when the fellow could hear it rattling around inside him as though flung about in the dryer. After all, if Hardy could hear his pursuer jingle, his pursuer could certainly hear the frightened jangle of his prey. Big brown bull's-eyed white eyes as advertised, toast-flecked, Nigerian maybe, skin dark enough to be nighttime, and like a crescent moon a confident and shiny smile. Hardy hated him. He could escape by turning into a store. And if he did? Shirts, ties, even hats nobody ever wore anymore were on sale, and Hardy imagined he'd see straight ahead at the rear of the shop a changing room he might scoot into to hide until the coast was clear. Her nipple stared directly at him, pink and perky in a brown pool that made his pulse hear itself in his head, hardly pounding yet, but audible to his reddening ears. The sheet was folded neatly in threes according to convention—Hardy always noticed that—and began with improper propriety: "Dear sir. I understand you have helped people like myself in the past . . ." Into the big pink palm he put his handful of nickels dimes and quarters. Good quality. Not a penny among them. Bless you, sahr, the face said, beaming. Sir was sahr now? Hardy hated himself for giving in, for being a coward, an easy mark. How did the fellow know? It probably took years or weeks and days of experience. To spot them. Him. The EZ mark. She called it the Cringe; he called it the Gratitude Game. He begged and then was grateful. She acquiesced and accepted. The arm was black not because it was bare and belonged to a very blueblack man, but because the blueblack man was wearing a black turtleneck and black pants and black-and-white athletic shoes. His hair was brisker than a cold breeze. He was . . . well . . . he was well dressed. The King of K Street. Requests came in the mail—

constantly. Scarcely a day at his desk and his secretary—if he had one—would have slit open some charity's appeal, just slit, since Hardy liked to throw away the slush himself, examine everything, the envelopes designed to look as if they contained a government check, at catalogues full of motorcycle parts, even ads for health insurance, so he would have her just open them—slit 'em—he imagined that she had a slick wrist—and pile them on his desk in a neat stack—biggest on bottom, next, next—for him to sneer or laugh or growl at before tossing them into recycle. National Preservation. The Heart Association. Multiple Sclerosis. Red Cross. March of Dimes. Give generously. Your contribution will enable us to make more mailings. Save the Whales, the Environment, the Seals, the Whooping Cranes, the Sea Turtles. Your contribution will feed a future thief for a whole week. Stop the Loggers. Defeat Cancer. Support the Fraternal Order of Police. The Salvation Army. The United Way. Your contribution will enable our board to enjoy luxurious surroundings when we next meet in Coral Gables. Protect and Serve is the blue-coat motto. Just who is the lucky recipient of this attention? The police themselves, my boy, who are never about when the panhandlers pan. He'd been shaken down at high noon, shaken in full public view, shaken till his change withdrew from an embarrassed pocket and fell out of his crestfallen paw. It was humiliating but she loved to have him lick her like a puppy. Why did he do it? He did it because he was a coward. He did it because she was better at being beautiful than any woman he would ever be likely to know. Broad pink nails, so striking on fingers so blackly barked. A coward a coward they called it a wuss, being a wuss, nothing worse. Miss Rudge, who will our food bags be given to? Why, a poor family, of course. But what one. You should say, Hugh, to whom. To whom, okay? Well, we don't want to embarrass anyone, do we? Would you like folks to know if you had to wear another kid's cast-off things? I wear my older brother's worn-out rags. She gave her body. He gave her gratitude. It seemed a fair exchange. But we're just asked to bring food. There will be—from the teachers, I expect—some no longer needed things. From good folk here and there. Items of benevolence added. Anyway, what if you had to eat leavings? Hardy had selected the can himself. He'd been told to. Pick out one we really don't want. Like these peas? Of course not, we love peas. Granny's Sweet Brown Beans. Let's see the label. Oh them. Take that one then. It's soup. With the dent. Or chili beans conless of carne. After all, we have to give so much to your father's homeroom, Miss Rudge will understand your modest compliance. Anyway, sweets are good, sweets are just the ticket; they've all got mouths full of sweet teeth rotted to their roots. Hardy knew his father's room had to sport the best—that meant most bountiful—box. The other teachers would admire—well, envy—how much more Hardy's father could extort from his kids, so much more than they pried from theirs. Out of others only modest contributions. He remembered midget Frigidaires. And cooling closets. You are such a silly, she said, letting her skirt slip past her knees. He went to his. Please. Please. Just a bit of change, whatever you have, bless bless. Damn black bastard's nerve. Neck hung with gold-colored chains. At least nothing hanging from his ears or piercing his nose. No scars scratched onto his face like some cosmetic hex. How could that be attractive? Hardy hurried on instead of watching where the fellow went when he finally had his handful. The homeroom of his father boasted a bigger charity box than the others. It held

hundreds of lemons once. Brought out year after year like a lawn-
mower. The box was married—but just—to a lid buckshotted with
little holes. Its regular reuse enabled the room to maintain a mea-
sured kind of gift giving, a steady match of one Christmas with
another, Hardy's father said, though he was forgetting inflation.
Everybody drowned in a sea of sympathy. An entire town smothered in molten lava. The track of the tornado. F4. Wind whistle.
No one in Africa has food. Even the stones are starving. Hardy
knew his parents liked to watch the box being unpacked, can by
jar, mitten by glove, bag by carton. As a surprise, there'd be a toy
ingeniously repaired. She lifted her bare foot free of the cloth
lifted her bare foot free lifted her bare foot. Gee. Oh gee, ". . . and
would like you to consider helping me at this time." That guy
hadn't looked as if he lived on a Metro grate. And if he were an
African with a smidge of sense, he'd never wear any kind of chain.
But they didn't think things through, did they? This guy lived so
much for show he wouldn't even pretend to be stricken and
shabby. More gun butt than pan handle. How Hardy disliked
D.C. The homeless were everywhere. Passing the time. That was
all. Waiting like plants for a little sun a period of rain a rewarding
response. In Santa Monica it was the beach, the Palisades with all
those fruit trees, but in Washington it was the plethora of public
buildings that drew them, the many benches in Union Station
where they were rarely run off because bigwigs didn't take the
train. In Santa Monica they were nuts and bolts. The nuts talked
to their reflections in store windows. The bolts waited till you got
near and then ran. Ran in an alley. Ran into a vacant lot. Made
you feel like a fucking leper or the local dick. Here they looked
cold and old whatever age and lay rolled in snaggy blankets on

grates and museum lawns. In Santa Monica they were fed by the city and without urging would sometimes gather in groups to chat, occasionally blocking paths and walks. Many of them had been nuts from their first Sunday. Don't make eye contact was the word to the wise. In the window a soulmate would be similarly gesticulating. See me see you seeing me. How did they like the way their stew was served on those loopy paper plates? Where a brown liquid ran from beneath the carrots potatoes beef like a primeval seep. He hoped his soup was okay though containered by a dented can. "I am a negro male senior citizen trying to cope with the following problems: 1." ONE. Hardy hated an empty day. Sundays. Below him, he could see souls on their stroll to church where a minister would try to make sexless love sound attractive to rows and rows of continuous semishiny seats. Sunshine on the caramel carpet. Bare brown walls. Otherwise empty streets. Sunshine on cement. Silent but for bells. Sunday, day of good deeds, the homeless were fed a hot meal at the city hall. Cardboard sign, nailed to a pole in Palisades Park, said so. D.C. was installing new hoop-shaped grates even a contortionist wouldn't find comfy. Where would they go when the seasons neared cold? There'd be Santas standing by grocery-store doors. Ringing a red bell. Rattling a worn clapper. Dang. Tending a red pot suspended from a tripod. Dang. Every damn day of the week. Dang. Those bells, Hardy thought, had lost their dings and had no dongs. It helped him to think that. So Hardy would go elsewhere and take his refusals with him—in effect, boycott the entire chain. That would teach them. But how forlorn and futile the single gesture always was. Still, show some guts. Never cross a pleader's line. Pots the size of sandbox pails. Because it was empty, Sunday seemed so large. By eleven, everyone inside their suits and silks, listening to the Lord's word, singing hymns with no names but numbers. Waiting for the gimme plate. Is that why singers said: I'm going to sing a little number ... ? Hymn forty-nine. Convict ten-oh-three. Hardy remembered reading about the dinky fridges the English cooled their ardors in. Like seeing the picture of a pygmy before you saw one in a sideshow. Couldn't store a lot, nothing large, consequently you didn't buy a lot, nothing large, didn't buy a lot because you couldn't shop with a car unless you could find a place to park which you couldn't, so you shopped every morning if you were a missus, you just walked to the store pushing the baby buggy sometimes, sometimes with a baby in it, visiting first a dinky butcher shop for red meat, internal organs, and muscular chicken before going on to where a clutch of bins were bunched on the sidewalk heaped with big sprouts and bigger beets and bigger yet cabbages to stuff and stretch your string bag, proceeding then to a dinky bakery to purchase tea cakes and tea buns and tea sweets and devil's foods whose frosting was hard as plaster, all the while making time with the butcher, the dry goods chap, or the sweetmeat dearie, passing the morning like a gassy emission, parking the kid in a braked pram outside the shop but in any weather—the fresh air was good for all and sundry—so the tot's slobber froze on his slobbered cheeks and made him look healthy forever because he, or—worse—she, soon wore little networks of faint red capillaries to prove she was ... they were ... well ... to prove they were hardy: that was the series of connections—the chain—what was it called?— the chain of inconvenience which held the society together, since it was your semidetached house with its annoying shrunken spaces that made you shop every morning, consequently requiring everyone to get to know everyone, neighbors very much in the neighborhood of one another, chatting away like chickens, hence everyone carried a string bag and tried to be genial, trudging from counter to counter with big British change that weighed too much for a pocket to hold for long—pence in the pants—so that even men, imagine, had to carry a purse and a wadded thing of string just to buy cigs; nor could a customer cut the connections and free itself by purchasing a big two-door Sub-Zero flown in from America even though it wouldn't fit against any wall except the one in the parlor, because you wouldn't be able to carry home enough potatoes lard and fish to fill it, on account of your car was of no use to you if you had to park it by the greengrocer's or by the baker's or by the fishmonger's and by the hosier too. The fact was that these various dink-sized things, spaces, human routines were knotted together very like string sacks imported from the Third World to make a social net, a net veined much like the ones he'd seen on a score of ruddy cheeks riding the Underground, the owners of the cheeks carrying bags openly abulge with cheap-peep purchases—this resemblance had impressed Hardy. The fact took residence in his mind where it served as a kind of universal pattern—a grid—to arrange his insight into things. A vast set of shabby supportive circumstances surrounded every newswrapped sleeper or pimp-appareled beggar or unwed widow with dollybaby at her bosom huddled at the door of a church to break your heart. He'd been accosted in New York by a trim earlymiddleaged lady several shades from plain—she had spotted him like a Shriner on the street—sir—always sir, as if he'd been knighted—well, hell, he was known to have helped deserving needy persons in the past—sir, she said—and then entered her spiel as if his slowing step had been a rising curtain. She needed money to get to Yonkers. Seven seventy-eight was what she needed, was with tax, the fare. His fingers failed of ten and gave her five, though afterward, walking away in shame in humiliation in a rage that reddened his face, he wished he'd counted out just the seventy-eight cents to help her evenly on her way. Coward. Lily-livered. Wuss. The Tree of Lights Campaign always fell short and was never declared over until February. Hardy's idea of how to lure new businesses to town was to promise that the Community Chest would leave them alone. Solicitations by phone: at noon, at six, when you'd be home. Someone on the other end pretending to be an old friend from the class of '88. For the honor of our Class. This phonathon's for dear old Alma, my second mother. Mother of my law degree. Listen, old pal, I didn't see a quad, a tree, a lawn, my many years in school—I saw only columns of the law, walls of heavy books, I saw only cheese crackers under fluorescent light, pages of opinion almost as blanched as bleached jeans—mock this, mock that—heard Jewish jokes. My class comprised scores of grinders just like me, as well as a few liberated ladies repeatedly unscored upon. Lived in a lousy little lightless room. Sat through stultifying lectures. Read boring books—boring boring books. And after all that got a so-so job. Don't Alma mother me. He should have given her exactly seventy-eight cents. If she wanted to pretend to precision that would serve her lying tongue right, to round her sum off and ruin its verisimilitude for the next sucker, though having the seventy-eight pennies she wouldn't plead for a simple seven smackers, would she? He still wished his tin hadn't had a dent in it. A nice man just gave me seventy-eight cents so now all I need from you, sir, is seven bucks to get me back to Yonkers. Yet who would stoop

to it—solicit, beg, entreat—who didn't need to? There, in front of
all eyes, on a public street? Still, only he—sap Hugh sap Hamilton
sap Hardy—had met her eye. Otherwise their entire transaction
was invisible as perfect servants were supposed to be. True charity
was anonymous, wasn't it? Handing her the tenner, no it was the
fiver, he and she turned into two stones in a stream, and pedestrians passed around them the way they stepped over sleepers on the
stairs to the Metro. Noli me tangere wasn't something Latin from
the law. This seeyounot hearyounever training was transcribed in
the genes and, paradoxically, transmitted by sperm that touched-
younowhereyouknewabout. Molly was not an appropriate name
for the Cleopatra whose breasts she permitted him to heft. A holy
office. Raising the fatty chalice to his lips. The Salzburg Seminar
wanted him to support it, the Folger ditto. Anywhere you had ever
been became an endangered place; everything you did incorporated itself as a not-for-profit foundation in need of funds; every
Cause followed you with open envelope. Dear sir . . . sir. She
offered herself—should he say?—fulsomely. Hardy waited for the
last kid to dump his donation but the last kid didn't budge, humiliation held him in his seat, he had no gift, he said, for the hungry
homeless poor, he hadn't because . . . because he'd just forgot.
Forgot the hungry homeless shabby needy poor. Well, that's all
right. Just bring something useful tomorrow. The kid's red hair
tried to creep under his scalp. Hardy had no name for him. Just
kid. He remembered the brand of his soupy beans but not the
name of the crestfallen kid who had embarrassed the class with his
embarrassment. Van Camp's. Help me through my struggle. In his
first job Hardy had worked for Hemline Associates, a big outfit,
big enough to hold a whole building captive, in an office park sur-

rounded by grass green as money. Hemline had sent Hardy abroad for his first time—to England to match the English sneer for sneer. At sneering he'd been a failure. He couldn't give looks. Giving was a significant thing at Hemline, part of your job, a definite expectation, Hardy found out, when he didn't turn in his promissory note to the United Way. It would have come out of his pay. As automatic as an electric eye, his bank account would open its arms. Like the seeing-eye door at the market where a padded Santa would stand, ting-a-ling-linging, giving you a stare-you-down stare. Hardy was metaphorically dumbfounded: here was a commercial fiction's fake representative giving you the once-over as you prepared to give a business your business—outrageous! you were the real creature after all—you weren't a shabbily costumed bad actor in a stupid play—and giving you the twice-over when you left. Once. Twice. Over. Not even Santa's red stomach was real. The belt was of cheap shiny vinyl. Donk donk went the ding-a-ling's bell. Hardy remembered the pennies which bad luck that day had brought him, and how heavily they weighed in his pocket; how he had received four cents in change when he paid for a magazine, four more on account of a small packet of staples and four from a frozen dinner, it wasn't fair, they bumped against his leg as if he were carrying a cosh made from coins, precious metals in a sock. Good idea. To clobber professional accosters on their noggins. Here's your money, dummy. They rang your bell, made you come to the door. Held your home up. Preyed upon your politeness. So they could rant, presume, even pray, while pretending to chat on your front steps as if they were leaving a party. Confronters. Beggars of attention. In pairs like police: one black one white. Halo-hoopers. Petitioners with clipboards as if they held the Tablets of the Law. A good cause is always a good excuse. Walkathoners. They ... the profiteers of philanthopyl ... they'll make use of anybody, children too, who skip rope in relays for hours to repair the sad plights of unwanted babies as though the bastards were rips in a coat. Trick or Treat runs through the same extortionist routine. Nowadays the kiddies offer you riddles older than the Nile—what's black and white and red all over?—presents that you, donning a clown's jolly surprised smile, reward with sweets bought in bags at the SuperStore: dwarfed bars of preserved glucose that coat the riddlers' stomachs and ruin their preteen teeth—that was meager comfort—instead of suffering the soaped windows of former times or the absence of patio furniture that's been hoisted without malice but for your inconvenience atop your porch roof. The chain had almighty many links, always: the candy manufacturers, for instance, who had captured Valentine's Day and had a leg up on Easter, sold during the weeks approaching their designated holy days enough sugar to make a capitalist of Cuba. If you gave a kid a healthy apple he might shit on your stoop in disappointment and revenge. You turn the trick, dear, and I'll enjoy the treat. Darkies came in dreadful droves to mug the smug in their suburban enclaves. They didn't even costume up or anything, just collected candy, keeping the economy healthy, their presence menace enough; what would we do without the poor to engage the gears? Yet what have we left them? Only a sweet tooth with which to bite down on their stale little pittance. A bit peanuttery, wasn't it? Hardy remembered the riddles and prepared an appropriate riposte: a nun, a chef, and a fireplug. Through eyeholes, down false noses, the kids stared at your answer as if at a bulldog. The worst doorknock nuisances were those prissily dressed pairs (white boy black girl) who wanted you to listen to their religious spiel, who requested the precious gift of their time, your attention, and received instead the absence of your mind and the anger of your soul. Nigerians have those wide noses, don't they? Splayed, but no nostril hair, never see hair there. Cowed. He'd been cowed. In Naples in Rome crowds of gypsy children crowd round you at the railroad station trying to steal your bags or your purse or your wallet or the package under your arm while you are hunting for lire to fit into all those grimy aggravating fists; thin-fingered they are, pale-faced though swarthy, greedy and grinning, inevitably skinny and in clothes patched from here to there, but dancy and darty, shifty-eyed and slick. Hardy was reminded of the insatiable appetite of squirrels. She didn't shave under her arms, was rather proud of the black thatches that enlivened her nudity. Matisse-ish. No. Modigliani. Ish. Long hair on ladies, Hardy thought, was a gift because it took some taking care of. Short-haired women weren't much for the giving business, in Hardy's opinion. Only interested in Easy Maintenance. In Maintaining a Masculine Image or the Business Woman Look. I'll do you if you do as you're told, Molly always said, with a smile like she'd already had her satisfaction. Once women wore layers of fat to be pleasing, were ample and rolling like verdant meadows and soft plump mattresses on pillowed beds. Warmly redundant. Like reciting Our Father in church. Dundant. The organ moaned an Offertory, a saucer-shaped basket would pass and mostly envelopes would fill it. Nothing so vulgar as a bill to prime the plate like hatcheck chicks line a glass so you could see what you should do. Beggars were apportioned—in Florence, in Pisa—one to a doorway. In Bologna, Hardy believed, charity was better managed because the Communists didn't permit poverty. In a just society compulsory generosity would be unnecessary. But our society was just social. According to the church, giving gave you good luck and a Christian blessing. Of some sort. Hardy wasn't able to believe in a deity precisely because of creation's constant need for charity. Well, he felt bad about the boy who hadn't brought—maybe couldn't afford—wasn't allowed—a donation, so the next day he filched a can of asparagus tips from the Hardy larder and tried to give it to what-was-his-name? its label said Le Sueur, before homeroom convened, but the kid—what-was-its-name? fancy French—Le Sueur, let's say—shook his nameless lankhaired head, wouldn't take Hardy's offering, dashed off, clearly unstuck from his seat. Disappeared around a corner like a sparrow who's heard a cough or a footstep on the gravel. Turned truant, Hardy was told. Were there a good god, there'd be no needy, Hardy's wise high school head said. Hardy felt worse about the shame than the truancy. Shame was like a sun rising inside you, wet and steaming from the sea. You grew warm, oddly feverish, your heart beat so fast it began to sweat, maybe it was like a hot flash, camera popping off to light your dark insides. And observing, sharing someone's embarrassment—secondhand shame—also brought blood to the cheeks. Was it the same blood, he wondered, that gave you an erection or was it blood from a different section of the system? Burn always with a bright shame-like flame. Yeah. He'd heard or he'd read. Eat from each edge. Flames meeting in the middle. One consuming the other. So giving charity or getting it: which did more harm? It certainly perpetuated problems, rewarded failure, indolence. How to keep the homeless homeless: feed them. Let them lie about on the warm sand, sleep in moist warm sea air, stare at the ocean until it turns into dream. Bless our happy homeless state. Hardy was in a happy homeless state, wasn't he? His apartment was as empty as a sunny Sunday. In any case, how much good got done? Were some givers given God's grace as a consequence of their giving, or did they need God's grace in order to give in the first place? He'd read that most of the money these charities collected went to the administrators of the business. To buy little red soldier suits and a tambourine, or to dress deadbeats up as Santas. Only a little found its way to the poor, the sick, the diligent researcher, the ill-favored poet in his garret, the painter supported only by his easel, the cold-fingered composer who's had to pawn his ivories, feeding dog food to his famished genius till it barks, and music blares out the horn of the speaker. All that the Boy and Girl Scouts did when they went scouting, as far as Hardy could see, was solicit for the scouts. Badges ought to be awarded for cookie sales and raffles. Hi. I'm Heather. I live down the street. Would you like to order some Girl Scout cookies? What kinds do you got, sis? Raisin oatmeal as always, I dunno, chocolate chip, of course, I guess, everybody's favorite, looking a lot like oatmeal raisin, ginger peachie it's called, I think, this year they promised to bake some of that hardasnails butterscotch. Hardy remembered peppermint with a certain fondness. Some would be so young their moms would have to follow in a car like FBIs tailing an actress. Apartments wouldn't let them in—one advantage of high-rise life. Except for the families in residence who roamed the corridors howling like Indians. KIDS AND PETS NOT ALLOWED was a utopian policy which had to be disavowed on account of those cowards in Washington, where Hardy, he was ashamed to say, lived, so he could enjoy being annoyed with his neighborhood, disgusted with his city, embarrassed by the country and its lascivious citizens—whose undisciplined offspring loved to button up and down on the elevators, to pester your floor, play hide and seek, and, fueled by giggles, race the halls until they located your poorly protected pad, where they would rap as resoundingly as the concierge you had given up expecting though the tap still dripped. At fifteen, at his home then on Greenleaf Street, Hardy would have to answer the door—Mom and Dad had sworn off that chore because—they lied—on the other side might be a complaining parent come to confront Dad with a D he alone had awarded and a D that would keep their stupid little squit out of Dartmouth—"answer the door" was the expression, as if it had asked, as if its deadbolt had made such a declaration . . . ah! and meet Heather—too undeveloped to be dated—standing on the stoop, but not dressed in her little Girl Scout skirt, or in her wide green sash where the medals were pinned, instead in a sack suitable for five-year-old grannies, sewn from a pattern better used to tile a floor. Hardy couldn't put a stopper on his youthful condescension (a more sincere if unmerited assumption of superiority), and inevitably succumbed to the temptation to tease. Where's your uniform, Heather, how do I know you're a scout without your uniform? She had an official paper in her hand. This was thrust in his face. Hey, he said, without your uniform you're not a scout, and without your skirt you're not a girl you're a granny. Her other hand held a folder depicting plates of garish-colored cookies in restful circumstances. The folder slipped open and flapped shut. Hardy laughed loudly and honestly at her. The stupid girl's mum gave his mom a complaining call, and soon both mothers were furious with a fury that flowed from them in fiery pinwheeling rings. They'd have to stop answering the phone or reading their mail, his parents said, and hard-ear any kind of question coming from the public sector. Hardy had hated scouts ever since . . . ever since Heather. Voice recorders were invented specifically to protect those who had fled to apartments to avoid salesmen, because now it was the phone that rang, not the front-door bell—"answer the phone" was the operative phrase—whereupon a heavily accented voice would try to give you something. As soon as Hardy heard the words "Congratulations, you've—" he'd hang. Or the phone would go deeple deeple deeple so Hardy's recorded voice could repeat: "This is Hugh Hamilton Hardy, I am sorry I cannot come to the phone right now but please leave a message after the tone and I'll get back to you"; whereupon a mechanical clone, turning a tin ear to his dismally conventional apology, would wonder whether Hugh was sure Hamilton was sufficiently insured by Hardy. Such solicitude from a machine should extract a tear from a hinge. However, Hardy loved the firemen's magical formula "weir raisin sum muny for the orfans." Raisin. Like bringing up baby. Or a ship from the depths. She would redden sometimes in the space between her breasts; he would praise her; she would shy a smile and run his hands through her hair. The firemen would infest intersections, holding boots up to your nose, if you'd been foolish enough to slow down while enjoying an open window. These were slicker-yellow boots into whose depths you were expected to cast coins of a number sufficient to rattle pellymelly on the way down since the firemen were always jiggling them as if absent legs were feeling a bit of bladder pressure and needed to water a garden. In Hardy's Midwest hometown, its admirable but underpaid defenders had gone on strike, and, in order to emphasize the public's need for their protection, had burned down a couple of empty buildings. Well, they weren't all empty. A pair of tramps got scorched. They burned—the buildings—very slowly, and many people came to contemplate their consummation. In Prague, because his window overlooked the street, Hardy had watched a master at work. A man, slightly portly, just past middle age, dressed neatly and rather formally, in tie, hat, and sweater worn like a vest, would come every midmorning to a slight indentation in the old buildings which so solidly lined the street, and fitting himself in a niche would simply stand in solemn impassivity with one open hand held at the side of his chest into which an amazing amount of small bills and change were deposited by passersby to whom he said not a word, nor did he wink or bow or smile. The hand would fall into his coat pocket and just as mechanically rise again, empty now, to resume its very discreet petitioning. That hand, so naturally positioned, could almost have been held where he held it as if it were being held there in idleness, without prior purpose. I am gentry, his dress, his expression, his posture said. I clearly don't need your money. Nor shall I try to elicit your sympathy by looking forlorn in any way; you'll hear not a word of whining, I've no sad story; you'll catch nary a look of anxiety or remorse, an imploring gesture; nor shall I close my fist on your florin, as if in a hurry, nor show, by bob or nod or bless you, some sign of appreciation. Hardy would slowly kiss her cute feet: toe one, toe two, toe three . . . She would grow moistly abundant. Resplendent, the thigh skin, stretching away to the mount. He thought just then of the Mount of Olives. Absurd the adventitious bridges between words. Yet it was astonishing how a sacrifice, a catastrophe could comprise a gift. After Cans for Kids had come and gone, the carton would remain in a corner of the

classroom, flaps up, waiting for its gaps to close. Indent. New
paragraph. "1. A wife suffering chronic osteoporosis for five years."
It was notable that after the salutation "Dear Sir," there was a
period incorrectly bestowed, whereas at the end of the presumably
heart-tuggy phrase "I am a senior citizen trying to cope," there was
a colon, properly disposed to herald the oncoming list of tribula-
tions: "1. A wife . . ." The typing, too, was flawless, and a local
address was placed at both top and bottom of the page: upper
right, then lower left below the signature, a Lemuel not a Gul-
liver but someone Tugge. Jeez. Lemuel Tugge. Really? He'd been—
lawyer Hardy had—denied the services of a secretary because, as at
Hemline, he was repeatedly on-the-road, in-the-plane, appearing-
in-offices-all-over-the-world with his case and his pale almost
painted smile, faint as those mural figures that have faded on the
flaking wall of an ancient church in dingy Sicily, his purpose in
suddenly showing up to quietly consternate a deadbeat, a behind-
hand supplier, an unfair competitor, a patent thief, a malingerer, a
physician who was practicing imaginary medicine. Hardy's passivity was perfect, he'd been told—although it hadn't gotten him a
raise in two years due to tough times, he'd been also told—because
it was not subservient or cautious or lacking in oomph, but gave
off an aura of calm confidence and certainty about the legal, if not
the moral, superiority of his position, a nimbus which could have
come from nothing but a clear and steady we'll-wheel-you-into-
suicide point of view, accompanied by a softly polished face, a
cuff and color odor as seductively alluring as perfume from a
scratch patch, yet a posture exhibited by the suit that resembled,
in representing the claimant's attitude, a volcanic cone only
momentarily covered with cooling snow. He had been left hold-

ing the can, so he put the peas—or was it corn? asparagus?—on top of the sack like an uneasy crown. Its presence was remarked the next day because during the night, Hardy supposed, it had toppled to the floor and rolled a short distance into a very prominent middle-of-nowhere. Miss Rudge merely swooped it up without a word and dropped it through a sack's ruffled throat. In contrast, Hardy's dad was aware of every open spot in his collection. Consequently, when laggards made up for their tardiness with late deposits he immediately took notice of them. Ah. Someone has had the kind consideration to bring us nearer to our goal, Dad the Good Samaritan would loudly announce. Splendid! More of such thought, if taken, will put us in the pink. The pink. Yes. Of extended palm. Hardy had to hurry off to his own homeroom where Miss Rudge effectively ignored her charitable assignment—Hardy was happy about that—so her solicitations scarcely filled two skinny paper bags. She picked up and plop-dropped his can of peas—beans—as mechanically as a sweeper. Miss Rudge's seniors didn't have to have Santas pasted to the twenty-four panes of their windows. They didn't have to have paper chains looped above the blackboard as though something above had given way. Seniors didn't have to make Christmas greetings for loved ones out of Magic Marker, doilies, and art card. They were grateful for their seniority. But they still had to contribute to Cans for Christmas. They still had to pledge their allegiance. No indent. New paragraph. "2. A grown daughter diagnosed as a manic depressive after an auto accident." Maybe, Hardy thought, he should offer to take her case on a split-the-settlement basis. Illnesses itemized. The sums required were accurately estimated and efficiently summed. Amazing. Nevertheless not unlike the exactitude of the lady from Yonkers. Which offered itself as a model. The letter was neatly typed and professional except for the dot after "Dear Sir." Personalized. "Dear"—meaning cherished? meaning pricey? meaning loaded? "Dear Sir." On some: "Dear Sir or Madam." Signed with just the right amount of incompetence. But a copy nevertheless, as his wet thumb drawn across the signature proved. Not even the suggestion of a smear. I need a secretary because, although I can walk into a Prague or Padua or Paris office and terrify the paperclips simply by saying hello and unsnicking my slick black briefcase, shiny as Mephistopheles's mirror, I can't face down a scheming beggar on the street. Coward yellow-livered coward. What did his correspondent want? Black too, called himself a Negro (yes, caps) (oHh the shrewdness of that nomenclature), well, this negro needed money to buy a house. A house. Hardy didn't have a house. He lived alone in a bare-walled caramel-carpeted apartment on New Hampshire. Where he met Molly. Who also lived conveniently by, in a building of the feminine gender. Where, after inviting him up, she stood barefoot on his back in front of an open window. Don't you dare look up my cunt or I'll trampoline your spine. She was slim as a hipped stick, still . . . her weight made him feel light. And durable. Even though his position was appropriate for the weak. Hardy let his cheek lie against the cool unshaven rug. He knew his passivity was regularly misconstrued. One could not insist too strongly: passivity was his strong suit. But it was—well, if not quite an act, an adoption—like a lie once told you are stuck with—a stray taken in—so you frequently have to add to it, feed it, elaborate on it, currycomb it and live by it. Day after day, on and on—prolonged. His penis would struggle to grow in the no-space between rug and belly. Worth putting up with because in a bit she'd step off and straddle, her feet like hugging hands against his ribs. Then Hardy would be allowed to turn over and look up. If that's what it took, take it, that was his motto; and right now it was a living, though he was weary of airports and the boredom of business class, the self-inflating chat of his fellow travelers, their predictable complaints, sly self-compliments, lies they had overtold by now until they were a part of history, bastards whom hope has made legitimate, and in his passive mode, in practice for his arrival in Providence or Buffalo, he'd listen, or rather nod, chewing airline chips to create a munch of protective static to insert between his ears and the babble of his seatmates. The garrulous travelers were not soothing the way a fountain soothes. They weren't squirting water at the sky and pretending to make rain, a rain so controlled it drew amusing pictures, pittypatters on the plane of the pool . . . Hardy emerged a moment from his reverie. His thoughts were being detoured, but the detours were odd because there was nothing under construction. Not plop—plap. That was the sound the dimes and pennies made when tossed by well-wishers into the basin where at least the copper glittered, a bowl cleverly designed to keep the donations at a depth deeper than a thievish arm, so that once or twice a month a man in fireman's boots and a hand rake, or in sandals if the pool had been drained, would skiddle or wade about collecting coins for what would be advertised as a charity—Children Without Stuffed Animals—some such—teddy bears for kids that cancer was killing, therefore comforts that could be recycled—a thought that made Hardy smile out his window at the university students hurrying through the streets to destinies much like his, though how many girls would grow up to have their toes kissed: toe one, toe two, toe five; or how often would a guy get the gift of a fleece like hers, ebonized, abundant, such as the long fall of hair that splashed over her shoulders, curled as though waiting to be wound around a finger? Hardy had a slow smile, he'd been told, one that scarcely cracked and barely widened during those silences which served, for him, as the customary response to a plea, and excuse, even a bluster, a smile that grew like a tree ring till his teeth finally showed, and continued on, at the close of the client's or the distributor's or the competitor's explanation, to open in a loopy grin of disbelief, genuine because Hardy was always surprised by the excuses his . . . well . . . targets thought up; their fabrications amazed him, the apologies they proffered left him gaga. No wonder the company never considered its suppliers, its contractors, its customers, doctors or their patients to be anything but liars, dishonorable deadbeats, incompetent crooks—multimalfeasors, his boss liked to say, multimals—consequently, Hardy (his calling card read: HUGH HAMILTON HARDY, RECEIPTS ATTORNEY, HEALTH AND HAVEN INDUSTRIES) was never cast in any role other than that of the Enforcer—Receipts Attorney indeed—his warm round innocently open face like a Gatling gun going off in a paneled office, no coffee from Sumatra thank you I've already had breakfast, no scotch from Glenquaritch thank you it's too early for me, no water from Vichy either thank you all the same I don't smoke so shall we solve our little problem now since I know your time is valuable, time is more than money it is life itself, our hours even minutes are, so yours must be. I'm (softly said) sure. I'm sure. Hardy presented himself as a man with no needs and no concern for politeness. Not that he was rude. Against his rules. There was never any reason to be rude. Brisk not brusque, efficient not inconsiderate. As a response to his adversary's hospitality, in reply to pleasantries, Hardy would return a quiet confident word of warning, offer a pithy phrase of godfatherly advice, a sentence set down like a sentence from the bench in place of the glass of Vichy on a doily or a cork coaster, a coaster so the glass wouldn't sweat where sweat wasn't wanted, coastered where the rocked scotch might have sat, or a cup of fresh and steaming Kona could have rested: beverages chosen to call attention to the company's taste, drunk to encourage a comfortable climate, placed to promote a sense of shared values, where instead Hardy's black brief smugly threatened. The niceties were nice enough though they—alas—did nothing for the supplier's lack of promptitude, nothing to alleviate the deep disappointment their corporation had inflicted upon those who had counted on reliable deliveries, or a certain level of quality in the product, or the promised performance of a drug or an instrument; who moreover suffered from the inconceivable inaccuracies in the offending company's catalogue, with its pages of barren boasts, the flagrancies of its invoices, its evasive personnel, its grudging responses; so, under the circumstances, Hardy saw no way to slow or soften Health and Haven's insistence upon mutually agreed guarantees which, were they not promptly honored, XYZ Plastics—the End-of-Alphabet Company's presently miserable business—would surely suffer final disaster, almost immediately feel the serious impact of just and proper punishments: ill will, loss of custom on account of damaging rumors and other dirty words of mouth, lawsuits, dumping, infiltration, fines, raids, maybe a takeover followed by sell-offs, foreclosures, bankruptcy ... and eventually, after futile but expensive payments to lawyers, there would be an unpleasant trial concluding with prison and, therein, a long stay.

Perhaps XYZ's CEO would one day be writing Hardy one of those begging letters that were finding their way into his apartment's mailbox. Hardy took time out seriously to wonder this, not aloud, of course, or as an oblique way of suggesting such a fate for himself, since, face-to-face, he never doubted his cause. His inner rightness glowed like the word of God . . . glowed. What Hardy liked about business was that in business nothing was known of charity. It was, in that sense, a genuine world. There were only—sometimes—projects undertaken to cultivate goodwill, because goodwill and a Samaritan appearance were both cash crops. "I've labored my entire life to be self-supporting and am embarrassed to have to ask for help because of the desperate need for money." "I have been fighting my battles for three years now without a break." "My physical condition is improving but my finances are completely gone." "My husband's job folded in January this year. He's still seeking permanent employment." "I was really having major problems breathing to the point on May 13th, 1996, my father carried me to the hospital because I was collapsing every thirty minutes while walking, cooking, doing anything." "Sold my home in 1993 to support family needs." "I am a retired Army enlisted person crippled in both legs, both arms, and I have osteoarthritis in my upper spine." During the time Hardy's head was being filled with pleas, he looked the beleaguered company officer right in the eye. Which he couldn't do when confronted by a faceless page. Implacability would invade his gaze, as if his eyes were watering from some irritation. In the middle of his whites was the big blue sky like a bullet hole in a paper target. Hardy's boss was decent, an older man, beginning to fatten, show gray, who had reached the stagnant level of his skills, and who, therefore, could never be advanced if management were to continue to be shrewd. He was a lawyer, too, but hired by the company to protect its interests. He was supposed, like a house dick, to keep the peace, and, at a distance, the police. But in the day-to-day of his vocation he resembled a ship's doctor, those architects whom contractors hire, or chemists who contrive perfumes or find ways, selectively, to kill weeds, encourage seeds, entice rain, grow wormless fruit. And, under him, Hardy had a similar function: enforcer for the H & H family. He was proudly aware of the comparison and how well he matched it. It even, one could say, monitored his heart. Yes . . . Hardy was well paid. Sellouts usually sold out for something. Yes . . . Hardy was good at his job. But sellouts lost faith in themselves, then lost will and were no longer effective. Hardy hadn't, had he? felt a weakening of confidence or commitment. So he wasn't a sellout, was he? Once, Pilip, his boss, Greg Pilip, had asked him—Hardy had just completed a résumé of one of his journeys—yes, it had been after a long and arduous trip to Prague to confront a company which had agreed to supply Health and Haven downlike comforters for their chain of Golden Homes—the down count was in question—and as a form of conclusion, between them, between the Boss and his Bully Boy, as after sex, there had occurred a moment of relaxation during which time Greg (as he was just then) had wondered: Do you know of . . . he had asked him did he ever hear of a gangster in the twenties whose name was Baby Face Nelson? Hardy hadn't, but the question sent him to the Net and its miniature biographies. Soon Hardy became acquainted with the Karpis gang, Ma Barker and Machine Gun Kelly, Dillinger and Capone; he saw Clyde die in a car that would consequently sport a hundred bullet holes; thus he witnessed Clyde die in more indomitable condition, on account of that, than a tattered flag. But he was a gangster of the thirties, a bandit for Depression times, and certainly unsuitable for the more exuberant twenties. In any case, he would never have corrected his Boss over one measly decade. The belief that Hardy was Billy the Kid and Baby Face Nelson, if not rolled into one at least identically twinned, had secured his job once he had obtained it, but the combination in his person of the two outlaws also guaranteed he'd be frozen at his present level, because such a skill—he believed management thought—had a limited market, and further, that if he were moved up—promoted for muscularity as a strong arm—his strength, when employed to push pencils, would be largely wasted; though as Boss he might effectively terrorize his Bully Boys into realizing their own inner belligerency, still . . . would that be the best use of Hardy's rare and inexplicable talent? His talent, few knew, was for docility, not a real docility which might be lazy and intermittent and taken for granted, but one which was the object of enterprise and effort, and therefore was always finding fresh submissions designed to delight, and subtle gestures of idolatry that, for instance, could convince Molly that Molly's calves were golden. O she did so want to believe! The wondrous length of her leg made Hardy's mouth pretend to water, though it did water, so where was the pretense? A lot of his life was like the line his tongue took toward its goal: eager yet enacted, planned but passionate, urgent therefore slow and deliberate. The important thing was, she felt his touch, his tongue's tip. Or did she? Perhaps she simply read his kisses and responded to their meaning, completing the circuits of excitement through her head instead of through her skin? Whatever, as our children say today. Hardy had a hunch—he clung to it—it was his only hope—that other companies might covet his particular skills; after all, every one he'd visited, every firm whose duty he'd reminded their corporate conscience of, would be aware of his worth; of course, they'd not be so indiscreet about their own shortcomings as to mention him in that connection, so his methods might remain unheralded after all, even when they should have won him wide renown, and increased his value on the market. Hardy was puzzled. It was a problem. He was afraid he might be mispracticing his profession. The law wasn't a gun to be held at someone's head, was it? Because, in a way, his practice of the law was prelegal, prior to any filings, arguments in court, judgments, or jury findings. A similar quandary amazed his thoughts about Molly and her apparent pleasure in dominating him. It was, he believed, only theater. She was as free from commitment as a leaf in the wind. Molly was very male that way: to enjoy her enjoyment was her aim and end. Yet which one of them was really in charge? Because Hardy knew that if he groveled, if he bowed as if utterly to her will, Molly would melt, and he would soon have the pleasure of her having him, settling on him very slowly, the way someone sore might settle on a cushion, giving him nearly the only thing in life which sustained his self-esteem, and allowed him to expire in a sigh which would have signaled sleep if they'd been making out in his apartment. She would pretend to rise and find herself unable to; we appear to be screwed together, she would say, pressing him into her. Whenever Hardy did toe three, toe eight, toe ten, Molly would get the giggles and pound on the bed with her fists. I beg your pardon, sir, but I unfortunately find myself in a bit of a predicament. My purse was stolen on the train, and I need to get back home to a hungry child, yet here I am without the

fare for a taxi, sir, you could surely spare seven seventy-eight. How
to stare in silence as if to a stone. That's all I need, I've asked that
driver there what his price would be. How to brush by a pleasant
person, so she seemed, with nary a reply, after she had sought him
out in the crowd, spoken to him in such a sad and anxious way.
Hey ... I find myself in a predicament too. I am glued to my
girlfriend. Her arms, which were holding her hands prayerfully
together, rose like parallel beams to point in perfect unison at a
Yellow idling near the curb. Like a fool Hardy fumbled for a fiver.
Couldn't be cold, couldn't be big about it either. Hardy should
have advised her to huddle in a doorway, put on an imploring face
and hold her famished Yonkered tyke to her shriveled bosom;
then seven seventy-eight in lire would spill like tears into the gray
cloth of her lap where a few prechosen coins might already rest to
signify charity's chosen receptacle ... and prime the pump the
way hatcheck girls do, cigarette girls too, as well as the indicative
flapped-over caps of sidewalk artists. And why, after he had fumbled up his fiver, hadn't he hung around to see whether she would
take her coconspirator's cab? to catch her in her lie? why? whatever for? Because Hardy knew it was a fabrication, and she knew
he knew, how could she not know, although it was a reasonable
way to beg without begging exactly, since she would simply seem
to be borrowing a precise sum for a specific purpose, in a natural
fix, could happen to anyone at least once, moment by moment
more mothers were being mugged on the Independent, even
though the cab was pulling away without any passenger, just as
Hardy was being washed down the avenue, borne on a stream of
pedestrians who did not enjoy folks like rocks lying in their way,
bumping him a bit about the elbows till he started slipping along

himself, in tune, increasingly, to the flow of traffic, another mummm in the hum of New York life. While the beggarqueen was already down a block soliciting ten twenty-five to return to the Bronx. Please, sir. Please? They infested the intersections. They . . . they . . . how many? . . . multitudes. Sometimes little girls holding gaily creped boxes and wearing a hot weary sorrowful expression begged at the stoplight, raising a crayon-created cardboard sign to a car window where a sour-faced honky name of Hardy sat in his sedan staring sternly straight ahead and tried not to notice not to care if the Rainbow girls got to summer camp or wonder what work the wonk would do—as he had advertised—for food, or bother to count how many kids the fat lass had. Had had, and would have. Hardy had a hunch that more than once a few young men of no special connection hung about with tin cans to collect a little action money. Sometimes the kids were ethnically disadvantaged, tiny and teetery, likely to back into the path or the side of a car; it would happen one day and who would sue whom then? or complain in some D.C. city council meeting of being struck for racial reasons. Hardy approached such lights with extreme care, sliding the driver's window up. He had learned to shrug like a pauper and smile at the approach of a paper-covered juice tin or shiny Crisco can. He imagined there'd be a problem getting the grease out: just how well were the pots washed? How well did they need to be? Or there would be a bevy of formidable black women peddling little sacks of chocolate candy that the candy company (enterprising as always) had especially bagged and tagged for sale by charities. They are turning the streets into toll roads, Hardy thought. Occasionally the solicitors were dressed in the uniform of some odd rip-off cult like what were they called? those alleged

African Jews, Yah ... Ben something ... one of the lost tribes of Israel, the beggarly tykes' mothers in white sheets and head wraps watching safely from a sidewalk, out of their own harm's way, while their offspring handed out leaflets full of illiterate racist propaganda which would provide some bang for the sucker's buck if he paid but otherwise remained wadded in the nongimme fist as if it would never be released ... wah ... yes ... yahwah; but mostly it was black boys raising money to buy basketball uniforms, or those Korean cult creeps selling rosebuds—what a racket—or once in a while a woman willing to work for food to feed her get—like the Yonkers con—the sole support of her entire unfortunate famished family, their lives hanging by a threadbare thread. Hardy didn't drive much, but he did object to being victimized, particularly when alone in his own locked and technically moving vehicle ... One time the children wore white T-shirts with the words HELP US TO HELP OURSELVES printed on the back in black. The organizers had made an investment in T-shirts. Hardy was impressed. He admired flagrant honesty. They were going to help themselves to the money in his wallet. If people gave to the government a quarter of what they throw to the charitable scams as if they were tossing Mardi Gras beads into the trees we could buy better bulletproof vests for the police and undertake small local wars without being noticed by anybody not even the budget. Kept next to the heart in his regulation lawyer nonlinen nonseersucker suit he was required to wear the entire D.C. year even when Washington was hotter and wetter than the tropics. Entirely unfair. Secretaries swished about in dresses shorter than shorts and thinner than flimsies. Molly was amused when it poked its head from his bikini brief. Coast clear, it is supposed to ask. The youngsters were dis-

tributing leaflets—explaining themselves, Hardy guessed, inform-
ing all and sundry why this or that motorist ought to have shelled
out, but offering the news only when, and well after, the motorist
had . . . shelled. His curiosity awoke the second time he'd waited
at that light (because life usually committed you, if to go . . . then
to return) where he'd been opportuned by a tyke no taller than a
yardstick; and this sad measurement provoked him into handing a
dollar out his window to the length of an elbow. He received in
smileless blessless thankless exchange a piece of poorly printed paper the size of an ordinary book page which he promptly tossed
on the seat beside him and forgot. Though Hardy remembered
now and then with a genuine shiver how once off FDR Drive just
before the mouth of the Triborough Bridge he had been approached
at a light by a thug with a brick and a squeegee—your window or
your reward—and Hardy was indeed scared by the prospect, especially since the off-ramps were lined with burned-out cars—it was
as if he had suddenly driven into an apocalyptic movie—when
nearly in the nick of time the line lurched forward and Hardy's
windshield received only a squirt of something no wider or wetter
than the spatter of a moth. Toe two . . . the little piggy that had
roast beef? . . . can of baked beans with real molasses . . . tomato
soup, very popular, homerooms would swap dupes . . . package of
pasta, something of use . . . like kissing a big beard, the beard of a
bearded lady . . . well, they all were . . . beard blessed . . . cellophane bag of marshmallows . . . her moan, he assumed, meant for
him to go on . . . do more . . . jar of peanut butter, package of pud-
ding mix . . . we shall grow old together, she predicted, pretending
to be stuck . . . packet of tea bags, box of macaroni and cheese . . .
toe ten. In D.C. if you were smart you stayed away from the edges

of downtown, but he had not thought of riskiness that noon because he was simply walking through the fringe, so he had not thought about how foolish he was being although after all it was broad day and there were plenty of people around even if he was walking through the fringe and the people were mostly dregs and drearies, so what was there to think about? When ching-a-ching ching-a-ching jeezus right near Chinatown's big fake gate the fancy-dancy boy with the wide white eyes drew his shoes up alongside and said with a grin made of steel teeth sir . . . so what do you do, she said smiling widely wonderfully at his—was it?—right ear, and something in Hardy said I go to dooz like this, that's what I dooz, which turned her wide wonderful smile into an enchanting grin that defined her full-lipped mouth and made it impossible to imagine she was unattached, nor was she, as it turned out, as her eyes enlarged behind her wine, because like so many in the city of secretarial love, she was the plaything of a congressman's aide—how was that for being near the center of power?—who, however, bored her and was only good for pop concert tickets, and who could be dumped with less than a moment's notice if a real improvement could be offered, which he offered over and over in the next few days, clearly besotted, a condition she easily perceived and a state that didn't do his case any harm since it was seen as a big improvement, because these secretaries were accustomed to being taken for granted and abused, driven by their ambitions to betray their bodies by lending them to men who, even naked, wore their suits, tight ties, and the arrogant faces of loan officers to the SleepEase of love, coming with no more sound than a rubber-soled shoe, though if their squeeze didn't squeal, didn't buck and sweat and play the whore, they grew mean. Once these stags got their balls racked, they skidded from bed like a book that's fallen from sleepy hands, withdrew into their underpants and were soon quietly closing the apartment door, fleeing the hall as if the building were on fire. Hardy naturally thought of SleepEase because it was a company he'd had to threaten, their mattresses were some springs short. You must think our old people don't move when they groove, he'd been inspired to say, this time to a lady too far down the pecking order for Hardy to be seeing on such a serious subject; it annoyed him a little so he was—in tune with his temper—a little rude. She was black to boot. How far down was that? Measure the inseam of that insult. Molly's man came back for more, of course, but he rarely bothered to ask her out, which was what she was fucking him for—to be seen in the scene with her squire. So, for Hardy, it was a ripe time. He was lucky. Her beau, who didn't know he had been xxx'd out, phoned a few times, discreetly rattled the knob of her door. Quietly: toe three ... toe three ... toe three. What's that? It's fureee. Let's see. A leg languidly ... lan guid ly ... At the intersection this time stood the rose peddler. Invariably in nothing but bud, long-limbed, darkly, redly petaled, the stems were inserted into a plastic water-filled baggie, the baggies boxed, the box parked on a median strip where the TwiceSaved stood. Hardy wondered what their supposed price was, these posies sold by well-scrubbed kids no more Korean than Grandma's cookies, not nearly as moony as he was, remembering her skin, her shoulders laden with hair, her rich-lipped grin. You don't know how to crawl, she said. I'll learn to squirm, Hardy had replied, holding her with a wink and a word as securely as dining out or disco did, his arms also in an enraptured twine. Hardy, however, was happy to take her out; he was proud to be seen with such a bust, and a smile that was bestowed on him like a promise; it made him proud because it made others envious. Hardy, unlike her other lovers, knew how to love her; he followed her desires the way a weathercock sniffs the wind. Hardy did dates, went to movies, held in the cinema's semidark no more than her hand and kissed her slowly before they undressed, softly letting her lips encase his, appreciating their width (toe one), appreciating ears neck and shoulders, in no hurry (toe two), appreciating her feet and ankles (toe three), calves and even knees (toe four), appreciating the long sweet streets that were her thighs (toe five), really in no hurry; and these were appreciations Molly appreciated. Because he didn't embarrass her with sitcom jokes such as How are the twins? To which she had learned to reply, Getting bigger every day. In public Hardy was polite and attentive. That's all. It led her to think he Hardy was in love. Though Hardy would have traded her in for a secretary. "Your reputation as a person who has helped people like me in the past prompts me to ask you to consider helping me now. I write this letter in need of immediate assistance for a travel opportunity which has recently been offered to me." "I understand you have helped people like myself in the past and I would like you to consider helping me at this time. I am a recently married young woman who is fighting for her life against cancer and debt." "It is my understanding that you do consider helping people like me that have a plan but do not have the financial means to put it together." "Hello. My name is Marvin R. Travertine. A little over six years ago my illness really started to take its toll. I was working all over the United States on our Hospitals, Major Electrical and Defense projects. I started having problems that intensified over five years to cause me to loose my business and work, to loose my

wife and kids, to loose everything." "Dear Sir or Madam: I understand you have helped people like myself in the past and I would
like you to consider helping me at this time. I am a creative motivated minorities person with a lot of invention design idea's, that
need to be researched, developed and marketed for the consumer
market." "Your reputation as a person who has helped people like
me in the past prompts me to ask you to consider helping me now.
I recently lost my job and am unable to find another one because
of age discrimination." Just how long did Hardy think his baby-
face would remain so threateningly fresh and cruelly innocent? He
worried that his work was leading him into a dead end. What he
was learning, he worried, was not useful. Whatever he was honing
had no future. Like a girl he examined his fresh face for signs of
lines, laxness at a level just below the skin. What if he did become
the perfect pickle fork? Pickle forks were on their way out; they
were being replaced by colored toothpicks for God's sake. Hardy
couldn't help himself. What was SleepEase thinking? What was
SleepEase thinking? To sic a secretary on him. A rank insult.
Though they did replace their sleazy sleepmaps, he remembered.
So whatever it took he'd take, including humiliation. Maybe he
could buy one of those T-shirts he'd seen and wear it for Molly.
HELP ME TO HELP MYSELF. She'd pretend to scream with glee. Hardy
fell more and more frequently into broods, and into eddies of
ideas, turning and turning around, a tightening coil of concentra-
tion sucking his sense of safety and accomplishment down out of
sight so he could no longer see with any degree of satisfaction his
face in the mirror or shiny desk at his office or his name on a ticket
purchased for him for a plane or on a paycheck received in the
mail since someone at work had started unsealing envelopes to

peek—one presumed—at what others were making. It was in just such a brown study, one noon, as he was driving to an appointment at Walter Reade—why was it always the lunch hour? he had munched through so many dismal minutes of meditation lately, whenever he was away from his work, and that was the reason—being off duty—he imagined, because then his mind was free to maunder . . . anyway, he was in a high-noon mood when he drew up to an intersection occupied by hefty yellow-slickered firemen helping yet another year the children stricken with impetigo to control their itch, when, without a thought, nary a realization, he tossed his half-eaten handful of hamburger pickle lettuce cheese yellow mustard meat and bun into a proffered boot as the light fortunately turned and his foot scooted his car through the intersection with such admirable though unplanned dispatch he hardly heard the holler behind him. Hardy couldn't have helped himself. His hand had had a will, for the moment, of its own, as unconscious as the sharpshooter of foul shots is supposed to be, eye arm aim and lifted limb, like that of a dancer, oblivious to the howls of the crowd, the taunts of the enemy, as automatically accurate as the strike of the snake or the escape of the grouse, more the latter, as Hardy zoomed with an incontinent squeal across the crossed roads and into an unexpected lack of traffic. Which he believed was a lucky thing, beginning to sigh with relief before he knew what he should feel relieved about, when he realized instead that it made the task of the car now following him an easy one. Here it came, with apparatus of a dismaying sort—like a siren or twin flashers—on its roof. One of the fire folk was after him—what could they do?—Hardy's hands began to sweat on the wheel, but now he didn't dare speed with a coplike character on his tail, closing fast, and—wait a minute—going around in a rush, with a luggage rack on the roof, not a siren or some lights, a condition Hardy would have recognized had he been less shaken—what could they have done, had it actually been an authority who then stopped him?—there was no law to his knowledge determining what you might or might not drop in a boot unless it was a bomb if the boot was held up to your nose, and without any invitation, if you were stopped legally at a light, minding your own thoroughfare; still, Hardy had behaved badly because he had let an impulse, without warning—the way with impulses—overcome him. Then he thought: foreign money. He flew to Toronto, Paris, Rome, Madrid, London, even Singapore and Hong Kong. And returned with unspent coins of their realms in his pockets. Heavy as his thoughts. What was he thinking? Why was he sweating? His hands, his palms, his thoughts, sweating heartsweat. Hardy saw palms crossed with coin. Have sum. Will travel. He of course saved his change: he piled it into margarine tubs for use another time the way he'd washed out the containers, melting the oil with very hot water, carefully, like those paper-coated lard cans must not have been, the coins in stacks arranged by size and therefore by denomination; so when he alit at Tegel and needed a nosh or a newspaper before he hit the Exchange he already had in hand a few marks. How they would rattle down the tubes of the Salvation Army's Santa—Hardy's savings—and drop to the money-littered bottom of Kringle's bucket—MERRY CHRISTMAS—or fill with their wish-fulfilling weight the palm of some arrogant accoster—GOD BLESS YOU SAHR—or sag the hat of the street entertainer, fiddling and singing sixties songs in a voice that was strangled by his nose. "At this time, I am recovering from two serious injuries—a near fatal head injury from an auto accident and a severe leg injury suffered while rock climbing." The margins of these missives were justified. That is: they were written on a computer. Issued in begging batches by a dot matrix printer. Poor unfortunate bastards. Hurt. Out of work. Overcome by obligations. Molly giggled quite a lot. Hardy kneaded her buttocks, then her back. You do like tending to me, don't you, she said. Don't you like to be tended? Hardy thumbed her shoulder blades. 'Course. But I enjoy it because it's so important to you, she said, turning and inserting him. Hours in airports. It was another reason why he was valued by his firm: he could travel without becoming rebelliously bored or worn out; jet lag didn't leave him irritable or sleepy; he was indifferent to the strangeness of strange rooms, even to strange tongues, money, towns, faces, food. He read *The Wall Street Journal* for practice, and, on long flights, *Business Week, Fortune,* or *Forbes* because they projected, like a few frames of film, a good impression. Hardy's garb was the sort you'd never notice. I like your clothes better off, Molly said; they're nice folded over the back of a chair . . . where his jacket kept its drape. He opened envelopes carefully so they wouldn't tear, especially after he began finding those begging letters in his box. One day he received: two. With a solicitation from the Kennedy Center Opera Company in addition. He could become a donor for fifty, a sponsor for a hundred, a benefactor for two Cs, a sustainer for five, an angel if more. Angels could go to rehearsals, hobnob with the singers, sip a glass in the greenroom with the first violinist. Angels flew through generous clouds of gratitude. They—the Kennedy Center Opera Company—would love to be named in the will of Hugh Hamilton Hardy, Esq., Attorney at Law. What could he will them, he wondered. He'd will them society women in gorgeous gowns to grace their glamorous intermissions. No, stay on top, I like it better. But how had they got the address of his apartment? His office would seem a more likely target, if anything about these requests was likely. And Hardy felt, as he gradually began to process and assimilate the many messages—he undertook to number them in an upper corner—that they were suddenly swarming and assailing him, creating a weight in his stomach with their carbon- or computer-copied sentences. On the back of one envelope, in pencil, were painfully printed words his lawyer eye read as Latin but, except for the "*Deo*," didn't understand: "*vero glutine ei conglutinature, id est caritate . . . adhaerens Deo.*" What in the world? He knew "*id est*" and probably "*vero*" too. There was a dogthrown bone bothering his belly though he hadn't swallowed it, just chased it: the memory of a horrid moment heretofore only his childhood knew. To pass through untouched had been his intention. As through airports, on planes, in enemy offices. "Glutinus"? In front of his own wide window where he could watch George Washington students, as well as secretaries, stream from the streets: he was . . . ensconced . . . envelope in hand, Latin on its back flap like a mystery motto. His father had once said he'd been "touched" for a loan, and Hardy had wondered for a while about what that was: was it special, such a touch? was it a secret society's secret signal? a gesture of intimacy? the call for an historic promise to be fulfilled? It was. In order to seem a bit more personal to those designated by a list to receive them, his mother wrapped certain gifts in white tissue paper because it was Christmas, but in white tissue paper, too, because such paper was plain and unprepossessing, and wouldn't too entirely intimidate its recipient, or advertise its offering as more valuable than it was. It was thought to give to the box a festive and personal touch, and possible because Hardy's parents

knew the name, the address, the sex and size of the family. A tag
might say: "for the boy." Women wrapped. Men undid. Wrapping
was only for toys and trinkets, not for common staples, or for
cleaning powders. There were a few of his father's discarded shirts
in the cache, a sweater that never fit anyone, as well as a hat with
a perky flower, a skirt of a length to encourage modesty, a box of
pencils which were not all stubs, and other useful things in seren-
dipitous variety—bridge club favors, for instance, that Hardy's
mother had happily received but hadn't liked. Then a bag of
candy—jelly beans or corn. Nothing—like the plain white wrapping paper—fancy. How abundant, how refulgently full of good
things, the big box finally looked. Hardy was made to admire it,
and his reluctance to do so was assumed to be the result of being
asked to give up some unemployed toy or two of his own to the
accumulating bounty. "From the Hardy Family and Mr. Hardy's
Homeroom" was printed in block letters on a large red-and-white
shipping tag wired to one of the carton's corners. Jackson Central
Senior High, the school's name, was writ small at the bottom of
the label, but was never an afterthought. The box, now precari-
ously laden, was placed very carefully in the trunk of the Packard
(a vintage car especially polished for the journey and felt to be
festive) and then they all prepared to go out and do good—as
sober in their selection of suit and dress as the choice of tissue was.
By now most children had left school to wait for a Christmas that
was only a week and a half away. Carols were relentlessly replayed
by the radio and saccharine movies by the tube. The day was cool
bright dry and brittle. The road seemed slow to turn, reluctant to
roll. Hardy had a heavy stomach. Full of what they called knots,
he decided. His father said it was like having a bone in your belly.

Molly moaned to keep him interested. In the middle of moving up and down on her like a pump handle trying to coax a little water, Hardy suddenly heard in his head—so long, so long ago—the title on the tag. From the Hardy Family and Mr. Hardy's Homeroom, he thought, as he thrust home. Afterward he rose as if setting, so weary he was. That was a change, Molly said with a light laugh of satisfaction. But for Hardy, something . . . everything . . . gave him, when weighed, a wrong sum; was amiss and out of place like a shoe in a sink; a sinister slope slid under and fought off his step. His father, of course, drove. As carefully as a driver's ed instructor. Seedy neighborhoods succeeded one another. His mother said: looks like rather a nice house. And then the car slowed before a front porch that sagged a little along the bungalow's short length. One door and two wide windows faced the street, the windows set off well to one side as if they were afterthoughts. Hardy looked hard for mice but didn't notice any. Paint clung to the clapboards the way insects cling—with expert indifference. There were no curtains in the windows, only tattered shades that had been indecisively drawn down. His father grunted and pulled the Packard onto two narrow strips of concrete that served as a drive. Did he feel like this when going to the dentist? Intestines might not grumble, they were supposed to be ropy, but how friendly was his stomach to the lake of lava it presently entertained? Are you sure these people need relief, his mother asked. They were on the list, his father replied. Homerooms just pick— you know—just pick a name. Well, you should have gauged the address. It must be a two-bedroomer, they're not cramped, moving into her hypercritical mode, and adopting a tone that made her son cringe: cool, cruel, inexorable. It was the same voice that discussed his report card. It was the same voice that listed his shortcomings as if being a son were a performance to be reviewed. It was the same voice that wondered who had left a shoe in the study—with a sock stuffed in it—where the sixth braid ovaled itself into the rag rug. It was the same voice. Hardy's father kept out of his schooling. Conflict of interest, his father said, a viewpoint that was baffling for a boy, but was quite comprehensible to a young man in the lawyer line. Bell or buzzer couldn't be heard, probably didn't work. His father thundered the door; his mother rapped sharply as though with heels. Hardy heard the din long after it was physically complete. At last the door cracked and a face could be seen through a former screen. Missus . . . Hardy, heavy in the plastic-coated armchair the apartment furnished him, couldn't remember, couldn't dredge up the name, ordinary as every day, a name he thought he'd never forget; well, he hadn't forgotten, just misplaced it, yet it was not on the tip of anything either. Missus . . . A pale face appeared, not at eye height, not even at his height, a little girl's face, though his father addressed her as Missus more than once while the kid stared at the alien invaders. Oz-borne. Hardy sighed, some would have said in relief, but Hardy didn't feel relieved, he remembered very vividly that Molly had said—he was about to roll off and slide under—had said stay—when they were in the midst—had said stay where you are, I like it better. Hardy's thumb remained forgotten in the open envelope that now lay in his lap. Memory was a spiteful monster. Going on then in the conventional way and reaching the middle of their journey—in some books supposed to be the best part—he read his father's homeroom off the wall behind the headboard even though the headboard was busy waggling. Saw it there as if that's where his mind's eye was. Not the number of Hardy's homeroom, to whose bags he'd brought his dented demeaning bean soup (maybe chili) can, but his father's, though the collection was their joint benevolence now, the largesse of the family, bounty that was presently trunked in the freshly polished Packard. Saw with his mind's eye, then heard it said in his head despite the action of his hips, which were pumping as though he were running no maybe climbing stairs. The words were as vivid as dreamed. Normally . . . normally? . . . normally after his devotional rites—toe two toe ten—she had settled on him, slowly as nightfall, teasing him in. Later, one leg through a panty, she said it was a nice change. No. *That* was a change, is what she said, sitting on "that" as though it were a sofa. Nice remained unproffered. She wore a satisfied smile to signal her approval. Did she perhaps mean doing it in bed? waggling the headboard? The kid went away at least her face did. Leaving to be seen through the screen a faint wall maybe not dirty. Hardy's father said don't, she's fetching her folks, but his mother drummed on. It was the same as a stampede in a Saturday movie. Then the empty screen drew back and they mostly went in. Hardy's father mumbled a minute if you please and went back to the car while Hardy and his mother hovered at the sill a moment before stumbling stupidly—well, Hardy did, he stumbled stupidly—into a dim room where there was a presence. Oh I guess we need some light, Frank, an air-filled voice said. Frank? Violet, get your father, thems from the charity is here. In a minute a man came to snap a shade up in one of the windows. There was a pause like that between distant lightning and its thunder. Hardy's father, bearing the box, pushed through the door. The room had no table, only a few chairs, so finally, after a hesitating turn around, Hardy's father bent to lower the carton with an almost inaudible grunt to the floor. The room, in its emptiness, neared neat. Frank was fat. One count for and one against then—on his mother's tally. The women . . . especially the girl . . . their daughter no doubt . . . was thin as hope, and her mother was slight too, wispy-haired, an Ozark mountain blonde with an Okie overbite, cheeks that had sunk under a now cool crust, and wearing a much-washed—would that be his mother's judgment?—pale, unfrilly—unfrilly was a positive point—what would you call it?—frock? Point plus. Point minus. Point plus. Point plus. Point plus. Good early lead. They stood around the box like mourners at a grave. There was no Christmas tree. There were no stickers on the windows pretending to be bows or bells. He saw no paper chains, no wreaths, no signs of lush living, which was lucky. There was one lamp whose shade was slightly askew, something on one wall Hardy never made out, four wooden chairs whose seats had once been caned—Hardy's father, during the inevitable postmortem, would surmise—where now scrap-shaped pieces of plywood were nailed. Violet of the thin arms held her mother's hand, and Frank, stout, solemn or sullen, who could tell?—Hardy's mother would be the judge of that—stood in the middle of the room as still as if he were holding up the roof. Hardy's father had a speech whose delivery would not be denied, not even by silence. And Hardy heard him as he had other years, during other dispensations, without admitting any meaning, suffered the schoolteacher's voice which came spooling out of his father's mouth, a voice specially created for educational occasions and enveloped by its tone the way the words which fill a cartoon balloon are encircled: lettered more darkly for emphasis here, light of line for contrast there, larger or smaller sometimes as its message required, and accompanied by exclamations stark as pines in an otherwise snowed-over field. But Hardy couldn't have repeated a single syllable. Memory was a sly monster maybe, and forgetting a fearful necessity; yet the fear was there, brought on by the experience of blanks, bothersome blanks concerning this or that, this or that that should have been available to be summoned like a servant. His father gave credit where credit was due, so much Hardy was sure of. Teachers knew what credits were and how they counted. The homeroom's number would be—would have been—reiterated. The importance of giving, particularly during such a season, would be stressed, though because of the separation of church and state, religious language, infrequent in his family any-way, would be excluded. These three: faith, hope, and charity—no, no, love; charity had been excluded—replaced or excluded. Hardy stared through the dusk at a few dark hurrying figures, late from work, on their way home. Lights came on in previously unlit buildings. Shifts were changing. Day students replaced by older hopefuls. Private life would now, for a night, be tried. And found wanting. Meanwhile he sat in dreamthought while his father con-cluded his pieties with words almost whispered they'd become so solemn, touching the box with the toe of his shoe to put period to all he'd said. Hardy's father seemed nervous, which was a surprise, because only after the speech was delivered did he remember to ask if he was addressing Mr. and Mrs. Osborne. Or . . . ? Neither said a word though Mrs. Osborne emitted a faint mewmaah. The rule was: the box had to be entirely emptied so that the carton could be retrieved. Hardy's mother said why don't you see what's there, or did she just say see what's here? Why don't you. Mr. Osborne peered down like a stone head does waiting for the water to drain from its mouth. There'd be can one, can two, package three, toy four, till all were removed and placed upon the floor . . . an eternity. Hardy's discomfort was not quite the same as that evident in Mr. Osborne. Hardy was wearing humiliation's second-best suit: his was the shame of one who shames. Mr. Osborne's heavy arms fell from his dun-colored shirt like further sleeves. In his regular line of work Hardy had encountered many liars, many spokesmen for the culpable, many criminals, and some showed, some even felt, guilt, occasionally they even inflicted their remorse upon him; but never had he seen shame, not in those well-oiled offices, not from hirelings who had patted the requisite powders on their blade-shaven cheeks each morning (just as Hardy did: foam first, palped into place, the razor moving as if it were mowing snow, then a blubbery rinse of the scraped face and a rough towel-off before the slap of skin-tightening bracer and the comfort of soothing talc); flunkies like himself who nevertheless had red-lipped, red-fingertipped secretaries to stoke the coffeepot and greet them in the morning with a steaming mug bearing a company insignia; because, having known both sorts of shame—having inflicted shame and suffered it—shame searing his soul so its skin smoked—Hardy knew the difference between a guilty conscience and crushed pride, between—in a shameless world—getting caught and being defiled. I like it because you like it, Molly'd said. She'd said so much this visit, which was not like her. Now and then she'd squeal, sure, often emit a sigh, or maybe give a grunt of desire or a moan of pleasure, but not . . . she'd not . . . make remarks. Look, Charlie, a can of beans, the lady whispered. Peas, Hardy's mother quickly corrected. They have black eyes in the picture. Like the Susans, Hardy heard himself, in painful sympathy, say. The little girl's voice had sounded full of false excitement, but she probably was excited a little. There were packages tissue had turned into treasures, after all. The girl had let go of her mother's hand when her mother had stooped to unpack the provisions, so she was free now to look at Hardy. My name is Susan, she said, but my eyes are green. Cans and jars and bottles were surrounding the carton like defenders come out of their castle. Susan's mother made low moos of presumably . . . affirmation. The resolution required for freezing Mr. Osborne's face left the rest of him as loose and dangerous as a slide of shale. While Hardy was looking at the girl who had decided to call herself Susan, Hardy felt her father—Hardy felt the heat from her father's head—and Hardy sensed their mutual embarrassments burning like beacons built to warn of reefs. Why don't you open this, honey, Susan's kneeling mother suggested. Pulling at one end, the girl immediately knotted the string. Let me do that, Hardy's mother said, scooping it up to untie the tangle with her teeth. Ripping open an end, his mother handed the package back. Thrust the package . . . pushed the package . . . he pushed his memory of the package back. Immediately that day that visit that intrusion what he'd seen through the screen—nothing . . . nothing—seemed to Hardy far away like the people passing that last moment in the street, and his fingers began to play with the envelope in his lap as if his mood had made his fingers nervous. It was a distance through which outcry couldn't reach. If a woman walking in the street below were suddenly accosted by a buck in running shoes and asked for change—wud do a deal of gud, ma'am—and a hand were thrust in her face so aggressively she started, perhaps cried out, seeing big eyes bearing down, suppose she screamed, the scream would seem no more to Hardy than a leaf let loose to litter the park. So pink the palm. Soft Mollypink the palm. Maybe it was his mother who shoved the whole scene like the package into his fidgeting fingers. It's some pencils. How nice. Almost all of them the same size. Mr. Osborne growled; it wasn't a word he uttered, just a sound, a growl a growl; but Hardy hardly heard the whole gruff rumble of it, his blood was hammering his head so, though a figure—it must have been his father—stepped back from the group as though startled, pushed. The fallback of his forces went unadvertised. Susan's mother continued to gallop gamely toward the cliff's edge. She shook a blouse from its wad for all to see. It had pretty pink buds all over it like the pustules of some disease. It was encouraged to billow out over the top of the box, to settle like a blanket of snow in a theater scene. Leave, roared Mr. Osborne. Take——stuff——this stuff——leave. Please, someone said softly. Suddenly that resolute face had become a face worn featureless by centuries of rain. Hardy's mother's hands flew into the air and Hardy's father, in a cloud of consternation such as a rejected genie might employ, caromed through the door still narrowly ajar. Hardy was suddenly in the rear seat of their rapidly retreating car without the slightest idea of how he'd gotten there. For hours he bore burning ears. No one ever spoke of it: not of the hoarseness of the outcry, not of the rude completeness of their dismissal, not of the Alpine height of the ingratitude displayed, not of the Hardy family's ignominious flight. Why should anyone speak of something that had never happened? couldn't have, consequently didn't. Hardy was haunted by afterimages, however. Of a small worn rug their gift box nearly smothered when the Hardy offering was set down upon it. A thin band on the thin finger of a thin hand. String struggling in the mouth of his mother. Who was, as a result of their commonly imposed Coventry concerning the subject, unable to compute the recipient's failing score, since the game had been called on account of catastrophe; because that's what she and his father usually did, went over the occasion like a lawyer and a client practicing Q & A: how did the house look? for it must be poor and run-down to provide proof of need, yet it should seem tidy and scrubbed to demonstrate character; were their manners appropriate to the occasion? neither suspiciously servile and gushingly grateful nor indifferent nor rudely unappreciative; how were their hearts? their spirit must be sufficiently downcast as to require rescue, but not wholly crushed and beyond restoration; did it appear that they would put their provisions to a proper use, that the clothes would be cared for and worn with a smile, that delighted children—Lily or Lilac—would play with their new-to-them toys? Above all, the Hardys wanted to come away feeling that their effort, and that of the homeroom children, had been worthwhile, that some injustice in this world had been set right, some suffering alleviated; it was the least the benefited could do, because it encouraged more giving, more help in the future to folks like themselves, down on their luck and needing a hand; for suppose there was no hand, suppose, as in this case, it had been badly bitten, and was held out no longer; suppose Mr. Hardy's kids collected cans without élan, that tins were stuffed into his father's homeroom sacks as they were heaped higgledy-piggledy in all the others—then what? for heaven's sake. The box had been left behind like an abandoned cannon when the Hardy family fled the field. There would be no box by which to measure next year's offerings. To make a match: that might mean no offerings at all. At last Hardy pulled the plain sheet forth, properly folded in threes like all the others. Postmortem, he thought. Appropriate designation. There'd been no postmortem. Yet he had just now remembered one. In which his father had held forth on the subject of—what? the repaired seats of the Osborne chairs. Yes. So had it happened? had there been a rehash after all, a family confab like so many others? or had he imagined it as he had imagined the words on Molly's bedroom wall? while headlonging into his pleasure. Molly may have been indulging him their entire time together, while he was equally intent on indulging her. Hey . . . maybe that was the definition of a decent relationship. Were he to speak for her now, he might just say: I am giving you what I imagine you want, while you are pretending to want it on my account. Well, little wrong with that, Hardy decided. It had not been a day of decision, but it had been a decisive day. T-day. The nightlights were lit. Yellow patches pretended to warm the streets. The company was sending him back to Toronto. Apparently his pleasantly delivered threats were no longer threatening. Toronto had done nothing to remedy their errors, although they had admitted them readily enough. They had even offered reparations, and Hardy had been gracious in his acceptance. So what had happened? Whatever it was, recalcitrance had occurred twice during the last three weeks—after each of his recent trips, in fact— nothing had happened, that was his problem—though Toronto was especially troubling because the sale of inaccurate blood-testing equipment was hardly a minor matter, not like those damn Mex-made hospital scuffs that peeled apart from toe to heel, or the porous plastic sheeting they made in Moline . . . man alive . . . manufacturing methods were poor everywhere in the world, but Hardy had held up his end—yes—up to now he had been almost a hundred percent successful in the intimidation department; his firm was spoiled, it had too high an expectation, Pilip had even thought it necessary to point out, at yesterday's rather tense meeting—tense for the first time—that Health and Haven didn't like buying the same plane ticket twice. Get your game face on, Pilip had urged, and go get 'em. Maybe Hardy had somehow broken the chain of inconvenience. He suspected the chain wouldn't enjoy losing linkage. Then the letter unfolded like something alive in his lap. Another petition for his collection. Hardy had to file his own stuff, keep his own records, maybe that's where the foul-up was, not in some weakness of his game face, not in his presentation of the grievance, but in a flaw in the paperwork which lay deeply out of sight like an intestinal worm. He didn't believe his own argument, however. Hardy's conscience didn't hear in his words the requisite conviction. He never believed anything said in self-defense. What was wanted from him this time? "Hello," Hardy read. Was that the way to begin to beggar? With hello? What happened to "Dear Sir or Madam"? As if his Hugh name on the envelope were of doubtful sex. "I write this letter in need of immediate assistance for a travel opportunity . . ." He—who?—Baltho—Baltho? Well, Harold Baltho didn't know the half of it, did he? He hadn't a job, no doubt, though Hardy hadn't read on and so he didn't know how Baltho had lost his last one, and therefore Baltho was not in a position to feel Hardy's own apprehensions, many of which Hardy had read from another letter, this one printed on Greg Pilip's tightly smiling face, sent by Greg Pilip's carefully entwined fingers, read off their display on Pilip's swept desk, a heavy gold frat ring on one hand, wed band on the other, thin file folder to his left, expensive rollerball resting to his right, well,

Hardy had a frat ring—Delta Tau Delta—he could wear it if he wanted to, but didn't because it might encourage some fellow feeling, a sense of internal alliance, just by chance, of course, in one of the deadbeats, you never knew, they went to college too, everybody went to college, college was as common as canned corn, even advanced degrees were without distinction. ". . . which has recently been offered to me." You are my sacred shelta, they might sing silently while feeling some stickum if not a bond with Hardy, a bond outside of business. "The trip is through Trinity College in Connecticut and involves travel and study in Tibet, Kathmandu, Nepal and Italy." Hardy could feel his travel bag where he liked it, crouched as an obedient dog might crouch, between his legs. In fact, the chair he had pulled to the window was very like those you find in an airport lounge, simply not welded to one another in regimented rows . . . well, the rumps wouldn't really be resting; instead, impatient and anxious and weary, anticipating hours of discomfort on the plane, where their owners would be squeezed behind a presoiled tray like an infant about to be force-fed a tin of stewed tomatoes or French-cut green beans, and fastened safely in a thirty-thousand-foot high chair by a stomacher—French-cut green beans would be too classy—and the rumps' owners would sit and snooze, or lie their way up the corporate ladder, unaware they were bullshitting Dick Tracy, that moment on his way to interrogate criminals caught trying to stiff Health and Haven with scuffs made of paper, maybe, or of passing off their sheeting as impervious to incontinence and protective of cotton, didn't they realize that mattresses were soakers? that mattresses cost money? especially ones short on springs? ones constructed of unresilient coils? moreover that when mattresses have been regularly wet they can't be reused as if you could simply rinse them out and wring them in knots like a gym towel, or replump them for another old bladder-blown shankbone to pee in his sleep on, the old goat getting out of his room and up to the nurses' station to complain about his applesauce while wearing cardboard scuffs and a paper gown designed on account of its inadequate ties to fall open so the sight of the patient's shrunken penis would not be denied the staff, and so that way they'd know where the wet patch had come from when they came to turn Old Bony from one bedsore to another . . . Oh, yeah, he'd have to say something of the sort . . . You could bet Hardy didn't find that spiel weak or unconvincing as he heard himself make it, because he'd have to throw a more threatening pitch than he normally did, once up north in Toronto yet again, though in words more genteel than those in his head: about HIV and the scandal power of the press, image damage and the costs of lab contamination including lawsuits the size of skyscrapers, of which Toronto finally had a few, but where you could find really good Chinese, not like in costly but cheapeat D.C., where there were more food poisoners, Hardy had after long experience de-cided, than elsewhere in this ethnickerized country. In D.C. secre-taries and their suitors actually sought out places where they would have to eat with their fingers and be given limberbread to wipe them on if they didn't seize the opportunity to lick their dates' digits: thumb waa one, pinky wee two. There were restaurants rep-resenting countries whose natives had never had anything to eat, newly unified nations where living and starving were one. Had he not recently received a "Dear Colleague" implorement?—here it was—from Unit 19a, Goldring Barn Est ("Dear Col-league"? . . . "est" was estate?), Henfield Road, Small Dole (were

they kidding?), West Sussex, that was headlined: HELPING OUR
CHILDREN IN AFRICA AFFECTED BY AIDS and that requested money to
support a fund-raising cycle ride across Tunis to Cape Town (had
to be . . . had to be . . . a deeply dumb joke). Hardy read that
Baltho had only been informed of his good fortune a week ago
and had only a month in which to find the funding for this "fan-
tastic adventure . . ." um . . . "unparalleled opportunity . . ." "We
will be traveling with an army escort through the Asian leg of the
trip" thanks to . . . thanks to "the Nepalese Ministry of Culture."
Took the cake, Hardy judged, first prize at the fair. ". . . deepest
regions of Tibet and India without fear of danger . . ." Health and
Haven had no deadbeats in either region so it was not likely Hardy
would have an opportunity to suffer exotic dysenteries anytime
soon, if he held on to his job, a worry that, before yesterday, would
never have bedeviled him, but did devil him now, even though he
knew he was being—what did they say?—too litmussy—no, too
prone to hives. For instance, these letters were getting to him, he
had to admit, even though he was receiving many cordialities with
which to end his day as if his day had come in the mail. "May God
bless you and my grateful appreciation in advance." Nevertheless,
Hardy was of the impression that large portions of the population
were ill with the dismals. "All I have done for these past three years
is try hard to get back to Happiness!" Rhonda has debt, depression, and cancer, a husband who is out of work and an eviction
notice from her landlord. Howie Towel is a motivated minorities
person, too, "with a lot of invention design idea's, that need to be
researched, developed and marketed for the consumer market.
Some of the ideas have to do with exercise equipment, and
safety-breathing apparatus like for swimming, fire, as well as for

gas mask, e.t.a." "While other young brides get a nice 'Honey-Moon,' I've faced nothing but hardship and pain." From the height of his own thirty years, Hardy wanted to assure Rhonda—Rhoda?—that he understood . . . that most young brides got just what she was getting, and suggest to Howie Towel that the heads of losers were stuffed to the sinuses with projects and plans which would never see more light than the handkerchief. Hardy would be that tough about it—the truth was a species of tough love to be sure—and he'd bring that news to his targets in Toronto too. Before now, however, he had never had to buck himself up for his job, he had just done it: walked in and wiped them out. Back to thought-less happiness. Yes. Had he been there, and had he enjoyed it? happiness? You always seem so happy, Molly had observed; was it because Molly's bare feet were giving him the Turk's massage that he seemed so? happy? Mr. Undemonstrative? A real Turk, fat as a harem eunuch, would have crushed his back like a biscuit. Hey, ethnic sex books—a new direction. The Bulgarian Blow Job. Reci-pes included. He could suggest such a project to Howie Towel instead of sending him money. However, none of this deeply dumb japery elevated his spirits. If Baltho had made the most outrageous request, there was Gerald Hepsmith to win the blue ribbon for directness: "I been working in a screw company for twenty years. I am now planning on buying a screw company. I am a little short so I had to put it on hold. Because of my financial situation. Whatever you can give me will be appreciated." But no God bless. Just an illegible signature. No date either. And the "r" of "Dear Si" had disappeared. Hardy thought he might mail an "r" to Carol Stream, Illinois. A very faint dot on the map, he bet. Hardy had so far—depressing phrase—had so far received requests

from McAlester, Oklahoma; and Moorhead, Minnesota; from Los
Osos, California; Los Angeles and Garden Valley, ditto; from
Leavenworth, Kansas; and St. Louis too, as well as Naples—
Naples?—Naples, Florida. The Brits had weighed in in the normal
way (only one was using the AIDS scam), but with letters too long
to finish and with signatures aristocratically scrawled. A letter
from London and another from Glasgow were identical except
that Mr. Akingbemisilu wanted a thousand more than the Scot's
three. One petition, the most outrageously distant, was from a
couple of retirees in Australia who desired to relocate abroad in
order, of course, to help people avoid the calamities that had be-
fallen them. They were experts in the mismanagement of money.
A woman living, she said, in the backwoods of the Sierra Mountains with her infirm husband and disabled son, wanted a ten-
thousand-dollar down payment on an apartment building located
more conveniently near their family doctor. For this she blessed
him richly. Then nearer his home (if his apartment could be so
called), Hardy had heard from Waldorf, Maryland; just a bit south,
he thought, on Route 301, as well as receiving the bad news from
D.C. itself, where Howie resided. Wash D.C. all you want, if you
want, the locals said, but washing won't remove the grime left on
the city's marble columns from smoke blown by decades of elected
officials. When D.C. didn't stand for Dismal Climate or Decay
City, it stood for Desperate Cunts or Dumb Congressmen with
Doubtful Convictions, depending upon whom you were laugh-
ingly achat with and into whose bailiwick the party was being
pitched. Hey, Mama, how are the twins? Cities you'll never visit,
Daddy. Hardy hadn't heard from Chicago, Detroit, Philadelphia,
or Cleveland; they were no-shows at his soup kitsch; they added

no hungry mouths to the breadlines. There was always tomorrow's delivery, of course, when another nation or another major urban center might be heard from. Pack lightly tonight for a quick trip, though Toronto was a long ride. No aerosol foam, no throwaway razor, no astringent, no talc because he'd count on an immediate turnaround and be back before his whiskers grew. Good tag, sharp description: back before my/your whiskers grow. Underwear in an emergency. He remembered being stranded in Sacramento. With a hole in a sock. Remember to reset alarm. Skip breakfast. Breakfast was always a bore. Anything in a bowl was a bore. Hardy's meals were mostly a bore because he had to eat them alone. Read and eat—not so easy. Taxi to the plane—a luxury because he could easily take the Metro. Hope the weather didn't decide to wet the runways causing underbooked flights to be canceled on account of wet wheels or other imaginary reasons, mostly mechanical so as to suggest a concern for passenger safety. One of the damn doors won't close. The nose wheel is flat. When, if the air ever brought him there—to the Tonto Medical Instruments Company of Toronto—he'd go straight for the jugular. Bloody their files, floor, and furniture. Buy a screw factory for Gerald. Return early evening. Ring up, should he? Molly. Wait a minute . . . wait. Hardy had what might be described as a secular epiphany. A letter he had received some weeks earlier, and which curiosity had encouraged him to retain, had been, he suddenly saw, the opening salvo in this barrage laid down on him by the needy. It had been from some godforlorn place in . . . Illinois . . . like Carol Stream. The room was dark now that night had sooted in, so when he rose he groped around the bowl of his borrowed lamp for its switch. In hotels he never could find them, but here, in his own . . . by now . . . he ought. Suddenly he saw his shadow so he must be real. The soft caramel-colored carpet made him kick off his shoes but the feeling was still sock. It was from a company or an institution and had an acronym, CETN, taken from the guy's name, the guy who was running the scam—here it was—Pecetnic. Avery Pecetnic. The letter was got up and laid out like a prospectus, with topic sentences in bold: "I'm offering you a personal open invitation to contribute to a unique solution to the problems that plague our youth today." Am I one of them youths? Maybe he'd be one of them plagues. Instead, maybe he—Hugh Hardy—came with the apartment. For rent: studio apartment, sofa bed and lawyer included, cost to you: no more a month than a maid. He had wasted his education and become a bully. He. Not even a big one. A Hugh. He struck terror only because of the mob-sponsored halo he wore. The black case he carried clearly contained at least one pistol proud of its caliber. His cool came from the confidence he had in his backup who was just a suitcoat behind him. He had a blackmailer's face, blank as a wall. He spoke his piece like a priest. They cowered and caved in on account of his neat nails, his starched cuffs, his tightly knotted tie, the slight crimp in his hair where you might have thought a hat had sat. But he had failed to threaten anyone at Tonto, Toronto. This was not a welcome out-come. Moreover, his love affair with Molly played well only for one act. He had no home, no pet, no lounge chair worn by his own butt into comfortable billows. Worse. He had no desire for any. He should feel bad about that. He didn't. His job was no more his than the hat he didn't have. Why should he worry about it? His shirts sat in a blond box made of layered drawers, the fac-ing sides scooped so they could look open like mouths: white shirts, all the same, ties with the standard slanted stripe, some red, some blue, and, as Molly said, his jacket looked best on the back of a chair. Toe ten. About clothes he didn't care, though he knew how to tie a Windsor knot. When he'd gotten his first job, his father had given him three pairs of links. Hardy felt far away, high in the sky. Flying without wings, he was barely visible, no more than the moon in daytime. Though he often complained, he ate whatever came to hand. No one could say he had preferences that put pressure on him or skewed his course. He didn't smoke, was the most casual of drinkers, only mildly interested in coffee, avoided vegans, serious sexual kinks, was rarely late for appointments. Hardy had no handles. Love or otherwise. He found he had a plan, though he would never have called it his "plan"—not until this nightfall when he saw the shadows of the furnishings on the floor. He wouldn't have known they were there until the light came on. His sweet round face might linger in his target's gaze like the blur of something bright; remain after he'd softly closed the office door behind him; but no one remembered what it was that gave their eyes, for a moment, an annoying afterimage. Hardy was merely an emissary from Tonto's own incompetence. That's what he should say: I'm Hugh Hamilton Hardy, and I represent your sloppy quality control. I'm the Ghost of Fudges Past. I am your Omissions. Hardy avoided giving offense, so why was he a strong arm in the delinquent-performance business? When he was utterly out of every social spotlight; when he was like the shadows that disappear during switchoff; when he was the way the world wasn't during naptime: why were these letters being mailed to him? "Provided you had the resources at your disposal, would you be willing to contribute ten thousand, five thousand, or thereabouts dollars?

Which category do you fit into? All that is required is faith and a minimum of twenty-five hundred dollars. We need heroes such as yourself to come on board to make this an effective vehicle for positive change." They had Hardy all wrong. Or had Hardy's address all wrong. His profession too. How little did these envelopes know him, even the ones with official-looking windows. They should be set right. Gee, he'd been all ready to give two thousand dollars, he might reply, but that sum was well beneath Pecetnic's required minimum. Hardy had no gestures, generous or otherwise. That was it. Molly, undulating her arms, shuddering her tits, swiveling her torso, shaking her ass, had told him straight out. Not only did he never waste motions, he never gave away his feelings by unguarded body language, through this or that subordinate gesture, so that nothing was conveyed—nothing—not geniality, not anger (not happiness?), while at the same time, he wasn't mechanical either, which, had he been, would have written paragraphs about Hugh, the man who was absent from the man. Such discretion was not easy to manage, Molly imagined, it had to be natural to Hardy, simply to move, sit, say without swaying or sawing or jiggling or hemming or hawing or twitching or showing nerves or even being especially slow, stiff, and monotonous. Hardy picked up his briefcase. Hardy hailed a taxi. Hardy turned on a light. Actions without adverbs. Hardy rarely hiccupped, coughed, sneezed, or blew his nose, never cracked his knuckles, tugged a lobe, rubbed or fondled the slopes of his chin, yawned, ran his hands through his hair, which was stiff thick straight and blond, although he did twiddle his fingers a little, did sometimes blink overly often, did occasionally say something out loud when alone, but rarely a huff or puff otherwise, though when he came he sighed. Molly said he said saaaah. I need to ask her what color her eyes were before she went to contacts. Should I answer one of these beseechers? That might be interesting—to find out what the follow-up message would be. Or better—he could hunt up Howie Towel, who had a D.C. address, turn up on his front stoop, beribboned like a fruit basket, himself the surprise. Such an action would be uncharacteristic, Hardy was aware; indeed that was its recommendation: in terms of tactics it was the way he did business, except this time he would not be on business. He would represent—what?—a local charity, that way he could seem to be on business. How easy it was for whatshisname in Carol Stream, Illinois, to create a philanthropic outfit simply by typing CETN on his computer, and subsequently darkening his fake acronym with an elementary mouse move—**CETN**—so it would be ready, by virtue of another click, to be transported like royalty into the center of the page, where, with still another elementary gesture, the initials could be highlighted in order to enlarge its size and increase its power to the shout of a headline—**CETN**. How easy to retain the nerve, after so swiftly simple a transformation, to allege the letters stood for "Continuing Eternally to Need." Hugh Hamilton Hardy could become a community caregiver with equal ease. Cast your bread upon the water in real life and it would sog up and sink for sure, if the ducks didn't snap it first; but this time, Hardy thought, he might appear at opportunity's door to demonstrate that what had been a crust when cast forth had come back by a miracle as a whole loaf, and he could hint that he'd be followed by a kingdom made of kaiser rolls—wouldn't that be wonderful? He'd be the bread all right, a loaf so soft, to make sandwiches, he'd have to be sliced by machine. Hello there, Mr. Roller, lucky guy, your

toilets are about to flush with wine. Hi Debbie—Malikowski, is it?
You can leave your dying grandma and her bedside to me, I'll sit
quietly there while you go back to work to support your three
preschool children and your feckless hubby, Earl, didn't you say
his name was? It did occur to Hugh, as he pondered with mounting pleasure the various agreeable responses he might make to this
wholly unmerited invasion of his life, that somewhere he might
have offended someone familiar with the scam, maybe some official he had had to spank, whose after-hours occupation was the
fleecing of the poor, saps whose luck had oozed out, so that they
were easily enticed into lying out of hope for a living: for a small
sum you will be furnished with a list of premelted hearts who have
a history of falling for stories full of hard luck and tough times; in
addition we shall supply you with a formula to follow when petitioning them (after all, D.C. is Grant City), so your sob story will
avoid mistakes of tone, errors in data, or slipups in the style of
your solicitation that may scare dear Daddy Warbucks away.
Attach return addresses, telephone numbers. Beg to be phoned.
"Wake me up, I don't care." Be frank. Promise to repay. Think of
it, sir, as a loan. Call on God but be conventional about it. Mention that you are the sole and sorry support of a family that of
course you love. "My children that are the most precious in my
life, along with my wife, see my everyday worries. I think they
deserve a better life. All I need is . . ." My God, Debbie—who had
addressed her letter with "Dear Sir or Madam"—needed only eight
thousand dollars to get back on her feet. Only . . . "I understand
you have been in a similar situation . . ." That last was perhaps not
a wise phrase. He, Hardy, hadn't been—wasn't—in a similar situation. Successful people often rose like cream, steadily, though

maybe oozily, yet gamely, to the top. And had never had a hitch come forward to be the hitch in their plans. Hitchless, like Hardy aimed to be. Without sin or snag, or hitch. He, Hardy, need never beg; he was not in a similar situation. Not by a mule's smile. Hardy made a list of the differences he imagined existed between himself and his petitioners, among them the fact that even were he to be in a similar situation he'd never purchase such a stupid list, or if he did he'd never write pitiful letters to anyone about his so-called similar situation, letters where even the commas kowtowed. Entreaty would not be his forte, he'd see to that . . . in the life he'd one day lead. Yet the expression "similar situation" suggested a complicity he couldn't towel off or comb away. Didn't he go to his knees for Molly's permissions, tongue out as a dog does, pleading for pleasure? Ah, but that was just act one in the theater of the flesh. So his and her arousals weren't for real? "I am taking the role of an insurance broker (licensed in the state of Ohio) and am seeking other licenses, honors, degrees and equipment, besides my career in tennis that I have worked hard for. I understand you may have been in a similar situation some time in your life." Debbie Daw, who lived on Tirmynydd Road in for god sake South Wales, wanted to get away from her mom, and wasn't that a situation similar to Hugh's? ". . . I need help to be able to look after my children properly and have a life of my own . . . As for my future, once my mother has passed away I hope to better myself by taking a course in floristry." Hardy intended to sleep that night deep in the recomposition of himself so that when the light that was whitening his windows woke him, he'd be full of remedy, resolve, and inspiration. He would be the . . . He would represent—no—not himself—an agency, why not? community caregivers incorporated.

COMMUNITY CAREGIVERS INC. COMMUNITY CAREGIVERS INC. He'd need to pack for a quick trip, though Toronto would be an overnighter now because he'd have to switch his flight into the afternoon. Pitch in a can of aerosol foam; add a simple throwaway razor, some astringent and talc, too, because he couldn't count on being back in D.C. before his whiskers grew. Fresh underwear for an emergency. Always a good idea. This new plan had merit. It would be, after all, better to stay overnight in a restful hotel in order to come on fresh in the morning. Hit Tonto then. Like a September snowstorm. When the Canadians are not quite awake and before they've bought enough salt for their streets. Hit Howie Towel the same way—this up-and-coming morn, front-stoop him. Make him wish he'd never been born. Or had Howie already said that? "I'm ashamed to say I sometimes wish . . ." He had . . . had written . . . someone had written . . . Why were they writing? . . . writing him? he? Hugh? The question followed him to bed where, fully dressed, he fell face-first into his pillow. At dawn of the big day, Hugh took off his shoes before getting out of bed, and tossed his rumpled clothes into a corner. He saw that it had been a moist night. The streets were wet and empty. He hummed through his shower. A happy noise but not a tune. It helped to have a purpose in life. Hardy was up and out and off far too early, although he was pleased that he'd beaten the can handlers to their intersections. Hardy cruised Howie Towel's neighborhood, one of worn red row houses sporting duplex stoops with corroded railings and crumbling steps. For his sort, these streets were still unsafe at any speed. Cruise and let them know I'm coming, he rather vaingloriously thought. Maybe I ought to honk. After all, I am a honky. But he drove out to a nearby urb and ate a dry egg on soft toast for breakfast, killing time with a *Post* he purchased from a sidewalk box, and toying with the counter's sugar shaker. Now that it was nine, it might be prudent to arrive. Hugh curbed his car three row houses from his goal, and let his case swing casually in his left hand lest he be spied. Indeed, as he approached, a young black woman and two milk-chocolate-colored kids came from behind the door of three thirty-five . . . and a half a—number Hugh could scarcely read. She stood on the stoop while the children pellmelled up and down the sidewalk, one furzy-head darting past Hardy on his briefcase side as if he weren't a paleface, the kid only concerned to enjoy his release, his happy flight. Hi there, good morning, Hugh greeted her, finding a morning use for some after-five joviality. She wore a simple loose cotton frock and straw sandals despite the coolish air. There was a slight gleam to her straightened hair. From the stoop she threw Hardy an intense but noncommittal look. My name is Hugh Hamilton, Hardy said, and I'm from Community Caregivers Incorporated. Don't want any, the woman replied. The wet night's gray skies were beginning to dissipate, and a line of soft light ran straight along the ridge of her nose to fall on the rich roll of her lower lip. I'm looking for a Mr. Howard Towel, Hamilton said, his tone agreeably deferential. Him? Hers was a stern fierce face, very sculptural, quite beautiful. Her eyes flickered, following the race of her two kids. For some reason, Hardy had got the impression that Howie Towel was white. Yes, ma'am. Mr. Towel has been in communication with our office, and—. Him? How? He don't phone. He wrote, Hamilton said, trying to sound matter-of-fact. Nicely typed. The margins were justified. She turned to yell at a child who was now getting a little too far away. Hamilton saw clean pale heels and slender calves. He shouldn't have said typed. He don't type. Oh. Well. It was . . . typed. I type. This was a militant affirmation. It was a letter whose looks gave a good impression, Hamilton said a little lamely. When I work, that's what I do—I type. Computer too. Git back here, Calvin—now! Clarisse! Clarisse, of course, stopped and looked back at her mother. Heedless, Calvin revved his engine, but, also careless with life the way kids are, immediately fell with a shriek on the broken and uneven cement. The young woman went calmly briskly down the steps past Hamilton toward Calvin's fallen form. Clarisse, dolldear, she said, don't you do that, that what your brother did. Dumb as a thumb. You boy. She shook her head slowly. Hamilton was left holding his case, now up near his chest. She pulled the boy to her and held his head against her thigh. Hamilton waited with a patience he had no need to summon. Then she led Calvin back to the steps. Calvin's nose wasn't runny, his eyes weren't wet. And he was almost immediately over his howls. Well I wonder if Mr. Towel is . . . at home now. Had he almost said "hereabouts"? He aint. She beckoned Clarisse. This aint his home either. Oh, Hamilton said, the address on the letter . . . He's gone for good, I guess, she said, looking at Hamilton as if she were really looking at him. Mr. Towel wrote us about some breathing apparatus, Hamilton persisted. He did ventions. The woman acknowledged that much. Calvin wiped his dry eyes on his mother's dress. Soon she had Clarisse held in her other hand. He was always try'n to improve the breath'n. Mr. Towel said he needed some financial help, Hamilton told her, trying to smile at the children with both corners of his mouth. The young woman swung the kids around and turned her smooth pale heels to him. He asked me for money, Hamilton hurriedly added. He would want that, she replied, for his ventions, but it'd be no use. They was just rags and wires. She let go of Calvin to take hold of the knob on the door. Maybe she was just a sitter; the kids didn't look hers, though they didn't smile back when he offered them his grin, so maybe they were the off-spring of Mrs. Stern the Smileless after all. Don't go in, Hamilton said. Please. She herded Clarisse and Calvin through the door as if she hadn't heard, her heels disappearing into an interior as dark as herself. Hardy self-consciously lowered his case and inspected the street. He saw unexpected anxiety. The door opened again. You can look if you like. Theys in the front room. The street was empty of everything except parked cars. Hamilton went quickly up the steps and slid inside. She shut the door through whose glass a gray light very faintly fell. A pale palm in a gesture which at the same time shuttered her silvered nails, and Hamilton turned left into—he guessed—a parlor where a pile of cloth bags with holes made for eyes were strewn (or so the holes seemed), and where wormlike translucent tubes were tangled. A piano bench empha-sized the absence of any piano. Straightened lengths of coat-hanger wire pierced the sides of tin cans that were sitting on it. There was an ancient exerciser in the middle of much confusion. Mr. Towel described himself, Hamilton said—suddenly remembering How-ie's letter t for t—as a motivated minorities person. He weren't, she said in evident scorn. But Hamilton wasn't sure whether Towel weren't a minorities person, or just weren't motivated. Here was the exercise equipment the letter mentioned, perhaps these woolly things were the gas masks. What would have been the underwater gear, he wondered. The amber worms? Hamilton tried to take in, to understand, the . . . burlappy bags? Could anyone have hoped these sorry contraptions might function for them? Your husband,

Hamilton began, but she interrupted. I aint married to 'um. Well when would he have written—ah—to my office? When he leff he leff his stuff was all she said, in a blacker voice than before. Maybe, Hamilton decided to hazard, maybe Mr. Towel wanted you to receive the money he wrote me to ask for. He dunt wunt me no more, or I him. Hamilton turned in the dim light toward her, caught a flash of eye, saw a flash of nail. He thrust his case awkwardly between his legs. Nothing was turning out as he had expected. He drew out his billfold and emptied it of money. I dunt wunt your munny, she said in a voice as flat and hard as the hand that subsequently slapped him when he pushed a fistful of cash in her direction. The sting went everywhere his bones went. He felt his feet as well as his cheeks warm. In a kind of blind consternation, Hardy, clutching his case to his chest like a shield, got into the hall, then stood a moment, bewildered, fist still stuffed with twenties. Calvin pulled the door open for him. There were a number of people on the street now—a baby carriage, a cat, some kids, a van. Hardy's car was as close as Canada. He was barely aware how he clasped his money or clutched his case. In his ears Hardy heard a heart hammering. He had hot elbows, hot knees, a hot nose. With hot knees did he dare to take a plane? He made a face that no one saw how horrible. To alleviate the sting, Hardy's blood recapitulated his every shame, and reminded him of the way he'd run after the red-haired boy with a can of—what? God, what?—held helplessly high in his hand. Then feeling mostly stupid . . . silly but unstruck. By his mother he'd been ass-chewed but never smacked. She bent over, brought her face close, and shouted up his nose. I understand you have helped people like me in the past. Helping those who have been trying to do right. By confronting deadbeats and cheats. Get away . . . get away . . . get away, the pounding in his head said. With care he stepped down steps that were steps well swept. Strangers who would remain strangers to him were in the street, unmoving, as if painted—their figures, their foreignness. Normal concerns were what he needed now. To restore the quo. Dare he call Molly when he came back still slap-cheeked from Toronto? Hardy promised to roll on the floor in an ecstasy provoked by her excellence. There was always more carpet. But would she ever love—or merely moisten for—a groveler? Around dawn the sidewalk had been rainwashed. It wasn't slick but it wasn't even. And the car—it seemed—so far. Or should he assume the supplicating posture of one dishonored . . . with its appropriate rush of blood in the wrong direction? Hardy had to be careful of the cracks, some of which were still dark with damp. Shift to slow, and be slow to go. Show courage. Though if he fell and dirtied his knee now she might rest his head against her thigh, and feel sorry for him, for a change, all night long.

Don't
Even Try,
Sam

Not that key.

Not that key. That's the yellow key. The one that hates to come back up. Once depressed, it is reluctant to recover. You know, dear heart, if you really want to play me, keep the pressure on evenly. It is never necessary to hammer. I take a hint better than a holler . . . I've been in storage you know. Not much call for my kind anymore. Not that it matters a whole lot where I stand. Most storerooms are more song and story than these movies I was made for. All I get to count as screen time is a little tinktanktunk in the sound track, a passing angled shot of the keyboard and my highball-ringed, butt-burnt top—oh, and then the lower half of whoever's sitting at me, with a finger or two from a fat-wrapped, shirt-armed plinkplanker visible, as if he were in action at the board—before the lens is away to frillyville and the muddy boots of the town saloon. The camera has to find its way through extras pretending to be a crowd, everybody moving their mouths faking monkey business—cocottes galore—and sitting on breakeasy chairs that could give way and dump their rumps in sawdust. What a bore. Bar as long as a Pullman car. Bar as long as a Pullman car. Not that key, honey. The key with the hairline crack. Yes, that one. Yum. My G-spot. So ask away.

I gathered from what I could glean . . . whoa . . . try that passage again . . . the hairline has a habit of—ever break a nail? It's like that . . . I gleaned from what I could gather of the plot that there weren't going to be any fistfights scheduled, shootout showdowns, or barroom brawls, though there's one close call—a lapel grabber, that's all. No one confides in the piano of course . . . Well, that info was a relief to my keys and strings—my keys relaxed, my strings sighed—they hate all those loose chair legs flying about. The piano player usually runs for cover as if anybody cared but the piano has to stay put so some klutz can get a laugh by chording the keyboard on his way down. Very funny, Charlie. But I understood this cheesy heart-tugger was to be set in French North Africa. The good guys would be wearing shoes. The way the on-set people were acting (beg pardon for the word), I could see they were about to shoot the entire film or damn near it on a single soundstage as if this were going to be a murder-in-the-mansion movie. Outside would be a city scene adapted from a previous flick. I had a moveable friend who kept me wisz. Oops. I remember . . . I remember the ashtrays. God, the number of cigarettes they burned up in the movies those days. The most emotional moments occur when smoke curls out of an actor's nose.

That was when they were starting to use girls as couriers because of the war, and young fems were scooting about the set like flies from fruit to roast delivering lines for the actors to learn on the spot, and fresh directions for the crew. Ordinary chaos would have seemed calm as a corpse.

I have a question. No one—not nobody—ever wanted to interview me. You're writing a book? About the Swedish Beamer? The magnetism of the movie? *Casablanca?* They're not thinking of another TV knockoff? For me it's a coming attraction. Hey, I've never seen a movie. I've seen movies being made. Parts of them anyway. Parts in. Parts out. Parts private. So, sure, I've noticed lots of hanky-panky. Even a little lick-the-dickie. Boots and Britches did his broads behind the set flats. During lunch. Beauguy really did like to play chess. What else do you want to know? What? Beau guy. I always thought he was French. Looked a little like Alain Delon. Could have been French, easy. Bogie. Huh.

I know why you want to talk to me. It's because everybody else is dead. Stars go out. Directors die. Companies fold. But some of the props get preserved. I've seen my friend the Vichy water bottle in the storeroom as wrapped up as the Maltese Falcon. We'd fetch a price now, wouldn't we? See, we survive, if we're allowed to live on our own. Even the sheet music that had to sit around looking as if it were about to be employed is still here somewhere. Waiting, like me, to be played. "Avalon" for god's sake.

They put me up a dolly for this flick . . . this flick you want me to give you the lowdown on. I rolled around like my shoes were marbles. I was supposed to sidle up to a table and once I got cozy the crooner would croon love's looney tune. Well, he would have, but the blounce couldn't play me. So for one shot I got to listen in while my bench carrier and the lab-coat guy—his name . . . ? you know . . . in the picture . . . ? I've got recall problems at my age . . . is . . . ah . . . yes, Rick—they go tête to tête at table. My man . . . Sam . . . he does say boss real well, very convincing. Has melting eyes. He's not the only one whose sockets seemed about to over-flow; I think it must have been the cig smoke.

I'll tell you the worst right away. You want to know the worst? You Q & A types always want to know the worst. The worst was—I have overheard interviews, *over heard*—so I know—I know what you want to know: the worst—well, the worst was when I realized this darkie couldn't play me. What a vile happenstance! What a remorse for me. After months of waiting I finally get a call and an opportunity to see some action, I'm working again after a long layoff, and the guy can't type, can't pluck, can't tickle the ivories. Not that *my* keys are, you understand. Ivory, I mean, or even bone. I wouldn't want anyone to think I was better put together than I am, but really . . . what a sorry résumé! What a downarounder!

I've got stencils though. Very cute. Cheap but cute. Stencil'd front, stencil'd side. Grandma Moses couldn't cliché better. This time around I'm dolled up because I've got a part to play. I'm at the goddamn center of things. This movie's got a key and that key is me! Oh yeah Rick's joint has got a band, a hoochie lady for the strumming, and a gambling den I guess: see what the boys in the back room will bet . . . There's a lot of sneaky people in the place, people with pasts, people without prayers. Like on a doomed ship or in the hotel of an about-to-be-bombed town. Fleeing people who just sit. Poor as churchmice, pawning their personals, but drunk on Champagne, Cointreau, and Campari. Ever try Campari? It stains. It has made me suffer. They sand out the rings and that hurts. Hurts the ego, hurts pride. They wouldn't sand a grand.

Oh sure, I've been on some pretty messy sets. I've suffered some scripts that were like unmade beds in flopbroad motels. You aint got a life long enough to listen to all I could tell you. I've endured real fights and genuine hysterics, clipboard romances and—Jesus—jealousies as big as forest fires, egos too, pratfalls that broke bones, real blood right at my pedals in a small pool of increasing congealment. But all the lines for this script were green as if they'd been grown each morning, script kids running around like waiters, might as well have dressed to play in the picture, which was set somewhere so exotic they could carry Captain Frog his words like shrimps under silver and nobody would be wiszer. Don't hit it again, please. Wiszer is a little off. I need a tuning. But for what?—a tune-up—what use for me these digital days? The hour of five used to be down there at the end of a hard day, you know, where it belonged. Dusk would have come into the piano bar. A jolly fat lady with a distinguished bosom is going to be warming the keys. And the martini arrives almost perfectly clear of vermouth. It aint right the day aint round anymore.

I heard there were complaints about my selections . . . which the darkie couldn't play anyway. And they—who are they? the invisible studio gods—the memo brothers—wanted a horny cottonclub girl to sing alongside, but I bet she couldn't finger me any better than Dooley, is it? who don't. You know what I heard about him? I heard he specialized in Irish songs sung in whiteface! That's worth a concluding chord! At sixes and sevens is where they all were. We had extras left over from the last French-fried colonial film parked at every table including gaming I guess, and Jews were doing Nazis like they wished they were. So why not a darkie who can't dance.

My selections were never my selections. I got no choice in the matter. I once played a stretch of Chopin. Not so long ago. In this cowboy bar my playing is going on, and some dumb cow comes over and wants "I Dream of Jeanie" or something likewisz, and he asks, rudely, what's that? what's that you're playing? And Doc Holliday says, thickly through a stuffy nose, it's a nocturne. But to be honest Doc can't play a note either, nocturne my stencil'd eyebrow, so he's faking it on me while another guy is nighttiming it up in a corner out of the camera's eye.

Twenty-two? Twenty-two is the answer to a trivia question. You don't have to have been there to know that, you only have to have been around bores. They're on every set that's supposed to be a bar. Another answer is: Chesterfields. Should have been Gauloises but that wouldn't have been American. Twenty-two. It's the number Helmut Dantine—I worked with him once in later years—handsome devil—it's the number he's told to bet in order to score at roulette. Rick, a real sog heart, lets the Bulgar newly-woos win the dough for their passage out of the picture. Like me, that Dantine wasn't paid to talk. I hear he got a contract just because he smoldered.

And working conditions. My strings were detautivating just waiting around in the fug, hot as the damn desert got. Why did they have to shoot the thing in August? though the people I worked for—Warmonger Brothers—were filming every minute of the day and half the night on account of the conflict. You could see shortages coming—of cellulose for film, cloth for costumes, rubber for tires, wood and metal and hair for wigs and crystallized sugar for those breakaway windows. Then actors would disappear, too, sucked up by their commissions. Of course I get no news in the warehouse. The world could've been coming to an end and all of us there would've just sat still for it. That is the life of a saloon piano. Sitting. It was what I was built for. Sitting. For silence, not music. To have patience, to be calm, to wait until a rollicking tune like "My Gal Sal" gets hammered out of me to amuse a bunch of layabouts whose delight is the sheerest pretense. If this is real life, real life must be a frigging fraud. It probably is. I go dum diddily dumdum but I don't feel dum diddily dumdum. People hear dum diddily dumdum but they don't feel dum diddily dumdum either.

Dumdum don't mean diddily to them. They've wiszd up. Oop. I warned you about wisz. The same goes for doodahday.

Like I said, everybody was running around crying complaints, ordering requests. You know movies are never thought out in somebody's head. No one has hold of a whole. There aren't even pieces. What would they be pieces of? And it aint a mosaic because in a mosaic all those itty bits fit into something—the big picture. No, this was more like, what do they call it? . . . collage. It's as if you made a lot of stuff just to cut it up and then you took some of the pieces and pasted a bunch of them back together. A few actors and directors try to control the movement of the movie they are supposed to be making, but helterskelter is what is really going on. Higgledeepiggledee in a pig's poke.

The cast? Honey—they're scattered corn. The dumped dame is off the set when the guy who dumped her cries or chortles or phones room service. Half the actors are playing golf. Al Wallis, was it? was walking around with a polo injury. I used to think that when the phone rang someone was there, someone was phoning, because the actors always answer hello or yeah or hi and then feign all ears, lobes awiggle as if a caller was bending them. They practice their reactions—I'm shocked, I'm surprised, I'm sad, I'm nervous, I'm worried—while Boots and Britches says why? why are you sounding anxious when you should be sounding confident . . . sound confident! I don't know how to sound confident, I can't do confident, I have never been asked to be confident . . . Okay, okay, try seductive, be seductive . . . My god, that's seductive? that wouldn't seduce a raunchy rabbit . . . Oh now, hon, see here, don't cry—George—let's start over, make the phone ring will you one more time. Makeup! We have eyesmear over here!

Oh boy, though, that short moon-faced shit was oily. Boy was that runt ever. With his nasal whine, with that shy smirky smile. He was all wheedle and a yard wide. That wheedle was worth a fortune. And she—she was a beamer. She was a ski slope girl, healthy as a travel poster. No wonder the wife of the star comes storming around the set accusing Rick, the lab-coat guy, of doing the bumpyhumpy with her. Beauguy. That's him. One of the two walk-of-stars stars. Ilsa the other. I really think she thought that Rick was uncouth. And he was always pissed off because the plot kept changing and he was convinced that was no way to run a railroad. Disremembering lines: I love you truly has been changed to I love you dearly, although tomorrow it may be that I love you deeply. Disremember this, a hit is like a miss, on squat you can rely . . . The stand-ins used to sing that . . . our fundaments get spry as time goes by.

And the soundman was doing banana splits because Beauguy kept muttering his cute little cracks so nobody could hear them, his back to the camera signing chits, and the writers would have been writhing if they hadn't been drunk in Toronto because he said them so soft so fast, too offhand, you know, like when this girl he's boffing but has no feelings for—sorry, it should go without saying—in this business you don't boff babes you have feelings for—if you have feelings for anybody you say I'm crazy about you—I'm mad about you—I'm nuts about you—as if Rick had feelings for anybody but Miss Visit Stockholm, the travel poster—as if Beauguy had feelings for anybody, certainly not the lush head he was married to, hey, even himself he aint happy with . . . Geez, we sort of trilled off the beaten track, didn't we? I never did do a note of Liszt. I regret that. And when they cast the TV series . . . shit, sorry . . . I can't forget—the shame—in '83, *Rick's Café Américain,* like a kind of coffee, did they contact me? My keys wouldn't stick for Scatman Crothers . . . I heard . . . I heard . . . yeah, he could play.

. . . oh . . . gotcha . . . back to boffing . . . um . . . the scene . . . you know . . . like when this girl—the girl he's boffing—asks him where he was last night ('cause she noticed his thingamajig wasn't up her) and he says I can't remember that far back, and then when she asks him if she'll see him tonight he says I can't plan that far ahead—well there's no drum roll for the execution of those lines, thrown away like a stubbed butt. Great stuff, I guess, if you aint chewing popcorn. Maybe that's why it got a lot of repeaters: girls trying to see through their tears, guys trying to hear what their Karmelkorn wouldn't let 'em.

Anyway, our hero, Rick, just shoves her—the boffee—out the door, don't he? Tough guy. Very sympathetic type. In a Western—I worked mostly Westerns—he'd get shot later on. He'd tumble from a roof to the mattress below. You can be short with the girls, indifferent, reluctant, ornery . . . but you can't shove them around and pretend to wear a white hat. I liked Westerns because they had decorums and I got to be played, even if there was always a rough house. That's what split my key. Bottle that was supposed to break like a clay pigeon in midair didn't break but flew past an aimed-at ear and hit me fairly square—just there—see . . . I got more wounds than Captain Frog's got medals.

Don't push down on me like that. When you surprise my keys they don't sound. I tell you some folks would set drinks down on the board as if it were stiff with rheumatiz. I could get drunk on licked lips, I've endured so many spills. Don't push down. I'm not in hearty operation, okay? And the leaners. Rick leans on me. Everybody leans. Let's go into Rick's and lean on the piano. Bogie, you know, had a lisp. Nothing about him was promising.

I thought I should try sounding like my music was coming through clenched keys, maybe then I'd get somebody to sit at me who could actually play, because taking away my sound and leaving me only stencils like I'd been made by Grandma Moses, with only a set of casters to show for my sacrifice—my being there—that was humiliating, the memory makes my hammers hard; only refugees from Bulgaria would have put up with it—because you felt helpless—because, when you sounded a discordant note, the soundman would say that's okay we're dubbing the piano in anyway. Sam hits me but he can't be sweet to me. The band plays while Sam sings "Knock on Wood" and he knocks me right enough, he can do that, though he always looks so concerned and friendly. Knock on wood. Konk konk konk. I must admit, though, I admire the choice of tunes in this movie. In my script it said that when the camera first comes through the door at Rick's Cafe, I'm to be playing "It Had to Be You" to harmonize with Rick's complaint later that of all the gin joints in the world, it had to be his saloon the beaming broad streamed into. Of course Steiner has to ham it up by wedging in "La Marseillaise" and der Führer's "Über Alles" in the Paris scenes as if he were rewriting the *1812 Overture*. He even called for a distant cannon to go off. I heard. Not the cannon. I heard he called. So she can ask, breaking up a kissy clinch: was that a cannon that I heard or my heart? Don't that epitomize the Queen of Corny?

Musicians who were there say the Paris script was pretty sticky, all right. And I guess I had a friend in bereavement in those scenes because Dooley couldn't play in Paris any better than he could in Casablanca, so another guy just out of sight of course played the theme while Dooley sat sideways so he could see what that other piano was doing, and pretend to ply—

Not that key either I guess.

The worst was—can I tell you now what the worst was?—the worst was when Curtiz in his costume of Boots and Britches staged the battle of the bands. The Germans come to town, okay? And act obnoxious. Of course. Then they start to sing, standing in a ring around me, what a nasty moment, but they start to sing "The Watch on the Rhine." "The Watch on the Rhine"? No one in the world but these guys is apparently supposed to know German. It's not a Nazi tune. They would never never sing such a thing. Niemals. Nimmer. Sooner they would warble "On, Wisconsin!" So they get the ubiquitous French anthem like pie in their ear. Why the smile? I know a few uppity words. You may have noticed. I got a range. And the French sing louder than the Germans only because they've got a band and all the Germans have is me. Okay, I say to myself, it's probably not a German guy playing me, but a Jewish guy playing he's a German. Geez. I finally get a chance to sound off and it's "The Watch on the Rhine." What a down-arounder!

The best time? The best time was the nighttime when the set sat in the dark with only the watch lights lit, each one of us looming—just bulks and bits—but the tablecloths glowing even in the general dim, and the glasses winking like a collaborator, the bar mirror tossing darknesses to and fro, you'd think shadows were cloaks and hats, the floor swimming in ink, our legs wading in it, all of us singing to ourselves, that little hum that comes with peace, when we worry only about where we weigh, released from all our day work relations, free to make our own connections, me with my bench, now stored upsidedown on my head like a crown, yeah, regal in my silhouette, the tables set for tomorrow's shot, the low light coasting through the Moorish arches, seeping between bottles, folds in the flats, and smoozing around my stiff keys like a healing lotion.

Bogie . . . I got his name defrenchified okay? sounds the same. Only looks different. I know pianos like that. . . . Anyway Bogie plays himself. I mean at chess. Now is that really playing? I call it doing the Dooley. Meanwhile I am collecting information. I know the name of the glass pattern they picked for the tables. The café set was pretty corpulent. But they probably rented everything. Took it all out of another warehouse like they took me. I can't eavesdrop as easy as Scheid—his name was—the sound mixer—you can imagine how Scheid was said—because he had every table every curtain every skirt and bra miked. He and Boots and Britches were pissed before they got to my point in the proceedings. Something about a buzzing sun lamp in a previous shoot. Pizzzzd. Don't hurt me, honey.

So if that theme was the center of the movie as some have said they think it was, then I'm there at the meaningful heart of things even if I'm faking it, but that's not my reason for claiming higher hierarchy here. I'm also the secret place where those travel docs get socked away for safekeeping, those papers the runt was going to chivy Laxlo to pony up for. You know, Stiff Knees. Follow him and walk the plank of patriotism. Anyway, Sam hides the visas under my lid. For most of the movie they would feel the vibrating strings of my heart. Me and Helmut Dantine were the quiet ones. He's the roulette winner and I'm the cache for the cachets. But we both smolder. Oh . . . there was a packet of papers on my lid earlier. Did you notice that? They disappear. Who knows what they were. I'm going to guess it was a little pile of sheet music that Dooley could pretend to read while he pretended to play. I think he really did sing though—to make it look real—in A-flat, in D-flat—but they probably dubbed his voice from a studio tape for the final sound track. In fact, there was some hugger mugger going on upon my top board, rearrangements that didn't make sense—sometimes a glass sits there, sometimes an ashtray, sometimes that stack.

And a mystery woman. There has to be a mystery woman, and it isn't always Mary Astor. Remember when everybody is gathered around me—Rick and Captain Frog and Captain Frog's three medals, with Dooley sitting at me with his seven grins—well, the papers are there then, on the near corner of my cover, and a half-filled wineglass and a half-filled stub tray too, but there is still room for the elbows and arms of a brunette in a white palm-treed blouse who's wearing one of those Shriner-shaped head pots, only this one has a floppy big sun brim. At the bass end of me is a local in a fez sitting next to his girl, and at the treble a swarthy in a turban. Back of all of us in a dark tie and whites is another fez. That's the scene. I remember the brunette's begging-your-pardon breasts pushing against me and the weight of her warm arms, though she's gazing at Dooley like she liked chocolate. Man, what a moment.

Right where that sheet music was, Rick hides the papers that the oily shmegegge has given him. An envelope is all it is. If somebody sneezed it would sail to Marseilles. In a manner ostentatiously casual, he slips it from a coat pocket to my purse . . . under my lid. The envelope is slim so Rick won't fumble the handoff.

But a prop that's not a prop—is what it is. A fake prop. Letters of transit they're called: travel docs signed by General de Gaulle the Sardine said. That's going to cut a lake of ice in Vichy France. Come on. I don't read history, but come on. A ticket to turmoil is what those passes would be. My friend and informant, the Vichy water, used to come in a respectable bottle under its own label. Anyway, papers like that might be persuasive in Portugal, but only Captain Frog's oft-bought signature can get the Heroic Stick on the plane—a plane I heard they built out of balsa and cardboard. Then serviced with midgets to enhance perspective for the screen. Might as well made me of balsa. Well, I am wood. But like Pinocchio I'm real. If hit, don't I cry? Am I not high-strung? Don't I have toes, feet, legs, sides, bottom, belly, cheeks, spine? You know what I resemble? I resemble a German make; my family is a distinguished German line. I'm from nobility like some are from Chicago. A Sauter is my kind. Sauter is a name due awe. Well, I'm not made of maple, and I don't have three pedals or the 2 Double Escapement Action of my model, no. 122, the Domino, and my compass is a bit constrained, not up to eighty-eight along the board there. I see you've counted. I'm a shorty, okay, but I can do ring-around-the-rosy with the best of them.

Not that key, please.

You're pounding me. When you surprise me I don't sound. Otherwise I am so—real . . . What do you mean I'm a mockup like the plane? Sure, they treated me like a toy. I can complain of their treatment, but—hey—I rise sweet in the morning . . . I do so have all the necessary keys. Maybe I don't treble up as far as some do, but you've just been hitting the wrong ones is all. The ones that have received maltreatment . . . That woman who plays

the tango—hell—she sways there strumming the handle of her gui-
tar. Might as well be a broomstick. And nobody minds . . . You
can't play either, honey. Scatman Crothers—I bet he could make
a plank plink.

The Ending? You want an ending? . . . The whiny creep—a
joker on every set, I hear—used to put out the cigarette that Boots
and Britches was eternally burning with an eye-drop of his urine
applied to its glowing tip. How's that for going out with a snizzle?
Yes. Yes. Vichy Water filled me in about the ENDING. It—the
bottle's label with the bottle on it—was taken to the hangar for
the dénouement—don't be surprised, I have a range if not every
key—music does not acknowledge the barriers of tongues—okay,
the climax—anyway did they blow that! Blow! Blow! Blow! Captain
Frog has been ordering Champagne cocktails the entire film—did
you notice that nobody finishes their drink but Rick?—you can
tell he cares about something—and Captain Frog brings his war
ribbons and a bottle of Vichy to the send-off. He celebrates the
moment with dead fizzy water? Nobody opens it for him, it is just
at hand like the U.S. marines. And we know why. So he can drop
the Vichy bottle into the wastebasket at a summational moment.
Vichy told me itself how the camera followed it into its hole like
a rat after cheese.

There were so many changes they had to use colored pages to
keep the actors' heads straight about them: blue, pink, salmon,
green. Now this you're going to like. This guy's name I'm going to
remember like I remembered Scheid because it's part of the joke.
Stucke. His name was Stucke. Like some of my keys. He brought
the pages to the set. That's why everybody knew the entire
movie was—. Right. And in that way, too—from stuck to stuck

so to speak—the production stumbled toward the truth of what they were trying to do—achieve a perfect mix of chauvinism and schmaltz.

Enduring qualities, you'll agree.

You want me to explain? Pianos don't explain. We riff, we run, we trill, we even thunder, but we don't explain. The inexplicable is the order of the day here. Chauvinism is reflected in the war of songs, ONE; in issues of duty, TWO; in Strasser's devotion to the Nazi party, THREE; in Ilsa's husband's selfless nobility, FOUR; in the Frog's subservience, FIVE; and schmaltz . . . schmaltz in the character of the conflict between duty and indulgence . . . where? . . . when they're at odds in the same official like the Frog, by the tug of war between duty and love in Ilsa, and betweeeeeeen love and indulgence in Rick.

Vichy said the scene was shot in a homemade fog. Rick and Ilsa are trying to enjoy a farewell clinch, and Rick says—Vichy swears he says—Rick is trying to be persuasive—he's been a real prick about Paris—so she loves him all the more—what a dumb doll—anyway—he says something like our troubles are but bubbles in this messed-up world, we don't even amount to a hill of beans—something like that—I say how high is the hill? how big are the beans?—anyway—then he says—Vichy swears he says—someday you'll understand that. That's what the condescending bastard says to a dame who's married to a freedom fighter on the run from an army of Fascist thugs. She'll understand that! I remember one night Rick sits in the set and drinks a fifth of 100-proof self-pity because his honey didn't leave her hero for . . . what did Rick have to offer? . . . his hill of beans. It's not a sad note. To end on. It's a sour note.

But Vichy says the movie ends happily with the two self-indulgent party pals, Rick and Frog, disappearing slowly in the mist, Frog rid of duty, Rick rid of love, both looking forward to a life of boffery and bourbon, or, if you prefer, complaisance and Champagne.

Don't run off, dear.

I've got an idea for a horror movie. Objects—see—in this movie—come alive. How or why remains to be worked out. They come alive and take over. I am this monstrous alien life form with a mile-wide mouth of teeth. When some ham hand lays a finger on me I bite it off. I just nip the tip. Neat as though it were all nail. Walk on me, will ya? And I scowl.

Whattya think?

Hey, I made a plink.

Try that one again.

With thanks to

Aljean Harmetz. *Round Up the Usual Suspects.* New York: Hyperion, 1992.

Jeff Siegel. *The Casablanca Companion.* Dallas: Taylor Publishing, 1992.

Soliloquy
for a
Chair

When we were born you wouldn't believe the fuss that was made over us: so many, so fit, so simultaneous. People drove by our mother's house and dropped off gifts and small change. We were tiny, especially when we were folded up. Crowds waited—patiently, I must say—to see us, maybe through a window when we were carried across the parlor, or during the few hours every day that people were permitted to walk through the kitchen to look at us lined up on the linoleum pretty much as we are here, only with not so much gray hair. Ha ha! I'm the only one of us with a sense of humor.

We're still together as you can see, even after all these years: that's Deadly Reckoning on your left, the one of us who received so much press; and Barry Buttock is next—we got around to calling him that on account of his constant complaining about the burdens he bore every day of his life, well, we were all weighed down from time to time (I always told him he hadn't a leg to stand on—ha ha!—he'd say he had four); then Overly Neighborly is on Butt's left, neighbor to me, always wedged in as we customarily were, but he seemed to enjoy it; then I'm in the middle—I was always in the middle—positioned below the paper pinned to a coat hook, the one that has curled like a burnt worm for being so long in a room moist with razor washings and shampoos; now we come to Commander Prince Paul who looks to me pretty much like the rest of us but one who fancied himself some sort of exiled African royalty, compelled for political reasons (that he pretended threatened his safety) to endure our life of required labor and enforced comradeship by parking against the wall of Walter's barbershop in Natchez, Mississippi, waiting, the guys say, like the taxi girls down the street, to be of use, but fearing (as the Commander insisted) to be found out and snapped into shackles on the spot.

We were all born together despite Prince Paul's preposterous mytherations, and healthy as bean sprouts, but Perce was without the entirety of his equipment—a front strut—though it never seemed to interfere with his duties which he carried out with as much enthusiasm as the rest of us . . . not much—ha ha!—yet an infirmity that sharp-eyed customers were bound to notice.

They'd pick up a comical magazine from Walt's rack to stay busy-headed while they were waiting their turn; then often leave it in Perce's lap when a barber became available, since some folks didn't want to settle down on a chair with no front strut. Perce wants me to say that all of us were fitted with those safety braces once but that Perce lost his in a terrible accident, and because of this unfortunate omission nobody would make use of him, just politely shy away and put their reading on his lap instead of lowering their anatomy. If it suits him in his heart to say it went that way, why not say it that way, say I.

The last in line, though he would hate to hear it put in those terms, is Natty Know-it-all, who got his name by being just the opposite, not quite there as to brainy particulars, and slow as faucet drip to learn or find, execute or opine anything. "I've half a mind to spin a top," he'll sometimes say—ha ha! It does make us laugh a lot cause he couldn't spin a top if his life depended on it. Just not built for tergiversations. Honest as the day is long though. Honest even all night. All night. The neons have a nervous flash. All Nite they bite air. Honesty's smaller hours go to those who pass them in their sleep. We have no sex life though we've seen plenty of yours, and we are greatful not to have to suffer the same miseries. If we continue to be of use, you will multiply us. Since many languages assign genders to things, we have voted to be pronounced "he," not "it" or "she," as if we were ships or fences.

Pleasure produced by frictions of various kinds, rubadubdubbing, and so forth—I admit—nervous kids have sometimes created it by sliding back and forth, sending pleasant little warmths rhythmically up my struts; and Prince Paul confesses he has enjoyed a few thrills upon opening or folding his legs. I find this hard to believe.

Nights get me. Neons or not. We sit amid our particulars but they are good as gone in the dark that washes through the front window smothering what little light we might have saved up for ourselves during the day and making for a silence that is peculiar to electric things and glass shelves. We die through use—we do—buttons into buttonholes—occasionally there's a trauma but mostly it is the quiet wear of unnoticed routines—life's a chair's hinge—our workaday seats are eaten by squirm and heat. But we also die during nights of inaction and enforced rest, when rust's slow debilitations pick at what we are and what sustains us with more repetition and determination than the woodworm. Yeah, when we close up shop a lot stops. Of course the sleep of metal has its merits, but I find myself missing the company of our daily things, now that the passage of people has ceased. During business hours we can overhear the shaving gear and the howzitlook mirror carry on a conversation, mostly about hypocrisy or vanity and such sins, or listen to a pair of sinks or trays of tedious utensils rattle on all day while clippers, scissors, toilet sprays yap away or buzz and bicker. Make your little noises, fellows, I let one weary leg say to the others now that silence seems total and only a flicker, reflected from distant headlamps, races across the floor like one of our mice. We've been called the seven dwarfs. I don't know why. People just say things sometimes.

All the barbers have their black vinyl chairs, of course. The head-man is always posted near the sidewalk. Perhaps you've noticed that barbershops tend to have the same configuration. Their façade is mostly made of window with a door set to one side. That door will have glass in it, too, so a passerby can see the row of us in a line like racehorses at the track, except that we shall face, not a vacant run to freedom, but the big bulbous dental armchairs where the hair is cut; where the beard is shaved; where the nails are filed and buffed; where the shoes are shined and admired. It is hard to like the three bears—that's what we call the barbers' chairs—they are so full of themselves and what they can do: "we rise and fall like empires," the headrest likes to say; "tilt and lift," the middle chair likes to put it; for the span, that is a leg's length, the repeated slogan is "lie back and take it easy."

Barbers used to draw blood and pull teeth. The pole, you know, advertised that. Back when the world had meaning. Leeches were kept in the white ball at the top while the bottom basin collected serum. The moving red helix mimic'd blood's downward flow, the white one twisted about the pole the way a bandage was wrapped around a leg or arm then, one fresh and clean the other soiled and soaked. But if you walk into such a barbershop in Chinatown you are likely to find an available girl.

By the way, all of us here speak Utile or Toolese, not just we Chairs, but the three bears too, the bottles of shampoo, the push broom and its pan. As far as I know, in this space, I alone—Mr. Middle—speak English, though I never spoke it to the barbers, Fred or Mart or Sam, or Winnie who did nails, or Archie who blacked shoes. I thought it would freak them out. So you will excuse me, I hope, if I make odd mistakes now and then. I rarely get a chance to practice the language. Beside, I've had to decide where to put my mouth. Of course, we all communicate by means of vibrations. It is simply that the link between a lamp and a scissor is so much more—may I say?—sophisticated, and more closely resembles your X-rays and ultraviolets and hi-fi. A few animals hear the vowels of Toolese now and then—it causes them to yowl—but humans don't have any ears for us unless we fall and break, or squeak and shout, or pop and whistle. Even then, you don't try to understand our exclamations. It's all right. We're used to it. Most of us—foot pads, curtains, couches, paper towels—don't grasp the meaning of your constant chirping and occasional singing any better than any of us does birdcalls and grackle cackle.

I shall be your translator, then, during this brief period of literacy. I am breaking our silence (in your regard) because many of us here in the shop know things about the Sam Bradford affair that you human beings seem unable to understand. After all, we were here the entire time. Yes, a few of us Utes shut down during the row; it was too unpleasant altogether for them; but most of us remained—how do you say it?—mesmerized by events.

But first, let me say something about our general situation.

The species I represent originated when primitive man made the first tool. He was looking for assistance from a rock, a fallen limb, a shell, a large leaf. And when that first man found a feather, stripped a stick to make it skinnier, or sharpened a stone, he was making something he hoped would help him out. Our philosophers (once-upon-a-time wine bottles trying to make a living now as vases for single blooms) speak of this as "the materializing of human purpose." Their celebrated analysis goes this way: the problem, which furnishes the stimulus, must be no small thing to enlist the form from a substance whose life is a continuous struggle. The instrument of solution, which is the tool emerging from the material of its making, must endure the painful lessons of error, trial, and luck. Versions of the tool are applied to the problem until the right nail is eventually smartly struck. The solution is signified by the creature's pleasure at his success, or his relief at the impediment that has been removed.

As an example, let's pick on a device that will clean and order human hair and whose need is obvious. The solution: a grid borrowed from a rake or a handful of fingers. This choice suggests that the cave dweller adapted one of the uses of the claw for other purposes—possibilities no doubt discovered when she ran a hand through her hair or undid knots or waited for a waterfall to encourage the tangled strands of her locks to float free.

Humans will have forgotten, but in those days the world and all its filaments were (quite correctly) thought to be alive: to possess a will, have plans, nurse grudges, suffer wounds. A heavy rock was heavy because it was resisting being moved. A hail of water might rush down the arroyo like an angry god. The sea was calm on account of Poseidon. A breeze might grow nervous, and the moon hide itself in a cloud. Thunderbolts were hurled from Mount Olympus at enemies on Etna. So when the toolmaker chipped at his flint, he was releasing certain powers already present in the stone. Right again. If he were smart he would cherish his tools because they were as alive as he. I am speaking proof that the things men have made are inhabited from material furnished by nature and by the energies and intentions of men.

You might have been wondering why a bunch of folding chairs would call their first employer "mother." Well, we do it just for fun, and because we like to display our wit and boast of the way our legs snap open. Fate was being ironic when it assigned us to a mortuary for our first full tour of duty, deeply so, since that's what mothers mainly do—give birth to an infant who will be able to restock the general supply and keep death ungratefully in business. The big black lady who fed the mourners cookies on small glass plates oiled our joints, because "around death, the quieter we be, the better, like those who have crossed over, it shows respect."

When we were cut out of our cardboard casing, we did not know how much of the world might someday sit down upon us or surround us with a selection of its business noises, but we were fortunate in fate's choice for us—a barbershop—since a barbershop was then closer to the center of things than almost any place readily available.

Six non-holidays a week, at eight in the morning, Walter would flip from CLOSED to OPEN the card that dangled from the doorknob. Then we would wait for the little ring the door gave out when the first customer came in. It was comforting, if business was brisk, to hear the snick of the scissors, the whisk of the hairbrush, and the skid of the barbers' razors when they were rubbed amorously along the length of their leather strops. Some guys disappeared behind the daily paper, others lost face in a roil of white lather; a few would immediately begin broadcasting their complaints about the behavior of other citizens and the ills of the nation. These routine moans and groans hid their features, I always thought, as successfully as the daily news. A regular whose name was Barney bewailed the condition of the economy, but told us little about his own perilously thin resources. The conclusions of Clarence's sentences were a bit shrill, as if his balls were being pinched, an explanation that pleased Barry Buttock, who first conjectured it. Clare would drift in most every morning before nine just to say hi! I wondered did he have a home or other friends or a place to hang his hat. Then our row of seats would begin to fill with customers, often greeting one another, their rumps already weighing—each in its own way—upon our crisscrossed legs. They weren't the only ones who felt the relief of leaving their feet so as to settle down upon Deadly Reckoning or Natty Know-it-all, often the first ones chosen because they were stationed in the favored end of our row, and had, in consequence, aisle seats, with only one well-sited shoulder. Perce wants me to say that he was superior to the rest of us because being built without a brace was like being born without an appendix. If it suits him in his heart to say it worked that way, why not say it worked that way, say I.

The murmur of the barbers and their clients, the clicks and snicks of implements, and the buzz of shavers were fairly constant and they were comforting too, reassuring the ear that all was well; and usually this carpet of clatter was punctuated only by the brief ring of the phone when an unheard voice asked for an appointment.

Our shop was mainly a walk-in. We were no highbrow female hair parlor. No sir, we weren't run by the style bunnies and their frightened hops into the latest fashions.

Early in our careers ... just a min ... the mortuary died a short time after we began working there, ha ha, we made rueful jokes about that, and we were stacked, roped, and dumped into a Goodwill without the least acknowledgment of the value of our previous service, which was exemplary even if brief ... As I was about to say, we Chairs sat at tables for a month in a small bar hereabouts, that's my only experience of bartenders, and we found them, to a seat, to be careless with their equipment and noisy at their handling, banging mugs about and crushing ice, but sullen as a bar rag, especially during the night shift. That's not our twenty years with barbers. No one could be more garrulous, gossipy, and outgoing than these guys at Walter's. It's not that they learned to talk to the talc (normally quiet, like unused bars of soap) or were inclined to toss their towels a chuckle ... no ... but once collected with others of their kind they'd be comfortable as a cushion—their tongues danced all day. With a little wax paper, Mart would play something he claimed was Irish on one of his combs—I was never sure which one—and then, energized, jig his fingers among his hair-dye dishes without bumping any.

Next? Ah. Master Robinson. You get to be the ghost today, Walter might say to a small boy who at that moment looked a bit apprehensive. Just climb up here, he'd say, where the clouds are. I'll make a ghost of yah. Then with a flourish the chalk white cloth would be pinned about the poor kid's body. Dad might be getting his own hair cut, and needed to assure his son, if it was a first time for him, that the scissors didn't hurt, these suddenly jovial men weren't dentists, and that the boy should banish fear and let his mouth water in anticipation of the flat round all-day sucker that would be his mouthful when his haircut was admired at last. Older kids, who were by experience now undaunted, might be rewarded—it depended on relationships formed on the street and outside the range of our observations—with a recitation of Walter's renowned menu. A few of its offerings were pictured on a cardboard sign like wanted men. The whole show went as I now render it, spoken in rapid-fire bursts followed by some explanatory pauses.

Hey honey bunch . . . hey handsome little guy . . . welcome to Walter's, home of all your desires. You want a part, a perm, ringlets, or a razor cut . . . an Afro? How about I give you a texture treatment? Hey, you want bangs, do you dearie, a beehive, or a blowout?—oh man, oh madam, right here—bob or bowl or buzz cut—you'll find their picture on row five—along with a bouffant doodoo . . . how about we do it up in a bun, then? So many choices, like chocolates, boxed by the letter B; *maybe a Caesar, a comb-over, what say? You're getting a little thin on top—no?—like a pond in a woods—no?—all right, no pond, no woods, maybe a few cornrows, a crew cut? We can just flat-out crop it off, straightaway give it a Croydon facelift (you know, that's a topknot); how about trying the curtained style, devil and dreadlocks, ducktails ass or a ducktails flail?* It's just hair, my darling, how can you get so fussy? *Okay honey, okay handsome, did you ever consider a Dutch braid, the false hawk, or the feathered look? All the rage; let's give you a finger wave then, a fishtail, a flattop, flipflop, French twist, fringe cut . . . or how about half a ponytail, half an updo? No? So you're that sort, a Hime cut, what say, okay? . . . Hi-top with a fade . . .*

Walter would make waves as if he were conducting the atmosphere.

. . . you know what, I've got it! A loose curl would look great on you . . . old liberty spikes . . . like the statue, see there—your hair is standing up like it was scared; *so a Mohawk, what do you think, handsome? Have you come to that? A mullet . . . a mullet?* Come on, honey, be brave; *do pageboy, pigtails, pixie cut—look cute—pompadour—look hip—full ponytail—look perky—whoa!* Knick knack . . .

Walter would rock as if riding an animal. A canopy of white starch settled over the barber chair.

. . . Is recon, rattail, or the notorious frat shag on sale? I know your head and how it grows: from pasted wig to when its amorously tousled; *we've got a full range; you could try a purely spiky look if you think it suits you, sure, or make your head into an ocean of waves, anything that floats; we remove short hairs, do nails till they cry uncle; we cut long tresses, trim beards—only as you wish, sure—schurre—we shave cheeks too, clean as a tin whistle—we will grease your mustache till it shines like a saloon sign—oh dear—you prefer the same cut as last time?—oh, yes, I remember—as it used to be—as it has always been.*

Hey, ask those chairs their opinion and they will tell you: your fortune depends on how you wear your hair, and what your shadow on the wall will say—those splotches where your heads rested . . . by the way, what did *become of you?*

Walter had the menu memorized. He would point imperiously to the faded poster on the wall while he chanted the shop's selections, though no one ever challenged the availability of his hairstyles, so I had no handy measure for the truth of his boast. The safely tethered children remained mum and wide-eyed while Walter wore a grin broader than the local river. The other barbers would applaud with a rattle of spoons in their coffee mugs.

It was a friendly place, a little stuffy from piped-in warmth through the winter, but blossoming with habitués at all times of year because, as every person not cursed by baldness knows, hair in plenty grows, through droughts and blights and snows, but not in tidy rows. Not them. Not those. Walter told his clientele that they were presently enjoying his garden, not theirs, and that he harvested head hair, ear hair, nostrils, brows, sideburns, goatees, beards, while cultivating the colorful blooms of fingernails, sandaled toes, and inked eyes. At her table at the back of the shop, Millicent manicured the ladies, but she took a little trolley to the chairs to tend the men. There they held out a shy paw and, bashful about such primping, hid their vanity in a din of rough male sports talk, political opinion, scandal, and local news, all in a language meant to impress one another and intrigue Millicent, who was immune to shock.

Prince Paul claims that Millicent (I never heard her natal name) dresses like a whore—long, thickly painted nails, piled hair, bright cheeks, ample bosom (a sample showing), a tight short sheath, and heels that double her height—but how would he know if none of the rest of us knows? and none of the rest of us, I can assure you, knows. We know nothing about clothes, only a blink about hair, nothing much about bodies, and only a touch about mascara, a few pomades, and some rouge. That's Prince Paul, though . . . he's good at pretending.

Behind those big businesslike barber chairs, several shampoo sinks interrupt a narrow glass shelf. There numerous bottles mingle among the mirrors like guests at a ball, frisking between shears, brushes, whisks, and fist-sized piles of moist and steaming cloths. Oils, conditioners, rinses, talcums, tonics, lotions mill about while, for stability, a more disciplined row of antiseptic and restorative bottles stand at brilliantine attention against a wall.

These are alleged to be good for baldness. I know them by their glints, their hums. Women, even more than men, will try anything to prevent hair loss. I was told the shelf resembled a bar but my only encounter with bars has been with wooden ones and these were burned by cigarettes or ringed by drinks and other ghosts of grief.

When fellows come to get their face shaved, their hair cut and hair oiled, they tend to sit in seats that represent their favorite speechifications. I am remembering one conk head named Harold who used to come in to have his fuzzed dome mowed for just a buck and who plunked himself down on Overly Neighborly to—Walter joked—"weight" his turn. He would sigh like a squeaking tire—Walter joked—and address those who were there—how many or how few did not restrain him—"So, did you know that one of the lost tribes of Israel was black?" This was greeted with the silence it deserved.

So much clutter . . . buttons . . . marbles . . . pins . . . Creatures called Human Beings by other members of mankind are turning the world into fuel, into furniture, into tools like my friends—utensils, kettles, cars—into towns built of wood, brick, and stone. Watch out . . . Those curling irons, holstered in a block of wood, can get hot . . . We hugely outnumber them now, this squanderous tribe of people who invented us, who use us, and will discard us in mounds set afire by our remains. Combs alone outnumber the heads they coif. Scissors are in the same situation, pens, coins, rings, buckles, guns. Most people have a couple. Even plants in pots or aunts in hoards can't measure up to the miles of tools shelved in stores, the unseemly tons of junk heaped in yards, knick knacks scattered like rice at a wedding. The entire surface of the world will be stored in pantry bins and furnish parlor tables. Assorted spools of stuff, in multiples and variations, boxed and bagged and trucked hither and yon—wires, pipes—yon and hither—are being displayed or captured, buried, sold, or stolen. When they dig our civilization up, and with those shards try to guess the rest, we shall outnumber the bones of Human Beings in offering clues. Think of it: the leaves of books may beat the leaves of trees in turning. And there are fewer cats than summer clothes.

Everyone enjoyed the soft blue haze left by the customers' cigarettes. The smokers were mostly men, though Millicent swallowed her menthols like someone in a sideshow. Chewers alone were frowned on. A wad in the cheek would dissolve in spit and soon the spit was oiling the floor. Which was made of squares of linoleum. Anyhow everyone enjoyed the haze left by lit cigarettes, smoky exhalations—they were thought—in a ghostly guise. The resulting communal breath seemed like a river of air that carried the fellowship of the shop from chair to chair. I know I never tired of our atmosphere: the smell of polish always pleased me, and the vigorous shine Archie would apply to some businessman's shoes made a nice noise, the way the smell of coffee stirs you folks to ride forth in the morning, eager dogs baying at the rising sun.

Our customers were a mixture of races, unusual to be found, I understand, in this geography; but the reality is that the population mix was thin and came and went as the neighborhood did, slowly shrinking as the whites took to their heels and the street's vacancies grew, swelling when poverty, like hunger, overtook its clientele. Serving such different heads was not easy. People born with hair bent like wire make a mistake to want it straight. Straights want swirls. Brunettes weep to be blond. Guys who have lots of it want their heads shaven and shiny. Learn, ladies, to be happy with the hue Our Great Maker gave you. Blacks who wanted to look white would come here on the assumption that white barbers would know better how to do it. As for my tribe of folding chairs—well, to us, asses differ only by weight. We ask two questions of our customers: how thin? how large? how small? how fat? how light? how heavy? That is that.

Every Front Room has a back room. That's where the joint's john flushes; where a restful rocker rocks; and an eight-place poker table swallows the central space. Barbers not on duty lazed there, playing solitaire, smoking one of the aforesaid cigarettes or reading the racing magazines. Walter took bets. On heralded occasions. For the Derby or the local track. And an evening game of poker took place, maybe once a week, sometimes twice, when a few friends dropped in and some chairs were enlisted to take care of the additional arrivals.

I understand and employ the word "herald," because I was sometimes placed, for an evening, in the doorway of the shop as a signal to knowledgeable passersby that poker was "on" at 10:00 p.m. "Okay, old fellow, you can be our herald tonight," Walter would say to me, though we both knew he was talking to himself. He likes to do that—be coy with a razor or angry with a comb. An occasional snarl would draw an expletive from him, followed by a small speech, all this for the amusement of the customer who was having his hair pulled.

Such outpost service is humiliating. You have been parked there, in the doorway, because no one will steal you, worn and rusty as you are, and there you must sit until the number of places for players has been fulfilled, whereupon you are removed from that spot to the poker room itself, your seat to be occupied by a nervous stranger from the street who has been brought to the shop by a friend and has, in any case, not come because of *your* ungainly presence. Regulars tend to be pros at poker and do not squirm in their seats like infants, though they may allow their eyes to wink and slide to one side, their nose to wrinkle and snort a swinish snort, their lips to grin or curl or smirk as if in commentary; and sometimes they like to release their grip on the cards for an expansive, apparently careless gesture, in order to mislead and deceive the other players. Meanwhile, I chatted with the chips in the pot. Boy, do they know a thing or two. As for me, I keep my lid on.

Doorman duty does pay some interest, face-to-face as you are with the street (seat to seat in our nomenclature) and brushed by the people passing, hurrying home after another warm day, with their anxieties safely snapped in their purses. Once in a while a funny thing will happen as it happened to Natty Know-it-all. Which is as follows: a little white truck double-parks in front of the shop and a guy runs to the rear of it. The truck, I mean. Then, before Natty can prepare himself, this hasty kid plops a large tub of chrysanthemums in Nat's lap. Well, I didn't mean a comical happening. Apologies if I mislead you. I meant strange. I meant odd. I meant mysterious. It was early fall, we all remember, at the very edge of evening, and the flowers were already half-lit, a pale pink, I think it was, the color of an embarrassed cheek, but, when fisted into a bunch by a determined hand, might be as perky as could be. Nat can't make a ring-a-ding thing about the delivery, since his back is to us and mostly out of sight in the doorway recess. Lordy, he would have said if he could have. Lordy, this is quite a different kind of ass than I am used to making room for, he would have said, I'm sure, given a reason to say, or a way to say it.

So he sat there as the few lights along the street began to glow. The flowerpot was damp and cooling. He says it felt nice on a warm night. But the mums were playing their part in a puzzle. Which was as follows: Sam and Mart should have gone home through the front door. Neither of them participated in the poker game. That was Walter's show. And when Sam and Mart left work they always ran their hands, in a kind of friendly gesture, over the curving blue back of whichever one of us was on watch. As far as I knew, the green metal door to the alley was never used. I mean the door opposite the john in the poker room. Which I refer to as the green metal door to the alley. So I say: how? how did they go in or out without spotting the pot, or the pot spotting them, for gosh sake?

In this way Natty passed his time that night. The moment the plant was delivered, the truck sped away. Some unknown person had parked before the shop, under the traditional red-and-white-striped spiral that had long ago stopped its dizzy spinning, a man, a young man maybe, had got out, was he the driver? did he take the pot from the rear of the truck or just come around the rear with it in his arms to deposit the—possibly a present?—yes, a gift. The street emptied. The bouquet (can we say?) sat in Know-it-all's lap. Shadows ran together like ingredients in a drink. The flowers were waiting, maybe, to have their blossoms shorn. Know-it-all didn't know it all, after all. The plant was uncommunicative. A place at the poker table must have remained empty because no one came to put Natty next to Perse. Hours passed. Darkness erased definition. That's how long the night was—as long as the letters *m* and *n* spell "me and my mind's memory."

On wagerless nights Walter would leave last, checking the lights and other equipment, locking the door with a brass key; and just before he began his hike home, he'd pause before the window to give it scrutiny while inside we waited for his image to be eaten by others. On poker nights the front door would be busy until eleven before Walt locked up from inside. The game would then begin. Walt's pick of folding chairs for back-room service was pretty random, though I was chosen often enough to learn the game. I thought I became rather good at it. Never play to win a particular pot, never become enamored of your pairs, because odds do not apply to particulars. Every deal is as unique as any other. Just keep track of the way the bidding breaks. Then follow the odds like a private eye. Fold when history tells you. Over the long haul you'll be a winner more often than not.

One of our regulars (for a time) was an undercover cop. He would slink into the shop at the end of the day, seat himself on Prince, and hide behind a magazine—*The Boxer's Monthly*, I believe—biting his cigar with yellow teeth. After a discreet interval, he'd stuff its dead stub in his mouth and slip away to the game. There, Walt would let him win one or two deals. It was a reasonable payoff. Some guys grumbled about it but Walt knew what he was doing. A little insurance, he said, against arrest. That's all. And a lot easier to give away than a free shave.

While dealing, Walt would sometimes hum mumble a tune—his "Auntie's in the Pantry" song. It really riled the other players. Mostly because they couldn't hear all the lines clearly and found themselves straining to understand something they didn't want to be bothered with. This is how his jingle went, as I made it out. His knees tended to knock.

What say you, mate,
as you accumulate
a stack from the dealer of the action?
Ante up, man, ante up.
Rattle your fist to simulate
the greed of the clattering cup.
Roll the craps, dude, shake and roll.
I'm twenty-one and lots of fun.
You can find me on the stroll,
wagging my hips, rouging my lips.
Ante up, mate, ante up.
I know how to flip an ace,
quietly fold or make a face.
Whatcha say, guy, whatcha got?
Threes are wild and I'm with child,
hid like a card in a lousy hand,
not at all as we had planned.
Ante up, man, ante up.

The fact that Know-it-all was doing an all-nighter weighed heavily upon me the way fat men, waiting their turn at the clippers, deepened the thin crease of my back. Dawn was arriving piecemeal, like a gift awkwardly wrapped, when the chrysanthemums—it must have been they—exploded, blowing away the glass front of the shop and hurling Natty out into the street, bent and spent, in a skid to the sidewalk opposite. Shards of glass rattled across the bare seats of those of us inside the shop, and slivers scratched our backs when we were blown against one another. Deadly Reckoning suffered a slightly bowed leg; Barry Buttock was seriously scarred; Overly Neighborly sailed out of his place in our row to strike Millie's table so forcibly its wheels would never revolve again; both Perce and Commander Prince Paul were pelted by chrysanthemum leaves and pieces of dirt; while I, Mr. Middle, rocked against Perce and Prince Paul, shoving them so intently their eight legs screeched in protest.

Leaves, petals, and pottery flew hither and yon, plaster dust settled on the barbers' chairs so abundantly you could write on them—and later, Mart would, with his finger, be inspired to reach eloquence. All of a sudden the place filled with police.

Who was this bomb intended for? we Chairs as a group or just Know-it-all, who could be an enormous nuisance sometimes, but still . . . ? perhaps the glassware?—jars and mirrors?—bottles or cloths?—of course not . . . only a few brilliantine bottles went pop; no, and it was not likely aimed at razors either, none of whom were injured, or any one or more of the heating irons, or the big chairs on which Walter wrote his boast, "I survived, bless God!" We first thought it had to be one or more of the human beings, but when the bomb went off all of them had gone home—we assumed—and were safe in bed. This crowd couldn't have played poker all night; the games were over—usually—about two. When counting casualties, they were without a scratch. Maybe the bomb didn't go off when it was intended to—but later than intended. Maybe someone—it would be Walt—was expected to see it sitting there in Know-it-all's lap and bring it in to be admired. Maybe it was meant for a late customer. By a sore loser. I was told that gambling parlors such as Walt ran were illegal, but the cop was fixed, and the sums wagered at the table, as far as I could assess them, were not as much as the true professionals played for, though pitifully more than any of these players could afford.

Most mysterious, most calamitous of all: we did not see any of the barbers leave for home, or stay for cards, or hear a late-in-the-day customer say, "Here! What's this?" and bring the pot in, or yell at Walt, "Hey, you got a plant on your front porch" while walking off to other business, innocent of evil intention in every alternative. Where, in the container, was the explosive placed? Was it buried in the soil or propped against the plant? Was it a firework, or vial of nitro, piece of plaster, or a grenade? Was propelling Natty so forcibly across the street a likely direction for an explosive planted in the soil of a flowerpot parked in the seat of a folding chair? The police didn't say much about anything, I think, because they didn't know anything. The victims—well, they were the shop and some of its fixings—the victims were about to complain to an insurance company instead of the cops but found both were impossible because the complainers were *just things*. Sam and Mart were annoyed they hadn't been hurt. Mildly maimed, mind you. Pleasantly pained . . . A few feigned mental fatigue but not for long; it was too tiring. Metal would have to do. The cops, for their part, picked up lots of pieces of burst dirt, blown plant, and broken glass that were reverently popped into clear plastic as they had seen themselves do on TV, protecting clues from con-tamination. They interviewed everybody in a human skin by ask-ing, "What do you know about this?" Otherwise, the Law stood around shrugging its shoulders and speaking vaguely about lab work.

Poor Natty Know-it-all could no longer fold neatly into a com-munity stack; could no longer stand ready to sit; he was an inno-cent servant of happenstance, and whatever remained of him was to be borne away in the rear of a city truck like the trash it had become. What were we doing, meanwhile? We were wondering—I must say, pathetically—whether this destruction would put an end to the shop; whether we should all be out of a job, and headed for Natty's junk pile. Oh sure, we knew that our bodies could be mashed flatter than a street, and melted like metal into metal, and thus revived for the doubtful pleasures of another life; but these conclusions were hardly palatable to us, not after our life in the barbershop—a good regular job, some appreciation, companionship, and—I would say—clean, even elegant, surroundings.

I now remember only one other act of violence in the shop over the years. I wonder whether there was any connection. I should think not. I should hope not. Of course not. Anyway, as follows: Walt and Marty were woofing around with a client who was undergoing a trim to his beard; Marty was pretending he was about to cut his customer's throat the way they pretend in the movies, grinning like kids up to something, drawing the blade slowly upward under the chin; when, with a noise that could only be called a growl, Archie stopped polishing Sam's guy's shoes, grabbed Barry Buttock by one leg, and flung him at Marty and Marty's customer's throat, and the razor too, I dare say. Barry banged into Sam's raised arm instead, so the blade did graze the customer's throat to the degree of a scratch. Perhaps. Mart's man jerked his head and swiped away the hot cloth covering his eyes, all and each with a howl of their own; Barry tumbled to the floor near a tin of polish, and Archie bulldozed his way out the door into the street.

I swear we never saw Archie after that. No one again polished shoes in the shop or hung up coats and lived on tips. Nothing was broken by the bashing. Nothing was said. Barry Buttock was examined and found to be sturdy enough to stand where he ordinarily belonged. Walt acted ashamed of something. He did say . . . he did say "geez." The customer, forever anonymous, wiped his face and the beard that grew there, and left without paying. He walked very carefully, looking down as if checking the polish on his shoes. We never saw him again either. I had forgotten all this until just now. Oh yes, Mr. Razor boasted to me that he had dulled his own blade to prevent any real injury. I never believed him. He was a well-known credit taker.

The way we are misused is no worse than any other. I am not like a lot of my companions, bitter about people, or despairing of my own nature, the way glass feels because it can be seen through—ha ha—nor am I surprised to have learned from knives that they have conserved their animus like juice in jam jars, waiting for dullness or—contrarily—the best time to snap, or how to hurry a finger toward the cut that awaits it. In the opinion of the barber guys, the way utensils are misused is no worse than any other treatment, however widespread, that the human species has inflicted on Mother Nature: hills are burrowed or leveled, lakes pumped dry, seas emptied of life, trees cut, forests burnt. It is no matter with men what damage they do, or their paved streets and ubiquitous cellars accomplish. They murder the very ground they walk on—it's all right—so why should we few chairs complain about a rusty pinion, a small tear, some slight impulsive knockabout?

After the bomb we collected our spirits as well as we could and endured the inadequate renovations that Walt could afford. Nevertheless, our reopening didn't bring our old customers back. No one likes to chance it. After all, there was no reason and no warning. Destruction just appeared like the ghost of broken dishes does during Easter or the Christmas holidays. The light that falls on glassware now is as tepid as wash water wrung from a strangled rag. It leaves, after it hits me, no differently than before, except that it departs more the way a sigh does than a joyous whoopee from a winner. The marks on the wall where our customers' hair once leaned will, I bet, be here long after we are removed to the scrap heap, separated from one another for the first time, and unable to feel the warm reassuring weight of a single human ass.

So we wait as much in daylight, as in the darkness of the shop, for the end of our adventures. On her wavelength, hardly heard, a lipstick is sobbing. Know-it-all insists that *we* were the targets—things were aimed at and the only entities injured. Those were his last sad words to me as he was hauled away.

If it suits him in his heart to say it went this way, why not say it went this way, say I.

The Man
Who Spoke
with His
Hands

AN EXERCISE

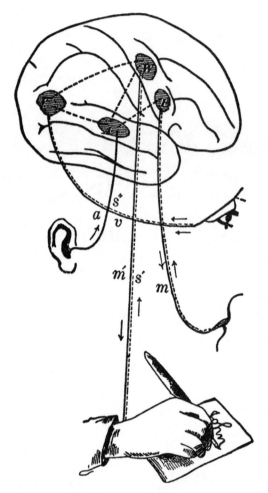

From William James, *Principles of Psychology*, 1890

The man who spoke with his hands was not deaf nor did he speak with his hands because he was communicating with deaf people. The man who spoke with his hands was not noticeably shy, therefore unlikely to say much, or be inclined to wait for a passing noise behind which to hide his remarks. He engaged in conversations with average frequency and ordinary ease, and employed for these everyday purposes a voice that was mellow enough to spread on bread; neither so low as to approach a whisper nor so high as to threaten screech. It was a voice as brown as his eyes.

The man who spoke with his hands did not gesture expansively, because he spoke with his hands not his arms and/or eyebrows. His hands tended to remain in close touch, mostly about mid-chest. His hands were made almost entirely of fingers. These were long and slim and supple. One thought of cigarette holders except for the supple. A cigarette holder is not supple. It is a bamboo tube with a coating of lacquer. Those who believe that smoke filtered through the stem of such a holder is less likely to sicken them are probably mistaken. According to authorities, they are being poisoned when they breathe such drugs. Smoking is a bad habit but the man who spoke with his hands did not appear to have any other habit than his hands.

The man who spoke with his hands had cheeks that were

tanned; outside of those two places—the left and right cheeks at the lower edge of the bone—his skin was pale. His fingers were exceptionally white and consequently easy to see, which is possibly one reason why he decided to speak with his hands, although nobody supposed that he actually chose his gestures; what made them so graceful and attractive was that they (his fingers for the most part) seemed to dance outside the range of their owner's attention. It is no longer fashionable to describe anything as "unconscious." The few who still employ the concept have probably been smoking too much Freud. Freud had a cigar habit, and we know it was bad because it killed him.

The man who spoke with his hands would, while speaking, sometimes move the thumb of his right hand gently (one might say with circumspection) back and forth, in and out, of a hollow formed by a downward curl of the left hand's lengthy fingers, as if they were lightly gripping a pole where the thumb slid. Professors Rinse and Paltry understood this to be a meditative moment; for instance, if he were saying that he hadn't taken any of the students in his History of Religious Music class to hear some famous organist who had come to Columbus yet again this year (it was the sixth occasion), they would take his hands to be indicating that he had debated long and hard about it. As Professor Paltry saw the thumb glide gradually out again, he thought of the trombone. Freud would have ascribed this habit to another practice that was equally compulsive and otherwise unspeakable.

On the whole the man who spoke with his hands created movements that were slow, as if they were distant from his words, and reluctant to leap to conclusions. Only when his forefinger, seemingly held back by the pressure of the thumb, sprang forward in that snap one uses to flick a crumb from the dining cloth did they call attention to themselves. This gesture meant—the Professors believed—that whatever it was he was discussing—an event, a meeting, a class, an opinion—was over and done with, was no longer held by him, was not to be taken up again. When he said: I just couldn't face another long bus ride with a load of noisy kids; there was neither snick nor snip, but a gentle, almost imperceptible movement of the fingertips, the nails in full view, as if brushing something away or warding it off, pushing the imagined thing out of his purview. Then he might conclude: so I didn't. The snip would follow this.

A gentle brushing of a tabletop with the fingers will roll crumbs to the edge and over it onto a ready palm. There is no need to flick offending grains of salt or sugar into space where they will sand up something else—a chair seat or the floor beneath your feet. A table knife will scrape them to a corner and fancy folk or attentive waiters in hightoned restaurants employ a silver blade just for this purpose. So the flick is probably a bad habit too. The flick removes a problem from your presence but does not rid it from the world. Indeed, the cloth from which the crumbs have been so casually ushered remains stained and abused, and the gesture that removes these ashes and these cinders also signifies an intention to renew the table's use as if it were new and its covering not in need of removal. Germs are not thusly scraped away and remain to infect the éclair and its brood.

The fingers of the man who spoke with his hands might mesh like the tines of forks, but gently and easily, for tines may jam. Then one could watch his fingers slide between his fingers like blending fans, again very gradually, so the hands were clasped, and almost immediately moved again, separating with the silence of cream, and thereby measuring degrees of commitment or withdrawal, of coolness or ardency, agreement or disavowal. His hands often assumed a prayerlike stance when he began to speak—pardon me, your humble servant, by your leave, sir—and then the right hand would withdraw, its fingers sliding very slowly down a calm left palm until the wrist was reached when they would hesitate a moment before rising up again or continue to drop on down to the wristband of their owner's watch.

Yes, the man who spoke with his hands could be nervous and impatient too, the fingers of his right drumming on the back of his left. That tapping reminded Professors Paltry and Rinse of the way his long slim white fingers flew on and off the holes of the flute, whereas if the left danced a bit on the back of the right, it meant, they calculated, expectation coupled with serene acceptance. Occasionally both hands would droop from their wrists like fresh wash hung from a rope, but this was not a feminine gesture, even though Professors Rinse and Paltry judged it signified: you win, I give up, you don't say. Unless, of course, the hands suddenly flew up again, when it meant a very firm: go away, take your topic elsewhere, little boy, run out and play.

When the man who spoke with his hands was confronting a knotty problem, or trying to be clear about a complexity that had hold of him, he would revolve his hands around one another, slowly or quickly, quietly or forcefully, as the puzzle was pursued. The knot at last untied, the left hand, palm exposed, might fly gracefully away as if to say: there, you see, or, it consequently comes to this. I liked particularly the definite but brief pinches one pair of fingers might make on a lower arm or the upper skin of a hand, or all the subtle tweezer-style variations, since he seemed to have a special role for every digit, and Professor Paltry particularly felt those fingers were very sincere about their business, well manicured and behaved, especially during geometric gestures, small circles mostly, as if one were twining one's hair, or unrolling an idea like a length of rug.

Occasionally, the man who spoke with his hands would add a little flutter, or some zippy propulsion of the right indexical toward the object or person he was addressing (the way one adds "-ed" to a verb or tacks on "-ly" to an adverb or attaches an "-est" to an adjective or "-ness" to a noun of which "saintliness" could serve as an example, or "livelihood" be an attractive instance, or "implicational" at least representative), thereby altering the assumed character of a run of silent remarks.

Rarely did the man who spoke with his hands permit them to touch his head, ears, or face, though Professor Paltry saw a forefinger brush his earlobe once in a gesture so expressive as to warrant applause. They never strayed below the belt, or roamed far or widely from his torso, or fell meekly like a coat sleeve to his sides. And despite all of this nearly continuous motion, the Professors hardly noticed them; took little heed of this habit; were not distracted as much by the fingers as by the light which rollicked from their owner's bald head, pale as paper. He was a man, compact and even slight, whom one could nevertheless pick out of a crowd as one would the most attractive piece of fruit from a bin. His hair would have been brown had he had any. The truth was, Rinse and Paltry talked more about the man's dark curly eyebrows and his bald pate than his shiny nails or their scintillating moves.

When the man who spoke with his hands performed, his colleagues read his gestures as signs, and Rinse thought his fingers danced, but Paltry heard an orchestra that the man conducted to accompany his words. Paltry saw the pick, the drum, the strum, the tweak, the pluck, the rub, the damp, the trill, the run of the instruments, the strain of the strings, as the man's nails flickered, and loose fists were formed only to relax like petals leaning back into their blooms.

Arthur Devise was the man who spoke with his hands, and he played the flute, the piccolo, and the recorder. When the death of Clarence Carfagno created an opening in the music department, Arthur Devise arrived to fill it. Professors Morton Rinse and Joseph Paltry held it against their new colleague that he had been chosen without consulting them; they held it against him that he was a friend of Howard Muffin, the President who had hired Art (as they would later affectionately address him), and a president whom the male faculty—to a man—despised; they held it against him that he was almost as old as they were and so as long a failure as they were (though they didn't immediately put their animosity in such terms); they held it against him that, as a musician, he was quite accomplished; Professor Morton Rinse especially held it against him that he, like Rinse, played the flute, the piccolo, and the recorder; while both men held it against him that Muffin had picked Arthur Devise because the Department of Music had always—anyway in Paltry's memory—had two members (there were three altogether) who professed the flute, the piccolo, and the recorder, and that it was proper to continue the tradition; the remainder held it against Arthur that he actually seemed a good sort and a wise choice, because they did not want to think the President ever acted wisely; Professor Joseph Paltry held it against

Devise in addition that he was a widower with an attractive daughter about to become a student of music in her parent's own college, in her parent's department, and might enroll in her parent's
class; they jointly held it against him that Devise agreed to teach,
lead, and pamper the choir and the chorus, and had them sounding splendid in no time; finally, they held it against him that he
spoke with his hands, and that, at first, neither Rinse nor Paltry
liked what he said.

The man who spoke with his hands, because he spoke with his
hands, was a quiet man, with a slow warm well-regulated smile, a
smile hard to dislike, and he chuckled deeply in his chest to the
point of an almost inaudible rumble, and the slow well-regulated
shaking of his ribs made his hands, so often positioned on what
would have been his stomach had he had one, rise and fall lightly
like a pair of drifting leaves—motions charming in their pacifying
consequences. It has been said that Saint Francis of Assisi used
such gestures to charm birds who would then perch upon his
extended arm and eat grain strewn artfully along it, though some
say they just flew in for the grub.

Dottie Devise was, in contrast, chipper, perky, cheeky, cheerful,
and squeaky as a toy mouse; perhaps her voice could be better
described as chirpy, high but thinly pitched, leaping from syllable
to syllable almost as if it came from a clock. When she bounced,
which was much of the time, her small breasts crossed the net like
tennis balls, and reminded Professor Paltry, unpleasantly, of the
way his sister's rose and fell in a manner most disturbing when she
had led cheers, her high school letter sweater leaping as if there
were small animals bundled behind the cloth trying to burst free.

MOR ning PRO fes sor Paul tree? The question was almost a

relief. I am fine, Miss Devise, as you can see. TEE hee, I am HAP pee to no tha TT. And howw arr uuu, Professor Paltry would particulate. FI ner than BE for. Holding books against her busy chest, Dottie (for that is what she chose to call herself) would flicker away at a half skip. Professor Paltry would sigh like a dying inner tube, shake his head as he entered his office, and each time think how terrible poor Devise must feel, having raised such a giggly flibbertigibbet almost from infancy, as the Professor had been led to believe.

He remembered the way she seemed when Art had first arrived at the college: quiet, demure, in a frilly frock, her hair tied up like a restless dog, since Art apparently could not teach combing. She followed her father when he walked her to her school, precisely five paces behind. Dottie was untouched by her future nature then and didn't jiggle.

The sorrowful story that President Howard Muffin so enjoyed retelling about the tragedies their new colleague, Arthur Devise, had been honored by God to endure—the loss of his wife, the loss, during the war, of his power of speech, which might explain those expressive hands—was just one more thing to hold against him, and would have been held had it been necessary, but there was so much against him already that, at least in the early days of their acquaintance, Devise had to go about bent as if he were leaning into a persistent wind.

The man who spoke with his hands remained on the staff long enough to earn a sabbatical if Millwheel College had granted them. Then he and his daughter disappeared without so much as a giggle of goodbye or an equivalent wave, though President Muffin announced that Professor Devise was leaving for personal reasons. This was regrettable. The bags beneath President Muffin's eyes swelled with something near tears. Professor Devise would be missed, especially his piccolo and his work with the chorus, which immediately fell out of tune. Bon voyage et bon chance. Don't forget us.

At the time of Art's departure, Joseph Paltry not only held nothing against him, he considered Art his friend; he appreciated his trills, rests, riffs, roulades, and cadenzas, and understood what Art had to endure from his daughter whose birdsong Paltry now heard as the cackle of starlings or the shriek of the shrike.

If one were thinking of the northern bird, this comparison would be inaccurate because its call is mellow when it isn't scolding. But the loggerhead's is as sharp and abrupt as a spill of tacks, and has a harsh complaining quality as well. Shrikes were not unheard of in this part of Ohio, so her appearance at the College was scarcely a miracle. They are predators, fierce to a fault, with bright white teeth often in a wide girlish grin.

Although she still lived in her father's protective shadow, Dottie was now a disturbing presence in Professor Paltry's class, the introductory Elements of Music, and she showed up for office hours more regularly than he had his lunch. She could play several instruments tolerably well and was far ahead of almost everyone else, a fact she let her questions prove. Paltry had attempted to move her to a more advanced level but both Dottie and her father wanted her to stay where she was. Now, in his office, she was provocative, showing leg, showing smile, standing close, tossing her hair as she'd no doubt seen in the movies, and asking increasingly personal questions.

On a day no more dismal than most others, Joseph Paltry was

approached, while reading in the faculty lounge (a large closet-sized space with a coffeepot, scarred wooden table, and few chairs where he liked to hide out and study scores because everyone else hated the ratty little room and found that it reminded them of Millwheel's tightwad president and their benighted condition), by Arthur Devise who had entered with his hands wrapped around a steaming mug in order that they should enjoy its warmth since the day was sleety, gray and cold, although no more dismal than most others.

Devise placed the mug rather emphatically in the middle of the table where some chiseler had scratched TEACHERS LOVE THE IGNORANT with a flinty-pointed pencil, its carbon darkening the line; and then he pulled up a chair near Paltry as a conspirator might, and allowed his hands to make his apologies.

Paltry shrugged his "no matter" shrug. Devise pursed his right thumb and forefinger, and snapped the clasp. I understand, he said in a tone level enough to encourage planting, my daughter Dorothy has been making a nuisance of herself. Devise's left thumb wiggled as if to say, I don't mean that. Instead, maybe the pursed thumb meant she is my dear girl who has never had an unclean thought. Perhaps the wiggled thumb meant that an innocent batting of her lashes has led to a misunderstanding. Paltry wondered how to approach such a confession.

Dottie had, of course, been making eyes at Paltry, embarrassing him past pink, but he naturally said, of course not, why would you think that? Both of Devise's palms slowly showed themselves as if they were aces peeking from a poker hand. Well, she has predilections . . . she . . . in the past . . . From a binocular position, the fingers tentatively disclosed the inner hand, then exhibited one apologetic spasm like tossing a toad from your grasp.

Ah, Paltry exclaimed, genuinely surprised, that's why you put her in my class. You thought I'd understand.

I thought you'd know I wouldn't do so otherwise.

Yes, otherwise it would be a poor practice.

I had to keep her near me.

A class with you, a class with me—that's near.

The hands of the man who spoke with his hands slid into a tangle of shame.

I think it's because she misses her mother. Well, not misses exactly. Because she has no mother. She's decided to be the mother she needs.

She doesn't act like a mother with me.

Ah . . . she . . . I'm afraid she wants you to make her a mother.

But anyone . . . nearly anyone . . . will do, I presume.

She has gone rather far in other . . . schools.

High school even?

Yes . . . well, other places . . . community colleges . . . She's gone rather far. Since she was thirteen.

Surely she would not promote such things with me?

Possibly. It's likely.

She has accused me of . . . you know . . . looking at her.

I am terribly sorry. She is playing the coquette. It's her subject.

But her speech . . .

Oh yes, I know, her speech is mechanical. It's made up. It is a complaint about mine . . . my hands. His hands were stitching cloth. She . . . you see . . . squeaks in protest.

I've noticed you do move your hands about.

I don't do it. God does. God moves my hands. I speak that way on his behalf.

This conversation had been so painful for Paltry that each

previous word had felt pulled from him like an embedded cork, but now almost every function ceased: his throat clogged, his face burned, so his blood must have rushed into his cheeks. They are both mad, he thought. Since he was able to make such a judgment, his mind must be operating. But he wasn't breathing. Never had he heard anything so preposterous, but such a statement, made to his face and meant for him, was like a blow to his chest.

I know that what I say must seem surprising, although our good President Muffin was ready to entertain it. However, I have become merely an instrument of God's, or rather, not I, but my hands have become an instrument of God's. They do his bidding and, when he's speaking, will not mind me. Since they often make their moves while I am speaking as I am speaking now to you, some people have concluded that they are accompanying me. Two fingers pinched and lifted the loose skin about the knuckles of his left hand. I have thought you might be one of those. The musical connection, you know.

Devise's pause made his statement a question. Paltry could not answer. He began to think, though, of what he might possibly say to this man who had become a threatening stranger—humor him, deny him, sympathize, chastise him, return the subject to his daughter's wayward ways? say I don't want to hear another word, bolt the room? Paltry's weight shifted. This was sensed. One of those hands touched his arm.

As if released, Paltry stood up. He thanked God he had grown a beard, and in that moment realized who it was he had invoked—already a ghostly presence if this testimony could be believed. Always a presence according to doctrine. He might perhaps ask how Professor Devise presumed to know that the gestures he involuntarily made were those of some other spirit than his own unconscious, but this would prolong a conversation he wished had never begun. Well, there was no conversation since he hadn't said a word. Maybe he shouldn't aid or abet it. He would just go.

I can't make out the signs they are sending; I cannot read their code; I just know; and I was never a believer either, before my wife was so terribly killed. Devise's smooth firm features looked to be dissolving in a solution of sorrow. He was swimming in tears, that was it. When I told Dorothy what had happened to my hands, she became hysterical. She accused me of leaving her as her mother had, though, of course, I hadn't, and I assured her that my mind was clear, sane through and through like—you know—paper that's one hundred percent cotton.

Paltry found this comparison almost as unsettling as his colleague's revelation about his hands. The man was mad. Did his hands heal? He had been touched but was it the King's touch? He had some warts ... perhaps if ... He had shaken this man's hands. What happened then? The man was mad. I shall wash my hands of him, Paltry thought. He has the whole world in those hands. They certainly were idle, but why was it only his hands? If he were a puppet, his legs should move too. When his head tilts, his eyes should roll. The madman ... Why was he—Joseph Paltry—a person who endeavored to stay in the background—why was he always the accosted one? the falsely accused? the rudely confronted? After all, he had only backed around his office desk, keeping his moral distance, with Dottie in salacious pursuit; and then, rid of her one more time, all he had done . . . well, he had locked up all his temptations in a steel cabinet and fled to this squatters' hole, a place forsaken by all until now when a crowd seemed to have assembled. The chairs were standing guard, the coffeepot was listening. No comment from the mug but steam. Paltry noticed that there were only six checkers left. Mostly reds.

I've endured the shame of her nymphomaniacal imposture; I've put up with all the jokes—

Jokes?

That I'm only going through the motions.

I—. Ah . . . Oh.

Professor Paltry, my friend, if you complain of her, we shall have to move on again, and we are running out of places to land.

I despise imposture, Paltry found himself saying.

I thought you might understand imposture very well.

Paltry did not reply because he was suddenly frightened. What was meant by that? Was there a threat? what sort? from what quarter? Devise had been last seen smothering his mug with both hands. Perhaps he was making a joke about the quality of its—what did one say?—mud. Led by his beard, Paltry retreated toward the door. Keep your eye on the hands, he implored himself. Keep an eye on.

I mean it is very hard to be honestly what we are. A finger, rooted in a fist, popped free.

Well, she better not. Dottie. Dottie better not imposture me. She crowds me, even in corridors. Where everyone can see. Paltry cracked the door and slid through. And from the building, he ran out.

Perhaps, after this, the man who spoke with his hands said less with his hands than before. Perhaps he kept his arms loaded with books. Perhaps he chose to participate in fewer social gatherings or to plan fewer accidental encounters. It was hard to tell. But for a time, at least, Dottie did nothing in class but cross her legs, and nothing after class but bob when he was carried close by circumstances.

Professor Paltry said nothing with his eyes or mouth, or evidenced anything in the way he walked, or gave his own hands leave to stray into oratory. He kept mum about God and God's signals; he kept mum about Dottie's—well—devices; he kept mum about his fears. Before the morning mirror he made certain to be clothed.

But he did practice flicking crumbs from the dinner table. Flick, that's gone, he would say his hands said. Get thee to a nunnery. Flick. As if it were a picnic and there were ants on the cloth. Flick. Let the air eat you.

If it is possible for a member of the faculty to drop out of school that is what Arthur and his daughter did. He disappeared and left his colleagues with four classes adrift like bottles in mid-ocean. Rinse decided to bus one bunch to Oberlin for the Fauré Requiem and regretted the ride. Buses, when a stranger occupies every seat, can be cheap, convenient, and restful ways to travel. Unless the bus careens over an embankment and tips, the bus gives the hits, the bus does not receive them. But when a bus is transporting what is called a group, there is likely to be singing and other forms of merriment—jokes, nips, makeouts, disorderly glee—and a weakening of the leader's position. It was unlikely that the man who spoke with his hands left by car because he didn't seem to drive. Perhaps his hands were too busy with their obedience to God's will. Perhaps he took a bus to Columbus and the train from there. Perhaps he had his goods shipped, whatever they were. His flute. His piccolo. His recorder. Dottie's clarinet.

The last time Professor Paltry saw Professor Arthur Devise the man was sitting on a campus bench like an ampersand. Paltry studied, from a safe distance, those hands, but what he saw was a very ordinary clench.

The Toy
Chest

Breast. Twin orbs. Check.

When I was ten I had a tin train that ran on juice. Juice was dad's word for it. The juice came out of the wall like pus from a pimple. The juice came out of the wall if you knew where the right places were, dad said, where light sockets lit eye sockets lit valleys and hills. Then you needed to squeeze those places until you forced juice to run inside a wire—a wire that was wearing a rubber protective suit—until the wire razzled across the floor in a frenzy of energy, and, in an electric ecstasy that all the same must have hurt like hell, forced juice to speed into a weighty little black box that was otherwise filled with the darkness of closets. And there it grew, dad said, like mushrooms in a cave, on stale air and mystery; there it hung on old clothes and weary metal hangers; there it mustered its resources until it showed it had some of t

That's all I remember about that sort of juice. Should I start over? There is such a lot of juice: orange with pineapple, pulp or not, vitamins added, shake well before pouring. Cider—not likely in this case—too seasonal. There's more to remember. T omato. Fits. Not an edge piece, though. Later in life, when the doctors put dad on a salt-free diet, we had to keep bottles of that thick red sodium solution out of his reach. He did love it. His doctors recommended cranberry. Dad mustered his patience—a drill

for which he rarely called the roll—diet, blood pressure, tempera-
ture, pills, and such. He swallowed the whole lot in one greedy
gulp. Cranberry was a fruit juice, he informed his physicians; what
he wanted was vegetable juice. One doctor—we laugh about it
now—had the gumption to tell dad that the tomato was a fruit.
The man was fired in short order. Well, not exactly fired. Not
exactly short order. Dad was a coward about most things if he
had to face them with his face. He just never went back to that
surgeon's shop. So I must have meant by "short order" that dad
had ducked the doc in three states: meeting, memory, or mention.
Dad knew the fellow was right about tomatoes, even the yellow
ones, and dad knew that we knew. Such a realization stung like a
sand ant.

he zip necessary to get my tin train going when I gradually
moved the handle that lay across the top of the heavy black box
like a hand on a clock's face. "Transinformer" was dad's word for
it. The word was quite heavy for so small a cube. Full of its
importance, dad said, but I was ready to give it all the importance it wanted. It had a name—the cube did, the word did not.
Dial-a-speed. He said it made the juice somehow juicier so the
juice was willing to shoot onto and through the train's tracks,
though you couldn't tell by just looking at them that anything
was different from one minute to the next; and the engine sucked
up the juice that was lying there wetting the rails, and everything
about how the train ran after he reached that point in his explanation, dad said, was like our Studebaker burning gas. Excep That's
all I remember.

t we got good mileage out of the old bitch. She was more reliable than my tin train. Tin train, tin train, come out and play, tin

train. It would go lickety down a length of track and then slow to a maunder as if there were a window it wanted to look through or a tree that stood out, funny reasons to groan to a stop. Even if Indians were chasing the engine or perhaps Pauline lay roped to the ties, it would utter a slow groan—hiss own, hiss own—it was always the train, the train that told the story I was dressing my world with. Toy train, toy train, toy train, let's take a trip, toy train. Dad showed me how to sandpaper the track. This made, he said, for a better contact. Your track's been gathering grime since last Christmas, he reminded me. He was so fond of reminiscence. Not because remembering was something he could do well because he couldn't do it well, huge hunks of his life had disappeared as if they had never happened, like those pieces that get lost immediately they are released from the puzzle box, and maybe they hadn't happened, but his life had possibly skipped a beat now and then; I know my life has holes at its elbows and its knees; it is a tatter of tales, mostly incomplete; my thin bones show. I know. I know. When our present date gets eaten, some crumbs, some smears will remain to mark the plate. Licked unclean. Unclean. Then the past that we've devoured, we excrete. This manure feeds the meat of a new moment.   Isn't that cheery?

Dad would with a smile ask me how many passengers had perished in the most recent crash of my train when it scampered off into the dismal swamps of El Gard beneath our dining table's drop leaf. He would smile because I would always reply: at true play there are no consequences, although I hardly knew what the two words meant. Not even broken bones? Maybe seven suitcases were flung about and their contents scattered. Wreckage of any kind? Few dishes were shaken even in the dining car when I picked the engine up. So I sent back his smart-ass smile. I didn't plan on staging an accident at the expense of my presently blooming paper lake.

I always hoped that a naked lady lay concealed beneath the countless connections I was supposed to make, but no luck, instead I possessed the most conventional box of jigsaw pieces imaginable whose garish colors clashed with their absurd shapes depicting a childish drawing. Green for crayoned grass, blue for cloudless sky, smoke for smoke—the clichés seemed essential to any childhood scribble—house with chimney, front walk that wiggles, floating stick figures except, in a corner, for no reason at all, one of the three bears, painted to look stuffed—the whole thing sawn out of some cardboard at midnight by a drunken tailor.

My parents could not bare me

My parents bore me

My parents brought me up to be their flogging post.

My parents used me for their flogging post. And would say now that I'm a whinery. I wrote numbers on the backs of the bear puzzle pieces—the nature of nature from none to five hundred. Now I can reassemble the damn thing in less time than it takes for you to type—oh—Seventy!

After I have been dumped on by dear ole dad, and there is a mildly broken spring to my walk, I spit on my childhood rendition of his face. Together they paint a pretty picture . . . the spill of spit . . . a pretty picture here . . . the swill of spit . . . a pretty picture there . . . the smear of spit . . . fragile as fragile glass . . . a pretty picture . . .

After every Christmas, when the needles of the spruce hurt the hands that handle them—ow! t inder!—I pack my train into the cardboard carton it came in: engine, cars, track, transinformer, station. Just so. There was no room for anything extra Santa might have brought. Those things—the recent gifts—were auntie-bagged. I remember about bagging. My aunt Nector made sacks from scraps of cloth and along their open edges threaded a drawstring that I pulled when I was hanging disobedient soldiers. Then I stashed the bags on the bottom and at the right-hand corner of the toy chest: artificial trees, alphabet blocks, a dollhouse bench, sign that said SLOW—CHILDREN CROSSING. Aunt Nector sewed me a small doll dressed like a pilgrim for Thanksgiving that I used to tie to the tracks, but the train would hit her and run off the rails instead of cutting her in two the way it was supposed to. A little more sanding made the tin shine like new-poured iron. Nevertheless, I found that the most rubbed sections of rail were always where the problem was. The engine would jump forward for a moment, then—look out—jerk to a stop—ouch—up and down the length of my entire train. Including all three streamlined cars. The Silver Star. It was a Streamliner a lot like a real one I'd seen in magazines. Out there where the air was clean. Excep

Aunt Nector was plenty stupid not to know when it was Christmas and when it was Halloween, when it was Easter and when it was Rosh Hashanah, when it was President's Day, when it was the Ruination of the World.

Tuh, that's it: t for me and t for you . . . damn if dad didn't do what he threatened to: he kept all the edges and threw the rest away. He said they symbolized forgotten soldiers but I think it stood for a penitentiary where thoughts that were both dirty and hilarious were kept, eating gruel with a spoon.

Everybody wanted to ride on the Streamliner because

Let me think.

Out there where the air was clear.

Out where?   There!

t   these little pieces are always the hardes t   though   my typewriter will double ells automatically   hardest   got it fi ts

In any case, the bags were easy ways to wrap presents and they could be reused every year like the same old excuses. My aunt liked to sponsor the second chance. Gift pouches she called them. In the kangaroo of Christmas. Hop a long way from the North Pole. Australians, my dad said, slept upsidedown like bats. They freed Aunt Nector from several concerns: now she wouldn't have to unwrap packages as if they were bombs; now she needn't fear of tearing the tissue paper or cutting the wrong string; it would no longer be necessary to iron the creases flat for me where, at each corner, the foldings had become crimped, so I could lay them away in an equally flat box saved for the purpose that was remarkably no thicker than a t ie, though i t was roomier in every other direction, as if it might have held maps once, instead of sheets of secondhand wrappings, and a cache that became a symbol of her penny ante thrif

t. They are all red as raw meat you'd think ... the picture should   begin to come in view about now   arty   image   hah   got one

How amazing, I always thought, that this particular green tissue, requiring exactly these folds, when they were used to wrap such fur-trimmed slippers safely in a shoe box, will finally suffer and endure Aunt Nector's healing iron to reach reusable condition—wow, what a disappointing conclusion—all this only to end up as a packing wad that will prevent jostling among the letters of my ink stamp alphabet box.

The Silver Star seemed to be moving while standing still. It hid its inner workings like a watch. It signified Ease. Grace. Luxury. Chic. Au Currant that juices the rails. To go with Airflow Pedal Planes, Airflow Pedal Cars, Airflow Pedal Trikes, Airflow Pedal Trains. Whatever bore the name: the trailer that's pulled by the Chrysler.

I begged her. Alice unbuttoned her blouse. I held my breath—deep, as you do for docs. She showed me. We were sitting right here alongside the toy chest. She said hers composed the toy chest now. They were moderate in size but round the nubbles were dark brown circles—a pond's pebbly curls. We were sitting close together playing touch me, touch me there. B lis s. We were sitting on the toy box playing with ourselves. I never again had a happiness so brief, so intense, so scared.

Ink pad   moistened with spit. I rubbed the noses of the letters forcibly into the black pad so as to stamp the headlines of our family newspaper—intermittently issued—I was the publisher, editor, printer, newsboy, and subscriber. MOTHER SERVES ICE CREAM AT BIRTHDAY FEAT fet oh well a ruined page.

t Denver. I remember visiting in the early fall, a yellow—yellow fog—a pall hung over the city, crawling nearly to the mountains. It was the latest thing in phenomena: the shape of a long-held puff of air. I would call out the times: the Silver Star will depart Chicago at 3 p.m. (if that was when I was down on my knees wiping track with a soft cloth to remove what sanding—I hoped—had loosened), or I would announce, in a voice made for announcements: the Silver Star is arriving on time from Indianapolis on

Track 3 at 5:49. I liked to brag when the Streamliner got all way round the Christmas tree and had done the papier-mâché tunnel, running on regular like the Studebaker did, a bitch in heat, not the car but the train was, yowling as if from the pain produced when the prongs of one piece of track entered the metal tubes of another. I had so many sections of straight and so many fewer of curve, I don't remember the number, but when prongs were completely hidden in their sleeves, my right of way extended from the tree right under the dinner table where the tunnel was too, a stretch of straight rail it had to be a stretch of straight rail since

for some reason dodge the table legs? dodge the crumb accumulations? March the troops beneath   hide   peer up skirts

I'll have to think about it. Why won't that damn blue piece fit something. I keep picking it up. My hand holding it hovers like a copter above the board. No fit found. Toss to the ground. So like blue. Screw you too.

every year, for a few years, I would get at Christmas several lengths

more sheets   of snowflaked paper

MOTHER SERVES ICE CREAM
THE WRONG COLOR

tissue-thin were our familial relations   You could see through our skins but make out only hinted forms   The real reasons for anything were not quite discernible My hands were two spooks

for some reason   oh yes   because I asked Santa for it on my first list, on my initial petition to the reindeered deity: please a section or so of track please a switch oh yes and a station and a station master who comes out of the station when the train passes a switch = one more reason I need a switch = oh sweety the wind in my window now makes the seed pods of our whitebud tremble, vibr

it won't be long and I'll be gone

they say a healthy breeze might bring it all back to me, nah, I don't believe so no life isn't like that

I won't be lonely in my state of death. There are lots of spooks on the other side pretending to be alive, but many more folks who are healthy as heifers pretending to be dead on mine. Sunk in silence are the graves of submarines. In my toy box I had two toy submarines silver as knives I had klept from the dime store. Safe on the bottom they rested, smothered by thoughtlessness. Finally, nobody remembered me living or me dead, ever again, no matter what. Even if—again—it never rains. Train rails hidden in weeds and cinders. No Denver. No Chicago. No arrivals. Hah. No departures. No God. No knowing. No ME DEAD AT FOURTEEN. Didn't I use that heading once, to scare an auntie? I devoted one issue to the sudden passing of my mom, another to the expected demise of dad, one more to the inevitable falling of relatives into the hands of pets

DEATH DAY EXTRA

Of pirates and other myth-making creatures

All aboard. I'd shout, and then place a paper person on the ceiling of the Silver Star—"roof" doesn't seem right—on top—and I would be that paper person clinging to the forehead of the train where the engine (during an escape by me and my minions following our robbery of the local bank) is; yes, is, okay, is, right, but wasn't I always in the hero's role? no, no I wasn't, I remember, I was a rogue, and a rapscallion, it was part of my business to outwi

t was the hero's role—t the local constabulary—to create crimes, to sei   ze the reins of power from General Chollop

Naughties/Misdemeaners/Crimes/Sins

A naughty was when I locked myself in mom's closet. A misdemeanor was when I stole the submarines. Crimes earned me a whipping. Only sometimes was I caught and sent to see the doctor. Sin was something else. Eloise (not Louise) was a girl from Sunday school I was trying to feel up for some reason let's say it was for information so I would let her read to me from a book dear to her father (why should I care about that old coot?) passages that were supposed to keep everything pure between us. The problem was I wanted to play doctor; she wanted to play church, the rules and results of which could be found in Sylvanus Stall's book *What a Young Boy Ought to Know,* which she showed me as if it were a family secret (what I wondered then was the D.D. that followed his absurd name?). Oh boy, I thought, this book has pictures too, explicit drawings, big disappointment, fish nibbling at bait and stories full of scares and frights and warnings such as "Satan has laid traps and snares all along your path through life, and you will need to be very, very cautious, lest you are ruined for time and destroyed for eternity." Well I wasn't cautious and I was ruined and I will be destroyed for eternity.

Alone though alive in the twilight of life far from any center of feeling not in my knuckles nor in the snot that's been blown from a nose empty of ideas and far from the center of any ceiling only alone like a speck-sized spider crossing a neglected wall where it will be smacked by my palm regardless of its record of good or evil or the smear we leave squashing it.

Sylvanus was against card playing. I didn't care for cards either, not even solitaire. Because   I crushed the cards that were not playable

   bent the corners   sIf you can't play with a plaything what good is it?   On a bet I threw that damn marionette down the back stairs, skidoo it flew, but the fool thing didn't break just got its shoulder string tangled with its shoe.

Even so, when I played, I played by myself; and mostly, when I played by myself, I played at war. And when I played at war I announced the whole thing as if it were a ballgame broadcast over the radio for the ears of eager listeners.

REPORTS FROM THE FRONT

I liked best the March Out. That was the moment the armies that were to be enemies in the coming war left their camps. One marched by land on a road the rug made—therefore down a woven band of burgundy to the beginning of its fringe. Another came (no not by sea because too few ships were to be found docked in the toy bin at the five & dime; no sailor soldiers were there, either, to man them) along the twisting foothill paths, over the slick glacial slabs, at last above the frost line, across the cracks between the mountains, and that meant atop blocks and small boxes, between pillows aslope to the plain of battle beneath the dining table, brave oh so brave in their disciplined lines of march, trucks as transport—putt putt putt—cavalry at a trot—clop clop clop—as well as airplanes zuzz bombing one another from above because I needed all my troops to participate and couldn't be troubled by pictures of former days when soldiers stood or knelt in colorful lines and died like blown-out candles, or recent times when they fought like worms ventilating the ground or, killed while they crept down burnt halls and peered around blurred corners, or kicked in doors, machine-gunning people in what were once their homes, in what was once a town. Boom. Reeeek. Poom. That noisy. Bullets whistling through a ricochet like a warbler's song. War is war I said and death the deity.

To this day I love lead red-coated soldiers picking meadows to march through, line up in, fire in, fall in   dumb shits   look out the artillery has opened up   I hear horsemen, the horns of the cavalry, the snap of banners in the wake of the charge, hoofs hammering the oak floors the refreshing way rapid water rushes against rocks   so much better than landmines

> The nightly news
> has repeated views
> US making war:
> We kick in doors.
> Our rifle butts
> them in their huts
> as we make wars
> and kick in doors.
> Those in cahoots
> our mighty boots
> kick in their doors
> and round up scores.

The world deplores
our frequent wars,
our lying leaders,
special pleaders,
as nightly shows
show how it goes,
when we make the war
they all deplore:
we kick in doors.

General Chollop is rumored to be marshaling his troops near the sofa. A thick and slowly rising mist reveals their numbers. Lucky Strike smoke. The breath of a visitor. What way shall they come? On TV they have machine guns shoot you down. On TV they make war on horseback airplanes tanks. The kids I won't have fathered won't have to imagine the cry charge, in protest the charge will be charged to him.

Ah, hah! happy horsemen will advance through the valley's meadows, waddle its creeks, and stir its dreams. The foot soldiers will follow but only two abreast. Then, assembling at the umbrella stand, the tanks will crawl over imaginary mountain roads covered by hemlock branches for camouflage, and groaning in protest as only metal can.

DRUNKEN MOTHER THROWS UP
AT BIRTHDAY PARTY

I believed whatever was read to me while I was being lured to sleep, so I was wroth whenever I ran into a wall and it didn't open like a shower curtain on a waterfall. I twice tried with no results but a bruise or two, and a puff of shaken plaster—similar celebrations for victory, and badges for bravery—were my rewards. My occasionally best friend Timmy said *wonderland* was behind the wardrobe, but when I climbed inside mine I was swiftly locked in, the latch chastised me, I heard its tisk, and I felt smothered by my own clothes, short in length as they were, and yet muffling quite completely most of my cries, which grew after a while more shrill as I became thoroughly afraid. I kicked and pounded till finally my mother found me there—she had been hunting me anyway since sonny was supposed to go to church with the whole family—and pulled the door open with a why are you hiding in here you could have smothered and spoiled everyone's day dear heaven how you've messed up your best coat I don't know if you can wear it to services now with those wrinkles exactly like the ones you leave me to wear as worry on my brow. Are you okay finally Mr. Snivel Root? I thought you liked church. Wipe your eyes and let's get this business under way we don't want to be late because it is embarrassing to be caught hunting a pew in the midst of the first amen.

Mother wasn't such a bad wad. She served ice cream of the right flavor. A bit of a tease is all. Kept the cone out of my reach until cream melted on the upper edge of her fist. I licked it off. That was my payment. Licking. I will give you a licking. I was given a giggle, sometimes a squeeze, before the fragile cone's crackle.

Bobby believed in Santa Claus but not in snowy wastes and imaginary landscapes. Presents shrouded in white tissue paper were piled into hills about Santa's farm and factory. There were so many people waiting for the Christ child to be born there had to be, if counted, hills of dead lead soldiers, piles of blocks, heaps of teddy bears, stacks of erector sets, and scheduled trains, whole ranges made of games designed to improve a slow kid's motor skills, as well as towers of books to be read from by fathers trying to sound like Riding Hood, Grandma, or the Wolf, each paint box and yo-yo in a snowy white disguise over which the sled slid when gathering them in sacks. What did they take kids for, these duped adults, telling them Santa's cheeks were rosy with frostbite—gee whiz—when they were obviously flushed as dad's cheeks often were with the brandy everybody left by the fireplace at the very edge and entrance to the Blessed Birth Day? Nevertheless, it was a yearly disappointment not to receive the slingshot, air rifle, or anatomically correct doll I had written Santa to request. My father says that Santa won't give me anything until I improve my writing. Mother says that when she was a girl she was courted by everybody including ferrets. She repeats this over and over. She has successfully hidden the gin.

The partly finished puzzle lies there like a partly ploughed field inviting every eye and then commanding the eyes' hovering fingers to halt their indecisive swaying in order to squeeze the chosen little knob into its chosen little notch. It won't fit. It certainly looked like a fit. How I hate sharing. I hate that hovering hand, uncertain, in the puzzle's airspace. I end up letting mom finish putting together a bowl of ripening pears, open shutters, reclining nude. Get the goddamned thing back in the box. I don't care if it's by Matisse. See how the pieces cling to one another like a clump of elderberries. None of this fruit is mine. Only the few puzzles I'm allowed to begin-middle-and-end, by myself alone, are mine.

How they once sat in that bowl so plump and pristine, so pristine and plump, their stems in the air to enjoy the ticklish strokes of the painter's brush. How they once sat fixed, defeated by disuse, in the bowl smeared on the canvas and waiting for the photograph's grin as if it were his penis going in. How many thousand copies of that stupid still life were made for the jigsaw to chew to pieces, all small all knobbed all broken into five hundred wiggly shaped shards.

The way you could tell it wasn't a chicken that laid all those eggs at Easter . . . the way was the colors they were colored. A few were speckled, but most of them were a wishy-washy blue or a smeary rose or a wrung-out purple or a yellow that smelled of pickle juice. And chickens had more affection for their eggs than to leave them any old place even under leaves or in a nest of crab grass. So a rabbit was a good guess, and Bobby believed that if he didn't eat those eggs—boiled as a precaution—there'd be baby rabbits grazing on every lawn until the mower got them or a dog. Easter was a funny day. You were given candy in a nest of shredded cellophane because God's son, after he was murdered by a cloud of thrown stones, pushed away a few rocks from the cave where he was hiding and displayed his organ in an unfurling of raincoat. What rabbits had to do with this was a mystery. Jerry said that it was rabbits because they were always fucking when they weren't eating and consequently constantly giving birth by means of those everywhere eggs, but Bobby said that such dumb stuff was for Christmas to figure out. Jerry said nevertheless rabbits were chosen to represent rebirth and picked because nobody was inclined on Easter to eat them with the eagerness that, for no discernible reason, they did ham.

I believed Bobby until I didn't. He messed up God and Goliath. He said God was four cubits and a span. And that Goliath came out of a hole in the ground. And sailed to heaven I n a kite.

Damn jellybeans. Curse of candy. The black ones are licorice. Beware. Damn licorice. But if lucky you found a nest with a chocolate bunny, hollow to the core, solid-eared, whose empty head you could bite off at the bow-tie line so that you could see straight down into the empty depths of Easter . . . If lucky. Something about worshipping the ceremonial sun. Nu nu nougat

A bun baked on Good Friday will never mold over and will last up to a year in the bed box curing coughs and ah hems and other people beside themselves with

Movement meant life so the rabbit froze in its toy tracks though the train was coming like death, more certain than shooting. This lack of maneuver was successful when performed among clumps of fiddle fern but out on the open grass it made them as obvious in their presence as a garden gremlin. I stood stone still once, in a similar fright at being surprised to see the bunny within a yard of me, oh what big eyes you have and why were you instinctified, or taught by your folks, to sit solemn as a breath held for the doc in a world of might-as-well-be water?

We say: toy truck toy theater toy train, why don't we say toy beer? This query has been written with toy words. Toy words are impossible. Here is another question. Why don't we say toy toy? I was pretending to pretend. I have been thinking about thinking. My toy train will have toy track, a toy engine, a toy station, but my toy truck will have real wheels. Ah . . . toss me . . . toss me a toy kiss. Can this caress be done with a real mouth?

My parents were ordinary. They wanted to murder me and I them, but only some of the time. I didn't know they were ordinary; that everybody had a pair of nags to make life miserable. I thought other people's parents were better than mine. Rather thine than mine. Could be sung. Into a sack. Like a breatholator.

I used to yell train times into a cloth bag. It sounded like a station must, its echoes muffled, woofed from far away. I remember now I dreamed of boarding a car as it was puffing out of all relation to have adventures I had read about—goodbye the magic of masturbation, no, "madness" The paper tunnel would be dark inside like the wardrobe was, but only for a brevity unless it . . . unless it . . . unless it stopped there in the grim of forest lurk. Wooh, I would breathe and rebreathe into my bag. The long low moan of a distant molestation.

I wanted to be the kid the neighbors said was so happy and sweet how could he have murdered so many while living next door just down the street in a neighborhood where such things were rare to never, and he mowed our lawns for a decent fee. Whoopee, we've made the papers,   our little subdivision has; and, although it owns only a few trees, it enjoys regular leaf collection, trash pickup and recycle bins, the quiet of banned motorcycles.

Actually, no one wants to murder anyone. If we would only disappear from the world—ma, pa, and me—I to a wine cellar to age at a vintner's pace; ma and pa—every relative really—sent like the mischievous to a blackboard, there to be erased.   But that's not disappearing from the world. Heavens to Betsy! That's name-dropping.

Today is one of my more lucid days. I put it down to the pleasure of unpacking my toy chest, no, the fun of finding my toy box, which was what Louise called her cunt when she fingered it just to put me off. Louise comes back to me, as if my memory of her had been waiting in my baseball mitt for me to recover it, the mitt soft the ball hard the autograph pale to the point of lavender, certainly not the indelible ink or the smooth warm thigh I signed and then drew like directions toward her furrow, she pleased as pink that across her creamy skin a caress left its maker's mark, an arrow heralding her muff, so lightly haired it still felt alive when I touched it, compelling me to scream, not the effect desired.

It was so. It was my firm purpose to flee this strange place. I did not throw her down, she fell, she told me so, her skirt flew up like a frightened quail, two birds brought down with one boom of buckshot blown into the center of the group by my gun, fired low as they were leaving in a shapeless cloud, a pair that makes a tasty meal served by a suited darkie in the dining car of—what did I call it?—the Silver Queen—one sleeper, one diner, one coach at the will of the transinformer my stream lie nerrrrr   my my my my my my my my my my my m

My toy chest was made of creamy wood the color of skin, and opened over the whole length of its back, and the entire width of its lifting, but boy, would you believe? its lid had a hinge that unfolded to prop the top—stay up, damn you—the way my father rested the Studebaker's hood upon a rod when he learned that the old car had flunked its final trip and had to be towed to town Whe w

w hen I had my rails sanded so they shone, when the juice drove the engine that ran the cars that bore my dreams, I liked my toy train better than anything that ever played solitaire with me.

A doll is not a toy and should not be flung into a toy chest like an old glove or used in fits and starts of interest as one might eat a meal. But I flung mine. A rag, it was dressed in spots of paint like a palette. I flung it so Nettie's head hit the lid and Nettie's neck snapped like a flag in a wind. She was wearing a pair of new jeans when I got her, everybody giggling when I stripped the gift of its wrapping and there she was—what a present for a boy!—who laughed loudest? hardest? longist? That would be Enid the Round Face, so fresh with a pale light furze on her cheeks like a peach has, yes, a peach-girl doll made of her clothes and wearing a pair of little knitted jeans. And an apron. Right. Both came off and on. Your mo

ve. Checkered like a chessboard where the armies of the white gather to glare their glare at the blacks who return those glares with outbursts of tongue as large as that of a Samoan lapping dog. Stomp.   I've seen them do. So. I said thank you very much for giving me one of your dolls, Eeeenid. Eenidd said, choking back a girlish giggle, I dinna give you a doll you dummy. But it's funny. It suits you. To a hee hee, said she. Suddenly I was twelve, or fourteen. After I came out of the closet af

They were just little hills of wool, well, cloth of some kind, over which you could stretch jeans in time, I was told, for atonement, i.e. a way of being barefoot only not bare because no one walked on stones anymore. Af

No leather, whether or not you care. So There.

Snapped her neck.

Soft furry sweet peach.   I would kiss it if I could. Munch me   made eating   celery and ice cubes

The train hove into view through the tunnel I made of papier-mâché for which I chewed the newsprint. My saliva. Really. You can briefcase it. I had a ticket for Toledo. A two bender. I'd take Enid with me to see Toledo.

By now I had a stack of tracks. Lots of curves for bends in the bed. Snap a neck on that giggling bitch who pretended she hadn't given me a rag for my tenth/twelfth/fourteenth birthday. When shame overcame me. She had so many necks. As many as Medusa had snakes. And I have excuses. Af

Let us sing the dolly song. There has to be a piece that will fit this corner; somewhere in this box of one thousand small knobby jigs there are four. Let us dance the jig the jig the jigsaw. Shit. There is always a missing one. Even when you have just opened the box and there has been no opportunity for a straight edge let alone a corner to fall on the floor and be swept beneath the so

> We wish to be stones, we do, we do,
> and feel as a path does the steps of you.
> We want to grow large like a gall on a tree
> and eat every word that's said of me.
> We do, we do, we long to be free,
> join with others in mayhem and song;
> carve the raw turkey, raise a red glass
> to the wind in the wood, my old beau, your ass.
> We strive to be sharp as the saw in the mill,
> and eat the heart of the game we kill.
> We lust, we do, though we fear the dark,
> Where we do what's done in a van we park.
> We fear for our lives, we do, we must,
> but not half so much as our lives fear us.

there   Father said   you have lost the piece that fits the corner of the earth   you have your foot upon it stupid child

I loved my mother at first

she helped me with my homework
she showed pride for me occasionally
and her best side sometimes, not her worst
she gave me Kool-Aid and bread and peanut butter after
school   and a kiss for a kiss   in addition
for learning the spelling of the word for the day
which was
go away

A NOTE ABOUT THE TYPE

This book was set in Garamond, a typeface originally designed by the famous Parisian type cutter Claude Garamond
(1480–1561). This version of Garamond was drawn by Günter
Gerhard Lange (1921–2008) and released by the Berthold type
foundry in 1972. Lange based his Garamond revival on a
combination of models found in specimen sheets from both
Paris and Antwerp.

Claude Garamond is one of the most famous type
designers in printing history. His distinguished romans and
italics first appeared in *Opera Ciceronis* in 1543–44. While
delightfully unconventional in design, the Garamond types
are clear and open, yet maintain an elegance and precision of
line that mark them as French.

Composed by North Market Street Graphics,
Lancaster, Pennsylvania

Printed and bound by Berryville Graphics,
Berryville, Virginia

Designed by Betty Lew